Sweetblade

A stand-alone Heretic Gods novel

Carol A. Park

Shattered
Soul
Books

Shattered Soul Books

Pennsylvania

Shattered Soul Books
2600 Willow Street Pike North
PMB 259
Willow Street, PA 17584
www.carolapark.com

Publisher's Note: This is a work of fiction. Names, characters, places, and incidents are a product of the author's imagination. Locales and public names are sometimes used for atmospheric purposes. Any resemblance to actual people, living or dead, or to businesses, companies, events, institutions, or locales is completely coincidental.

Cover art/design © 2018 Brit K. Caley
Interior illustrations © 2018 Andrew Park
Book Layout © 2017 BookDesignTemplates.com

Sweetblade/ Carol A. Park. -- 1st ed.
ISBN 978-1-7321491-2-0 (paperback)
ISBN 978-1-7321491-3-7 (e-book)

FOR MY FAMILY AND FRIENDS

Who have suffered or still suffer
with physical, mental, or emotional pain,
no matter how "big" or "small,"
whether I know about it or not.
You are loved.

Contents

Acknowledgements

I never actually meant to write this book.

It came out of my struggles with refining the character of Ivana from *Banebringer*: I ended up having to write part of her backstory to get the character right.

Once I had gone that far, I figured I might as well flesh it out and turn it into a spin-off novella. 90,000 words later, *Sweetblade* was a full-length novel. So much for a novella!

That being said, I'm grateful for those who were part of this process. Without my "production team," this book would lack polish and visual flourish, so I'm grateful to my editor, Amy McNulty, my cover artist, Brit K. Caley, and my interior illustrator, Andrew Park. I'm blown away, once again, by the atmospheric covers Brit creates, and I'm still giddy about the seventeen (!) progressive chapter icons in Part One.

My stalwart beta reader, Tam Case, must have read and critiqued three different versions of the manuscript, which is no small order. I'll also thank Wes Allen for trying, even though life circumstances prevented him from giving detailed feedback this time. He's the reason that I know some people might find this book just too darn depressing.

Of course, my husband, Calvin, reads my drafts so many times that he occasionally argues with me about something I changed in a previous draft, forgetting that he advised me to change it last time. He deserves an alpha/beta reading medal of honor!

I'll be honest: this was not an easy book for me to write. It's dark in a way that *Banebringer*, which has also been called dark, isn't. *Sweetblade* might even be called a tragedy when read on its own—which it certainly can be. **There is also material that some might find disturbing: most notably, an emotionally abusive relationship and references to/depictions of self-harm.**

The story beyond what I originally wrote gave me fits, yet for some reason I felt compelled to persevere. My final thanks go to all of you who pick up this book and likewise persevere!

Part One:

Ivana

Chapter One

Ivana huddled against the side of the building, but all it offered was shelter from the wind. The stone wall was cold, shadowed in a narrow alley and thus prevented from soaking in what little warmth it might have gained from the sun.

Ivana blew into her hands and, from her own place in the shadows, watched the fur-cloaked passersby on the thoroughfare before her. Their heads were tucked down and their hands were shoved into pockets or gathered beneath the warmth of their cloaks as they hurried toward their destinations at the end of a long day—for most, a warm hearth, a hot meal, and a cozy bed.

Her stomach clenched and she flexed her fingers. She had never expected it to be so cold so early on in the season.

In retrospect, she should have. Her father had included Setanan geography in her lessons, after all. She knew the cold came sooner than it did at home here in Carradon, the capital of Cadmyr.

Yet another bad decision in her long line of recent failures. She would have been better off heading south.

But the thought of staying longer than necessary in Ferehar, the place where everyone she loved had died because of her…

She shivered and pulled her threadbare cloak around herself, determined to try again. There had to be *someone* who needed a copyist.

She tossed up a brief prayer to Temoth, the Conclave's god of luck—what could it hurt?—and stepped out of the alley onto the main street. A woman with three children trailing behind stopped to read a notice on a community board. Ivana approached her, trying to look as pitiful as possible. She was sure that wasn't hard; she looked pretty pitiful without even trying.

"Please, Da," Ivana said. "I'm looking for work. Do you have any need for a tutor—or even a copyist?"

The woman spun toward her. "Oh!" she said. Her eyes flicked down over Ivana. "I…No, I'm so sorry." She averted her eyes and drew her children closer, as if they would be contaminated, and started to move away.

Ivana bit her lip and swallowed her pride, as she had many times in the weeks prior. "A coin, then?" She held out her hand.

She didn't need to work to make it tremble. She had watched how the street urchins squeezed pity out of otherwise unconcerned people—and learned. "It's so cold, Da." In silent agreement, her breath puffed out frozen clouds with each word.

The woman paused. Her gaze darted around the street, and then she plucked a coin from inside her sleeve. She pressed it into Ivana's hand and hurried off, children in tow, without another glance.

Ivana touched the coin. A single selma. A sixth of what used to be her monthly allowance. At the tavern back home, it would have bought a mug of steaming cider and a thick slice of warm, buttered bread; here, in the city, she might be able to buy a hot bun from a street vendor in the poorer districts.

Would it be wiser to save it for a better cloak, or boots, or gloves?

Her stomach grumbled.

But that could take weeks, and she was hungry now. Death by starvation now, or death by frostbite later.

The choices before her weren't promising.

"Hey, rat!"

She spun around. A city guardsman was headed her direction. Begging was illegal.

She curled stiff fingers around the selma and ran—like she always did.

Ivana may have had no luck obtaining work, but that didn't mean the day had been without value. She found a street vendor who was trying, at the end of the working day, to get rid of the remainder of the buns he had made, and she purchased two for the cost of one. She began devouring the first one as she headed back to the space she had claimed in one of the slums, in an abandoned alley that no one seemed to want.

The stone wall she slept against must have had a furnace on the other side because the wall was always warm rather than cold to the touch. As a bonus, the house at the end of the alley kept a lantern hanging outside most nights, providing enough light to keep her sane.

It had been hard to find that spot. The others guarded their spaces like they had bought and paid for them, and they didn't trust her yet. Every once in a while a beggar would be willing to share their garbage fire for a night.

All that being true, she could hardly believe she was the first one to stumble across such an ideal location, which could only mean there was something else wrong with it she was too inexperienced to know about—or perhaps that her mind was too numb with cold to work out.

So she had managed to claim it—at least until someone stronger than her ousted her.

It wouldn't take long for that to happen.

Sure enough, when she arrived at her stretch of wall, she was disappointed to see a human-shaped shadow disappearing into the dark end of the alley. It seemed her spot had been found. She waited to be challenged, but no one stepped forward.

Instead, a voice spoke from behind her—from the lit end of the alley. "Whatcha got there, girl?"

Damn. She shoved the rest of the half-eaten bun in her mouth and clutched the other to her chest before turning to face the newcomer. "Moffin," she mumbled around the bread.

The man leered at her. "Sneaky lil' sprite," he drawled. "How about you hand over the other, and I'll let you alone?"

She eyed him. His cloak was tattered around the edges but intact, and his gloves had holes, but, burning skies, at least he *had* gloves. If he wanted that bun, he'd have to pry it out from between her teeth.

"Go to the abyss." She swallowed the remnants of the first bun and stuffed the second, whole, in her mouth.

Anger flashed across his face, and all at once the gravity of miscalculation hit her. This wasn't another beggar trying to pinch her food. He was drunk, and he was itching for the excuse she had just given him to expend his pent-up aggression.

She hadn't known it was possible for her to feel colder than she already did. But it was.

He lurched toward her, and she lunged out of his reach, but he caught the edge of her thin cloak. He yanked her down to the ground, and she scrabbled against the hard stone to push herself upright as he dragged her back to himself. She strained against the strangling hold of the cloak around her throat, fumbling with cold-numbed fingers to release the simple pin that held the cloak together.

Never had she hoped that the cloak would rip, but she did then.

It didn't.

She struggled in vain as he turned her around and yanked her to her feet so he could breathe his hot, liquor-drenched breath into her face. "You think you're better than me, eh? You deserve that more than me?" She opened her mouth to scream, but he backhanded her cheek, and the sound died as a sob wrenched from her throat. It wouldn't do any good anyway. No one would come to her aid even if they heard her.

She flailed in time to her racing heart, hoping for a stroke of the luck that had abandoned her.

He fought to wrest her thrashing body under his control, bruising her arms and wrists in the process, and he was winning.

So finally, in a last-ditch effort to at least gain enough distance and control to be able to ram her knee into his groin, she dug her heels into the ground and pitched all her weight back against his grasp, forcing him to try to yank her back with all his own strength—and then went limp.

The sudden release of the tension caused him to stumble backward.

And then, it happened: Temoth looked upon her with favor once more.

The man's heel caught on something. He tripped, and as he

lost his balance, he let go of her—and fell backward.

She staggered away, regaining her own balance, and prepared to run...

Until she noticed that he wasn't moving.

She froze. *What...?*

His eyes were frozen in wide-eyed astonishment, and no breath formed in the air in front of his parted lips. Her heart still hammering, she crept closer.

A jagged stone stuck out from the side of the wall near where he lay, and the end of the stone was smeared with a dark substance. After a moment of hesitation, she rolled the man over. His hair was wet and matted. She touched the back of his head with a trembling hand and turned her fingers in the light.

Blood.

Burning skies, I killed him! Her recently devoured hot buns rose in her throat on a tide of acid.

She swallowed hard, determined to keep the little food she had where it belonged.

Her mind raced, and the thought flipped over into a new light. *I killed him!*

She hadn't done it on purpose, of course, but no one would care that it had been an accident, or that she had acted in self-defense. If they found her here with a body, the consequence would be worse than being hustled off to a workhouse for begging.

She frantically wiped the blood off her fingers onto the man's own clothes and ran.

A week later, huddled against a less friendly wall, she was cursing herself. Why hadn't she stolen his gloves, his cloak—his shirt even? It wasn't as if the march of guards had been imminent. For that matter, he might have had coins in his pocket.

She still wasn't thinking enough like one of *them*. That was why she was barely surviving.

It was a bitter irony that her exceptional education was apparently useless to her now.

She dragged a finger through the grit on the ground, starting to trace the Xambrian word for *cold*, and then thought better of it and drew her hand back under her cloak.

The weather had turned even more bitter this week. Her fingers and toes were growing numb as the temperature had fallen along with the night. The cold seeped into her so thoroughly that she could even forget the hollow ache in her stomach for a time.

How did the others manage it? If she didn't find somewhere warmer to sleep, she would die out here, for sure, sooner or later.

She touched the pocket of her trousers, where her sister's necklace had traveled with her all these months. It might buy her gloves and food for a week. And she would still be shivering on the streets.

She clenched her fist together and pulled the necklace into her lap. A last resort.

When she thought she couldn't bear it anymore—were the workhouses so bad, really?—light flooded her corner of the world.

She blinked, eyes watering against the suddenness of it.

"Are you cold?" a male voice said from above her—presumably the person holding the lantern. She couldn't see any more than that blinding light.

She shrank back against the wall, the memory of what had happened the last time a man had spoken to her still too fresh in her mind, and then she sprang to the side and half-ran, half-stumbled down the alley. She put as much distance between him and her as fast as her frozen body would allow before realizing that he wasn't following her.

She turned a corner, stopped, and pressed herself back against the wall. She didn't hear any footsteps. Indeed, he hadn't even made an attempt to grab at her.

Another few moments passed with no sign of pursuit, so she peered around the corner.

The alley was dark.

She closed her eyes and breathed out in relief.

She heard nothing. No scrape of a boot against the stones. No rustle of fabric. Not even the soft whisper of breath.

But the darkness within her eyelids lessened. She opened her eyes. Light spilled forward, casting her own shadow and that of someone else on the ground in front of her.

Her heart thudded double-time as she dared to turn. The same man stood behind her, this time closer.

Where in the abyss had he come from?

He made no move toward her, spoke no other words. Just stared at her, holding that same blinding light. She crept backward, as if there were some insane chance he hadn't noticed her, until she was out of his reach. Then she turned and fled again. This time, she ran for longer.

She finally stumbled to a halt, hands on her knees, breath coming in short, misty gasps in the cold night air. She sank back against another wall to wait for her heart to slow but kept her eyes wide open this time. She strained her eyes to catch any sliver of the yellow light, but only the half-lidded moon in the sky above illuminated the alley.

At last, she was convinced that she had lost him. She straightened up again, turned—

And ran right into the man, who had snuck up behind her in the darkness, his lantern now shielded.

She recoiled, but he grabbed her arm and held her fast—though he made no further move to thwart another escape attempt.

Instead, he flipped over her arm and forced her frozen fingers open. He ran his gloved thumb over the fingertips.

The burst of energy that fear had given her drained away and immobilized her instead. She was now unable to do anything else but watch him as he caressed her fingers as though they—her *fingers*—were a long-lost lover.

Finally, he dropped her hand. He unshielded the lantern and she flinched back from the light once more.

She squinted at him. "Who are you?" she managed to squeeze through her chattering jaw, though her lips were so cold it came out more like, "Huahyu?"

"Are you cold?" he asked once again.

What in the abyss? Was he mocking her? "Of course I'm cold," she answered at last.

He didn't seem to care that he was blinding her. Instead, he regarded her silently, long enough that her eyes adjusted, and she could finally see the stranger clearly, though his face was shrouded in the hood of a fur-lined cloak. The ensemble was complete with sturdy boots and the thick fingers of gloves wrapped around the handle of the lantern.

He looked so *warm*. Annoyance spiked through her fear. Were the slums offering tours to wealthy folk now, so as to assure them that they were in no danger of descending to these depths? "What do you want?" she asked. "Do you intend to stand there blinding me with your lantern all night?"

He looked at his lantern and then back at her. "You don't speak like a street urchin."

Why in the abyss did it matter how she spoke? What was wrong with him?

When he still didn't move, she gathered herself up and made to move away. Maybe if she didn't run this time...

"Where are you going?" he asked.

She turned. "To another cold wall to die in peace."

"Come with me." He began to turn, as though he expected no protest.

She laughed, though it sounded more like a hiccough. "Right."

He paused. Without turning, he said, "My house is warm, and I will feed you."

Her body shuddered and her stomach ached at the words.

No. Ivana, no. It was profoundly foolish to follow a strange man with no way of knowing what he really intended. Hadn't she already made enough foolish decisions for a lifetime?

He walked away.

But what were her other options? To freeze to death on this bitterly cold night? To give herself up to the workhouses and hope to Temoth that she wouldn't be skimmed by slavers or pimps? Even if the stranger had no better intentions, she would be no worse off. Right?

Against her better judgment, but without other recourse, she hurried to catch up with him.

Chapter Two

The stranger led Ivana to a modest house near the southern wall of the city. The neighborhood was near the sprawling commercial district that encompassed the docks, far enough away from the slums Ivana had made her home in that she noticed a change in the ambient odor in the air—or lack thereof.

She had become used to the stench of rotting garbage. It followed them for a while until she realized that at some point she smelled herself.

A middle-aged woman met them at the door, which alleviated some of Ivana's fears. His wife? Surely, if his intentions were malicious, he would not have brought her home to his wife.

"I have a guest," he said without preamble once the door had closed behind them. "Prepare a late dinner for her." He held up a finger. "But first, draw a bath. She stinks."

The woman eyed her but curtsied without comment, which

dispelled the theory that she was his wife. More likely, a house-keeper. Still. That seemed normal, right?

The strange man disappeared, and the woman did as he asked.

The bath felt heavenly. Ivana hadn't had such a bath since she had fled home. No, since before they had left Kadmon's estate. Ten, eleven months?

Had it been that long?

It was difficult to tell if the ache in her gut intensified because of that thought or because her limbs had thawed enough that she could now pay more attention to the emptiness of her stomach.

She might have preferred to eat first and bathe later, especially given that the housekeeper provided her with only a clean, soft robe when she was done drying off, but in either sequence, *his* orders had satisfied—or were about to satisfy—her most pressing needs.

The housekeeper led her to a dining table that could hold six or eight people. An empty plate and clean cutlery had been set out at one end. It was the promise of a meal to come, which her stomach was eagerly anticipating, and noisily, now that she was warm. The man sat at the opposite end of the table, but he had no place setting; Ivana supposed he had already eaten.

Ivana lowered herself into the seat across from him, and the housekeeper scurried away.

He watched Ivana. Silently. In fact, aside from his terse commands when they had entered, no one had spoken. Not even the presumed housekeeper, who had been more concerned with carrying out her employer's orders than conversation.

She didn't dare speak first. So she shifted uncomfortably under his gaze and fingered her sister's rose necklace, which she had fastened around her neck when the housekeeper had made her change out of her filthy clothes.

Finally, the housekeeper brought out several silver-lidded platters and a pitcher of beer.

The smells wafting from the platters were almost too much to bear, but she held herself, waiting for the man's leave—if only to prove to herself that she could still act like a civilized person.

The housekeeper lifted off the lids, prepared a plate for her, and then stood back. "Dal, by your leave? I'm later than usual," she said.

The man held one hand up in vague dismissal, and she curtsied again and disappeared back through what Ivana assumed was the kitchen door.

Ivana watched her go with dismay. Now, she and the strange man were alone. No witnesses. No one to hear her if she screamed.

She almost laughed at her own melodramatic thoughts until she reflected that her situation was actually that bad.

There had been no one who cared about her screams for a very long time.

She stared down at her plate, her mouth watering. This wasn't just a meal. This was a feast, especially for mid-winter. Rare roast beef with braised turnips and sesame oil, sweet barley cakes, and boiled eggs. Was this how this man ate all the time? Was he some middling noble who chose to locate his city home near where he did the most business?

That thought was almost worse than her previous. She had suffered more than enough at the hand of nobles; what irony would it be that her supposed benefactor was yet another?

"Are you not going to eat?" the man asked, breaking the long silence.

She looked up to find him still watching her. "I—by your leave, Dal?" she stammered, unnerved by his scrutiny.

"Obviously."

She swallowed and inclined her head.

Her manners and the man's gaze were forgotten the moment the food touched her tongue. In no time the plate was empty again, and she filled and emptied it twice over before she began to feel sated.

The man didn't speak to her while she was eating, and as she finally slowed, she became conscious again of his gaze.

She flushed and wiped her mouth with the napkin set on the table above her plate. *Now I find out what he wants with me,* she thought. He didn't seem the type to pluck a waif off the street out of the kindness of his heart, and if his purpose were carnal—or *only* carnal—why feed her first?

She hesitated and then lifted her eyes to meet his. For the first time, she studied the stranger more closely. The tone of his skin was the creamy medium beige of native Setanans, so that told her nothing more than that he was likely from Cadmyr, Weylyn, or Arlana. His hair and eyes were dark brown to match. He was of average height for a man and had a medium build—from what she could tell, given his loose-fitting clothing—and, indeed, he seemed middle-aged.

Everything about his physical appearance was unremarkable.

Except his eyes. They were penetrating, as if they could cut right through her every thought. He didn't look away at her scrutiny, and the continued silence became once again uncomfortable.

Finally, she couldn't take it anymore. "You've been uncommonly kind," she said. "Thank you."

He didn't respond immediately, in word or gesture. When

he did, it was as if she hadn't spoken. "Why were you on the streets?"

She hadn't expected that question. Her name, perhaps, or finally an indication of what he wanted from her, but not that. Was he a slaver, perhaps, looking to make easy money by abducting beggars who looked like they could be nursed back to a salable state?

And where did she even begin? "I-I-I don't—"

"Don't stutter. It's irritating." His eyes swept over her. "You're from Ferehar."

She swallowed. An obvious enough observation, given the deep amber-bronze tone of her skin. "Yes, Dal."

"A long way from home."

Was he trying to determine if anyone would miss her?

The food in her stomach was heavy. There was no one. None at all. Not anymore. Because of her own foolishness.

She found herself taking a few gulps of air in response to a tightening feeling in her lungs. She looked down at her lap and curled her hands into fists. She had lived with the struggle to meet her most basic needs for too long. Now that they had been met in full, at least temporarily, the reminder of how she had ended up here swept in to fill the void—and she didn't want to have this stranger prying and prodding her about it. "Let me save you the trouble, Dal," she said quietly. "My father and mother are dead, and my sister—" Her voice broke, and her hand went reflexively to the rose pendant again. "If you intend me for ill use, there is no one alive who would rise to my defense. Please, may we skip the feigned pleasantries?"

He was silent for long enough that she felt the need to look back up at him if only to see what he was doing.

He was doing nothing. Only watching her, his face impassive and unreadable. "You're afraid of me," he said, not quite a question, but almost.

She had been. She still was—a bit. But right now resignation and despair were competing with that fear—and winning. But how could she explain that? "Wouldn't you be?"

To her surprise, he chuckled. It wasn't the sort of chuckle one might expect in response to a jest; instead, it was low and soft, as though to himself, and he wore no smile to match his supposed merriment. "What's your name?"

She furrowed her brow. She didn't understand his game. "Ivana," she replied. Not Ana. She would never be Ana again.

"Ivana." He rolled the name around on his tongue, as if tasting it. "Ivana. You may be assured that you are quite safe from *ill-use* while here." He stood up. "Follow."

Once again, Ivana felt as though she had little choice but to follow the stranger. With a lamp in his hand, he led her down a short hall and to a room that was barely large enough to deserve the moniker—it was more of a large closet.

He ushered her inside. "You will stay here," he said. "And you will dine with me when I am home. When I am not, my housekeeper will see to your needs."

Ivana was speechless. He didn't intend to mistreat her—or so he said—and had opened his home to her with no conditions, for no apparent reason? "I... What do you want from me in return?"

"Nothing," he said. "But perhaps one day I'll find a use for you."

He secured the lamp to a bracket on the wall and turned to leave.

"Dal," she said.

He waited but didn't turn around.

"May I know your name?" she asked.

There was a long pause and then, "Elidor." With that, he disappeared into the darkness of the hall.

Ivana turned around once in the tiny room; there was room to do little else. The only pieces of furniture were a cot, on which someone—she presumed the housekeeper—had laid out a clean dress and a nightgown, and a small stand holding an empty washbasin with a cracked mirror above it. A single step would take her to the cot, and the step she had already taken into the room had brought her in front of the washbasin. The half-shelf above it held a clock, and the shelf under it held a pitcher of clear water, a chunk of soap, and a hand towel.

And then there was the mirror. She took a step back and bumped into the cot. It was the first time she had seen such a clear reflection of herself since leaving Ferehar. She hardly recognized the gaunt face and hollow eyes staring back at her. She looked every bit the part of a beggar, except cleaner—now. The gods only knew what she must have looked like when her face had been filthy and her hair tangled, and how she must have stunk! It was no wonder she hadn't convinced anyone to hire her.

The rose pendant that hung at the end of her sister's necklace rested beneath the hollow of her throat. The bright, delicate flower was out of place against the canvas of her leaden countenance.

She was tired. She wanted to lie down and, frankly, never get up again. She sank down on the cot, propped her back against the wall, and crushed her knees to her chest with her arms—as though if she could only compact herself enough, she might squeeze the aching in her chest right out of herself.

It didn't work. Instead, she stared at the pitcher of water and the light flickering on its glazed surface. She wished the lump in her throat would break and provide some sort of imagined release through tears.

Except that never worked, either. She cried, and nothing ever changed. No amount of tears would bring back everything she had lost. Her sobs could never erase the terrible mistakes she had made that had ruined them all.

The futility was maddening. Something inside her urged her to scream, to lash out, to punch the bed, or even the wall—as though that would somehow release the pain. But that wouldn't work, either.

Why had she fought for survival for so long, anyway? What had been her goal? To restart a life for herself, empty and alone?

The light danced a different step for a moment—an unfelt movement in the air, perhaps, or a piece of the burned wick falling down. But it caught on something on the floor, under the lower shelf of the washbasin—a glimmer, a reflection on a polished surface, perhaps.

She sat up straight again, reached down to feel under the shelf, and pulled out a small blade, like one a man might use to shave.

She stared down at it and turned it around in her hand. She didn't want to die. But neither did she want to exist in this wreckage known as her life.

She ran her thumb over the blade lightly, absently, and recoiled as it bit into her skin.

Stupid. What had she expected?

Blood welled up from the cut, and she grabbed the towel to press it against her thumb for a few moments.

She peeled it away, examined the tiny wound, and then nodded in satisfaction. Barely a paper cut. The pain had lasted but a few moments.

There and then gone. So easy, so quick. If only her life could mimic that little cut.

She drew the razor gently across her forearm. Blood beaded up from the cut once again. So...*controlled*.

It was hardly even a conscious decision that drove her hand to make another cut and then another. The screams inside fell silent. The aching in her chest, instead of threatening to rip her apart from the inside out, seeped from her skin. It was...comforting. While the cuts were stinging, she could forget.

I'm going crazy, she thought.

As if to prove to herself she wasn't, she wiped off the razor and put it on the lower shelf. She then lay back down on the cot with the towel wedged between the inside of her arm and her body, and finally fell asleep.

Outsider

A year and eight months ago

*I*nterestingly, Old Fereharian does not appear to be related to any of the other languages of the continent. Of course, having no written form, it is difficult to—

"Ana, look at this."

Ivana cradled her forehead in one hand and shifted to bring herself closer to her book and farther from the disturbance. *—it is difficult to compare as one might—*

"Ana?"

Ivana blinked. *Oh.* She tore her eyes away and lifted her head to see what her father was looking at. He had one eye pressed to the end of a wooden tube and was peering through it and down to a thin pane of glass that rested beneath.

She sighed but smiled. His latest project: the microscope. They were relatively new, and only a handful of scholars at the universities around Setana had them yet. Her father had no hope of purchasing one himself on his wages, even had they been easy to obtain.

So he had made one.

When she didn't get up, he looked up from the device and gestured to her.

She placed a bookmark in the book, set it aside, and went to her father so she could see what had him so excited this time.

"Go on," he said. "Take a look."

She obediently looked through the tube, stared for a moment, mystified, and then slid the glass out from under the tube to see what the sample was. It held a segment of a thin leaf. She put it back and looked again. *Burning skies.* Hundreds of spidery lines surrounded dozens of orderly boxes. His microscope had never shown this much detail before. "We've studied leaves before," she said. "What changed?"

He grinned and slid a thick circle of glass—a lens, he called it, like from a pair of spectacles—out of the body of the microscope. "I finally perfected the glass lenses," he said. "Isn't it amazing?"

She had to admit it was. "Have the scholars at the universities seen this?"

"Who knows? And even if they haven't, they aren't going to listen to a personal tutor with his crude, homemade microscope." He glanced at the clock on the mantel. "Oh—" He set aside the notebook he had just picked up, no doubt intending to make a note, and instead picked up his hat and set it on his head. He gave her a kiss on the forehead. "Can't be late for the young lord's afternoon session," he said with a wink, then left.

Ivana shook her head. She picked up his notebook and flipped absently through it. A year's worth of notes and discoveries, the latest of the notebooks he had made over the years. He had dozens of them locked away in a chest in her parents' bedroom.

His talents were wasted on those brats. By now, he ought to have been at one of the universities researching and mentoring other promising young scholars and disseminating his discoveries for the benefit of all Setana.

He had started on that path, but he had given it up when he'd married her mother and she'd become pregnant with Ivana. Now, he was here, in their home region of Ferehar, tutoring the four children of Lord Kadmon.

He had a family to take care of and tutoring for a noble paid better than being a fledgling scholar.

The front door swung open, and she set the notebook down quickly, afraid it was her father having forgotten something—he was protective of his notebooks—but it was only her younger sister, Izel.

She flew in the door like a bird before a storm. "Ana, are you still in here?" she chided. "It's a gorgeous day, and I'm walking to town for some cider. Come with me!"

Ivana looked toward her book, but Izel moved between Ivana and the table and picked the book up. She paged through it and raised an eyebrow at Ivana. "You shouldn't leave these lying around," she said. "If someone were to search our house..."

Ivana snatched the book out of her hand, removed it to their room, and locked it in her trunk.

When she returned to the living room, Izel made a face at her. "I don't know why you even take such terrible risks."

"Mama says you can't understand a culture until you understand the people's language."

"We're not *supposed* to be learning other languages," Izel said. "It's forbidden, if you recall." She tugged on her arm. "Come on, before Mama comes in from hanging the wash and finds some chore for us to do!"

Ivana sighed. She supposed she could use the chance to stretch her legs. She had been cloistered in the house all day, and a frothy mug of cider at the end of a brisk walk would be nice—especially on one of the first nice days since winter had begun to lose ground to the creep of spring. She retrieved her coin purse, tucked it into the pocket sewn on the inside of her sleeve, and joined Izel, who had already opened the door again.

"Good," Izel said smugly. "I would hate to have had to threaten you."

"Threaten me?" Ivana asked, following Izel out the door.

"Yes. With telling Mama and Papa about your thing with Cern."

Ivana halted, flushing. "What? How do you know about that?"

Izel rolled her eyes. "*Everyone* knows about that."

What rumors had Cern being spreading exactly? She shouldn't have let him kiss her. But she had just wanted to feel, for once, that she wasn't an outsider among the others her age on Lord Kadmon's estate and in town. For a few minutes, she had felt appreciated.

Ivana set her jaw and marched forward again, trying to cool her cheeks by force of will alone. "It wasn't a *thing*," she said. "It was a little bit of kissing. That's it."

Izel smirked, but she wisely said nothing further.

Until they reached the clothier, that is.

Ivana hung back as Izel pressed her hands against the glass window and gazed at the dress displayed there.

"It's so gorgeous," Izel said with a sigh.

Ivana eyed the gauzy dress critically. With winter finally giving way to spring, the other girls had been anticipating discovering what that year's new summer fashions would be. Ironic that Ivana would end up being one of the first to find out, considering what little interest she had in the subject.

The sleeves came down to just above the elbow, where they split and hung free for another handspan. The shoulders held up a plunging neckline, and virtually no back. "Where's the back of the dress?" she asked, incredulous.

"It's the latest style from the cities," Izel said, a hint of reproach in her voice.

"It's a wonder it stays up at all."

"Oh, please," Izel said. "If you were a noble, you'd be wearing one, whatever you thought of it."

"Well, I'm not." Ivana craned her neck to see the advertised price. "And nor could either of us ever afford such a thing. Do they raise the price in correlation to how little material the dress contains?"

"It would look fabulous on you," Izel said, looking Ivana up and down.

There was the tiniest bit of jealousy in her voice, and Ivana found herself flushing again. Ivana wrapped her arms around her bosom, which had blossomed rapidly in the past year—far beyond that of other girls her age.

"Let's go," she said. "Staring at it isn't going to make it more within our reach."

Izel moved away from the window without further comment.

Ivana, however, found herself glancing back as they continued down the street. It would look good on her, wouldn't it? The way that neckline plunged...

The thought of the attention it would draw from *real* men gave her a tiny thrill, and she shivered.

Foolishness.

The word was in her father's voice.

They walked in silence for a moment until Izel looked at her out of the corner of her eye. "So," she said. "How was it?"

"How was what?"

"You know. With Cern?"

Ivana glanced at Izel. She appeared to be perfectly serious, even *eager* to hear the details.

She frowned. "It was all right, I guess."

"All right? *All right?* That's not how those silt novels you've been reading make it sound."

Ivana's eyes widened. "What—how—!"

Izel smirked again. "I found one under our pallet. Fascinating stuff."

"You shouldn't be reading those filthy things," Ivana said.

"Oh, and you should? You're only a year older than me, Ana."

Ivana swallowed. "A year and a half. And it's research."

Izel snorted. "For *what*? Future encounters with Cern?"

Not on her life. "All Cern and I did was kiss a little bit. Besides, Cern is a child. The men in those stories are..."

"Experienced?"

"Different."

Izel harrumphed and appeared to be ready to belabor the point when a long whistle sounded.

"Ana! Heard about you and Cern. Got any left for us?" Whooping laughter rang out from a group of boys loitering on the street ahead. One of them made a rude gesture near his groin.

Ivana's fists clenched tightly. "Tell Cern," she said, once they had approached, "that if he spreads any more lies—"

"You'll what? Suffocate him between your melons?" They laughed again

"Come on, Ana," Izel said, tugging on her sleeve with one hand and fiddling with the rose pendant she wore around her neck on a fine chain with the other.

Ivana turned away, her face red from more than embarrassment. Stupid, childish—

"Aw, Ana, don't be mad," another boy, named Tavil, said. "At least you *have* something." He snickered.

Izel flushed, ducked her head, and hurried forward.

Ivana whirled around, and before she could think, she punched Tavil square on the nose.

He yelped and stumbled back, then yelped again when blood spurted from his nose. He glared at Ivana, but she had achieved her goal; he and his friends dispersed.

Ivana rolled her shoulders and flexed her hand. That had felt good—but burning skies, her knuckles hurt.

Izel gaped at her. "Oh, Ana—you shouldn't have! If Mama and Papa find out—"

"They won't. That idiot isn't going to go spreading a story of how a girl decked him." She sniffed. "Come on. I could really use that cider now."

Ivana and Izel chose a table near the door in The Golden Chalice—the nicer of the two town taverns—and ordered a single cider and a plate of honey cakes to share. They split the cost—one selma each, a sixth of their respective monthly allowances. It was an expensive treat for them, but worth it every once in a while.

As they waited for the server to bring their order, Ivana eyed the mistress of the inn. She was hanging a notice on the door. Once she moved out of the way, Ivana read the notice. Apparently, they were looking for extra help.

"What's so interesting over there?" Izel twisted round in her chair to follow Ivana's gaze, and then she spun back, her eyes alight. "Think Mama and Papa would let us work here? We could earn some extra coins..."

"I doubt it," Ivana said. Still, she eyed the notice. The idea of working was appealing. It would distinguish her from idiots like Cern.

The server plunked the cider and honey cakes down in the middle of the table, and at the same time, the door to the tavern swung open again.

The man who stepped through could have stepped out of one of those silt novels. He was tall, young, and handsome, and he had a creamy beige complexion with a layer of bronze underneath—typical of someone who was only part-Fereharian. He stopped for a moment, his eyes scanning the interior of the tavern. They flitted over their table and then roved back. His eyes met her gaze, and, incredibly, he smiled at her.

She turned around, certain that he must have been looking at someone else, but when she turned back, his smile had grown.

She flushed, gave him a tiny smile back, and ducked her head, embarrassed to be caught staring.

To her horror, a moment later he had approached their table. "Ladies," he said, his voice as warm as his skin. "Only one cider today?"

Izel's eyes were wide and her mouth open. She swallowed. "Uh—well, we can't really afford—"

Ivana kicked her under the table, and Izel swiveled her head to look at her, her brow furrowed.

"No reason to overdo it," Ivana said, conjuring up her most mature voice.

His eyes twinkled. "Indeed," he said. He smiled again, rapped the table with his knuckles once, and moved on to the bar.

"Burning skies," Izel said, staring after him. "What's he doing in a place like this?"

Ivana frowned at her. "Stop gawking," she said. "This is a respectable tavern; why shouldn't he stop on the way to wherever he's going?"

Still, Ivana had to force herself not to turn around to see what he was doing.

It didn't matter. He was being kind to a pair of girls, that was all.

Except then, her head jerked up as he reappeared at the side of their table.

He picked up their mug of cider, set it directly in front of Izel, and set down another mug in front of Ivana. "Hard to overdo it on cider," he said, amusement still in his voice, and then he returned to the bar without another word.

Ivana was perplexed. Had he *bought* them another drink? Surely he must know they couldn't pay him back.

She took a long drink of the cider, then coughed and put it back down, her eyes watering.

It was cider, but made stronger than she ever drank it.

"Something wrong with it?" Izel asked.

Ivana steeled herself and took another long drink. "No," she said. "It's just fine." She did turn, then, to look at the stranger. He was watching her, and when he saw her glance his way, he winked before turning back to the bar.

What did *that* mean? Had he given her his drink by accident? But no, he would have figured that out by now. She stared down into the mug, feeling a little nervous.

Izel began chattering away, the incident forgotten, but Ivana was quiet. She finished the cider, not wanting him to think she couldn't handle it—though, in truth, it burned her throat and stomach.

The handsome stranger didn't stop to speak to them again on his way out, but he did favor Ivana with another smile before leaving the inn.

This time, it went straight to her gut, and her stomach

churned in a way it never had before. Maybe it was the alcohol.

"I think he likes you," Izel said.

She turned back to look at Izel. "What? Oh, don't be ridiculous. He thinks we're sweet little girls, that's all."

Izel downed the rest of her cider. "Didn't smile like that at me," she said into her mug, and then she stood up and winked at Ivana. "Come on. We should get back."

Ivana was still too shaken to consider the irony that it was her little sister dragging her home.

Chapter Three

Elidor's eyes were on her again. But they weren't always on her face, and she had never seen him look at her body, not like other men she had encountered did at least. Right now, his gaze was on her hands, as it often was when he was home and they ate together. Watching as she cut through eggs. Buttered bread. Pushed food around her plate.

She shifted, making sure the sleeves of her shirt covered her forearms and the wounds there. They were covered, but she felt self-conscious about them anyway. She didn't want to have to answer questions.

Her desperation for food and warmth had lessened even after only a few weeks of living with those needs met at Elidor's home, and with it, her desperation to take her mind off her isolation had grown. Each night, her internal state was only mirrored and magnified by the darkness until she lit her lantern and reached for the blade again. It helped her calm herself enough to fall asleep; the past few nights, she had stopped even trying to fall asleep first.

She existed merely for the sake of existing, with only herself for company—and her own company was dismal. So she had finally determined to ask a question she had been avoiding—maybe because she didn't want to know the answer.

"Dal," she said, putting down her fork, unnerved once again by his gaze. "Am I allowed to leave the house?"

He raised his eyes to hers. Impassive yet probing. "You're not a prisoner."

"So...that means yes?"

"Where would you go?"

"Well, I was thinking now that I look a little less like a starved beggar, perhaps I might try to find work again."

His eyes drifted to her hands again. "Work? Doing what?"

"I—my father—" She halted and drew in a sharp breath. It was the first time she had said those words aloud since...

"I am well-educated," she said instead, "and have some skill with science and language. I thought—"

"Language?"

He sounded intrigued, and a spike of fear went through her. It was illegal to learn foreign languages. It didn't matter whose house she lived in. The Conclave would gladly drag away any commoner professing to know languages other than Setanan. So she clarified. "Reading. Writing. Grammar." She cleared her throat. "Of course." The words sounded unconvincing even in her own ears.

But he didn't press her. Instead, he settled back in his chair. "So you think to hire yourself out as a tutor—or copyist perhaps?"

"Perhaps."

"Those who can afford tutors hire learned adults, not children."

Ivana pressed her lips together. At seventeen, she was hardly a child. "But perhaps those who can't afford a learned adult might settle," she said stiffly.

One of his eyebrows twitched.

Thinking the conversation was at an impasse, she redirected the course of the conversation. "On that subject, I noticed you have a library."

Elidor had provided her no means by which to occupy herself. She had explored the house as much as she dared and had noticed the small library the other day through a windowed door.

When he didn't reply, she forged on. "Since I am unable to do anything more productive, might I borrow some books?"

He raised an eyebrow. "Books?"

"Yes. Books. To read. Something that both learned adults and learned *children* enjoy."

His facial expression didn't change—it rarely varied by much—but it took him a moment to answer. Almost as if he were turning over the pros and cons of allowing her free reign in his library. "Very well," he said at last.

Thank Temoth. It would take her mind off her troubles, anyway. Assuming they didn't instead remind her of that time a lifetime ago when she would sit with her father long into the night, reading while he conducted his experiments.

"You might find Barthen's latest treatise of interest," he said.

She furrowed her brow. His sudden conversational tone was unnerving. "Sativola Barthen? He released that two years ago." Not long before everything had begun to go wrong, in fact.

"I see you're already familiar. What did you think?"

Barthen was a renowned scholar at the University in Weylyn City, known best for his work with plants. His latest treatise had forged into new territory. "He should have stuck to categorizing plants," she finally replied. "The idea that because something can't be seen with the naked eye, it must not exist, is ludicrous."

"Really? And what leads you to that proclamation?"

She looked away, not wanting him to see the tears that sprang to her eyes. What conversations she and her father would have had about Barthen...

They had never had the opportunity.

Elidor let the silence fill the room, then waved his hand and spoke as if he hadn't mentioned Barthen in the first place. "You may certainly try to find work. But when you fail, come to me. I may have found a use for you."

Taken off-guard, she just nodded.

He stood and left without a word, as he usually did, leaving his housekeeper to clear the table, and leaving Ivana alone.

He was...strange.

And yet, he had made no moves to hurt or misuse her. He had never visited her in her room. In fact, she rarely saw him except at the occasional meals he insisted she share with him.

The housekeeper, who she now knew was named Da Veryna, took her plate, and Ivana nodded her thanks. Then a thought struck her. Would Veryna have any further insight on her odd employer? She was kind but didn't speak to Ivana much. She seemed as confused by Ivana's presence as Ivana herself was. "Da," Ivana said. "How long have you been in the service of Dal Elidor?"

Veryna turned to look at her. "About five years." She nodded, as though anticipating a follow-up question. "He's a strange one, I'll give you. Keeps to himself mostly. Sometimes makes unreasonable demands. But he pays well, and since he's gone so often, I can't rightly complain."

"What does he do?" Ivana had wondered, but she had been hesitant to ask Elidor himself. His demeanor didn't invite questions.

Veryna wrinkled her nose. "Something for the government," she said. "But I don't know what."

"That's all right." Ivana paused. "I was thinking of going out tomorrow. Is there an extra cloak lying around here I could use?"

"I don't know, but I'll find something for you." Veryna hesitated. "Some might call him unkind, Da, but he's never laid a hand on me, not ever, to this day, and he's always composed in speech." She twisted her apron in her hands. "I don't know why he's brought you here. He's not given to charity. But I think you're safe." She nodded. "I think you're safe."

Ivana gave her a tight smile. "Thank you."

Veryna curtsied and left with the dishes.

Was that reassuring, or not? If he didn't intend to harm her—and as Veryna noted, he likely hadn't rescued her out of the kindness of his heart—why had he brought her here?

Her brief conversation with Veryna raised more questions than it had answered, and Ivana retreated to her room to face the darkness again.

Now that she had Elidor's blessing, Ivana determined to begin her search for work the next day. She bundled herself up in the cloak Veryna had found and struck out.

She began with the places most likely to need a copyist: the library, and then a bank, and then a solicitor's office. But all professed to have no need of help—though the amusement and sometimes scorn in their voices told her they wouldn't have hired her even if they had needed it.

She moved on to shops, entering each and inquiring up and down each street in the nearby commercial district until she had almost returned to where she had started, with no leads. Finally, she came to one of the last shops, looked up at the sign, and was surprised to find that it was an apothecary.

She hesitated on the stoop, staring up at that sign and the apothecary's mark: a lush, fern-like leaf. It seemed simultaneously eons ago and only yesterday that she had stood on another apothecary's stoop, but not here in Carradon.

"Can I help you?"

Ivana stepped back and blinked, startled. A young man stood in the doorframe, a quizzical look on his face. She had been so lost in her own thoughts that she hadn't even heard the door open.

"I...ah...was looking for...um..." She couldn't get her words out clearly.

His quizzical look changed not to irritation, as she might have thought, but a gentle amusement. "The apothecary? Then you've found it." He opened the door for her to enter.

Not knowing what else to do, she nodded to him mutely and moved into the store.

Her nose was accosted with a riot of smells. Rose and citrus, from a rack of petals and peels in the window, drying in the sun. The earthy smell of roots and saffron, the tang of cumin and cinnamon, and the unmistakable unpleasant odor of aloe.

She wrinkled her nose. In fact, the aloe was particularly unpleasant here. *Was* that even aloe?

The young man rubbed at the back of his head and shrugged. "I, ah, sorry for the smell. A little experiment of mine went a bit wrong."

She turned her eyes toward him. He was wearing an apron and had stepped behind the counter, so she assumed he worked here. "Experiment?"

His eyes brightened. "Aloe and star-leaf," he said. "It didn't turn out well—or at least it doesn't smell too well. See, aloe can help relieve labored breathing, and I've found that star-leaf has similar properties, so I wondered what would happen if..." He flushed. "Well, I guess you're not interested in the details."

"Star-leaf? Really?" she asked, curious.

"Yes...I, uh, not that I spend a lot of time inhaling it or anything." He coughed, and she hid a smile. Star-leaf was best known for its recreational, not medicinal, properties.

"It's also a phenomenal pain-reliever," she offered.

His eyes widened. "I've never heard that before."

He wouldn't have. Her father had discovered it.

An ache welled in her chest, and she clenched her fist so that her fingernails dug into her palms. *Remember why you're here.* "Are you the owner?"

He shook his head and laughed. "No. She's out right now, but I can help you with most purchases." His eyes swept over her once. "I don't think I've seen you in here before."

"I'm new to the city," she said. "Actually, I've been asking around, trying to find work...but I guess you wouldn't be the one to ask."

"That would be Da Grania. But I can tell you she doesn't need any help." He gestured toward himself, an apologetic smile on his face. "She keeps a constant flow of apprentices for that."

Ah. An apprentice.

That would have been an interesting line of work, had her life not taken such a swift turn for the worse.

"Is there something I can get for you?" he asked.

"No, that was all. Thank you for your time."

At least he hadn't looked at her like she was a blob of wayward mud on a freshly cleaned floor. In fact, right now, he was looking at her as though he were downright intrigued. "Feel free to come back anytime." He flushed again. "That is, I'd like to hear more about what you said about star-leaf." He fiddled with a piece of that same leaf that had fallen on the counter. "You can ask for Boden."

"Ivana," she replied politely.

Ivana. Somewhere, somehow, along the way, she had stopped being "Ana." She had never given that name again, not since she had told Airell her name was "Ivana."

Boden inclined his head and then gave her a sheepish smile.

His sweet and bashful demeanor made it almost impossible to remain in the darkness of her own mind. She couldn't help it. She returned his smile.

Ivana trudged back to Elidor's house, her head down and her hands grasping her cloak tightly around her, and almost ran into someone leaving a shop.

"Oh!" she exclaimed. "Your pardon, Dal."

The man she had run into waved his hand in front of his face, as though she were a bloodsprite that needed swatting away, and hurried on his way.

She glanced at the door he had appeared through. The sign hanging above it was shaped like a horse and proclaimed the establishment not as a shop, but as The White Stallion Inn and Tavern.

And a *help wanted* sign hung on the door.

Her heart sped up even as her stomach sank. She hadn't had any luck finding work, and now the possibility of work had fallen in her lap.

An inn. She couldn't. She didn't even want to enter.

She gritted her teeth. That was ridiculous. Did she want to try to provide for herself or not? How long would she rely on

Elidor's charity? How long would he let her?

She took a deep breath and shoved open the door.

Dinner hadn't been served yet, but the inn was still busy—and warm. Both men and women warmed their hands near the fireplace and laughed over pints of beer. Serving girls, some looking not that much older than herself, delivered drinks and received sly winks from men who had had one too many.

She turned away, feeling sick.

"A table, Da?"

One of the serving girls stood in front of her holding an empty tray at her side.

"Uh. No," answered Ivana. "I-I wanted to inquire about the notice on the door."

The girl nodded toward the bar. "Have to ask Dyric about that," she said, then started to move off.

"Is it so bad?" Ivana blurted out. "Working here?"

The girl followed her gaze to a table where one of the other serving girls was leaning over a table, pushing a mug toward a man who was admiring the view.

The girl shrugged. "You know. You get used to it. And Dyric says being good-natured about it keeps the customers happy." She flicked a glance at the bar. "Sorry, Da, I need to go." She curtsied and scurried away.

The man at the table made a comment to the girl serving him, and she flushed but laughed it off—at least until she turned away and irritation flashed in her eyes.

The air in the room thinned; Ivana's chest burned and her head swam. She couldn't do this. Not every day, not all the time. Back home, it hadn't been like this. There it had been a friendly small-town tavern owned by a middle-aged widow. Back home, it had just been one man. One mistake.

Bile rose in her throat, and she turned and rushed out the

door before she drew more attention to herself. The cold air settled her stomach, but not the ache in her chest. Only one thing would do that.

She hurried back to Elidor's—and her razor.

Ivana had been defeated. She had tried for one day, and she wouldn't try again. Not after the inn. But she had to find something else to occupy herself, so she ventured out to find Elidor, ready to see what proposal he had for her. A few odd jobs to earn her keep, perhaps?

It was the first time she had sought him out. She had to go looking for Veryna in the kitchen to ask if Elidor was still at home, and if so, where she might find him. Veryna directed Ivana toward a door that Ivana had always found locked. Apparently, it led to Elidor's study.

Ivana didn't know what to expect to find there. As she walked down the hall, her imagination ran wild. Did he keep shrines to the heretic gods? Cages of bloodbane kept for experimentation? Torture devices for undefended waifs that he and Veryna, actually partners in wicked deeds, lured here?

By the time she reached his door, she was trembling, which was ridiculous. He was the one who had told *her* to come to *him*, after all. Nonetheless, her hand shook when she raised it to knock.

She received silence as an answer. She fidgeted while waiting. Veryna must have been wrong; he must have left his study.

She started to turn away when finally the bolt turned on the door, and it opened. Elidor stood at the door, regarding her with those strange, probing eyes.

"I-I—" she began, and then she remembered his admonition about stuttering. She forced the words out, plain and to the point. "I had no luck with work today, so I came to you as you asked."

He was going to send her away, she was certain of it—but finally he stood aside and gestured for her to enter.

The study could not have been more dissimilar to her imaginings. It was small and nondescript, with nothing strange-looking to match Elidor's personality. A large desk filled half of the room. An overstuffed chair sat in the corner to her left, next to a filled bookshelf. Directly across the room from her was a metal door—probably his safe room.

The only curiosity in the room was the painting on the wall behind the desk. She recognized the scene as one straight out of Setanan history: the execution of the last Aife, remembered by history to be an iron-fisted despot who had eventually received what was coming to him. Three men looked on, expressions fierce and triumphant. These were those who would become the first three Ri after they divided the land as it existed then between them. Beyond the Ri were indistinct masses, arms held high in celebration of the victory for the common people.

At least, that was what she had thought it had depicted. She had only ever seen small charcoal illustrations before, but the painting was full color and large. Those who had been faceless figures now had faces, and she could see their expressions—not of celebration, but of horror. Because of the execution of the Aife? No—behind the headless body of the Aife a line had been drawn in the sky, which was in the process of splitting into two lines, like a seam being ripped apart, and black flames licked out of the gap between.

She caught herself gaping at the painting. "What...?"

Elidor, who had continued across the room toward a row of cabinets while she'd halted to inspect the wall hanging, turned.

"Have you never seen *The Execution of the Last Aife* before?"

"I have," she said. "But not like this."

"Copies can be altered."

"*Altered?*"

"To fit the narrative, of course," he said. "*The Execution* was painted long before the Conclave's rise to power."

"The Aife was a Banebringer," she said, suddenly understanding.

He shrugged. "Can we know for sure? Perhaps it was thought so at one point, perhaps it's symbolic."

"But...why would that not fit the Conclave's narrative? An evil man, executed in a coup for his tyranny, turns out to be a Banebringer? Of course. That would make perfect sense. Evil begets evil."

Elidor paced closer to the painting and stared up at it, his hands behind his back. "You're missing something crucial."

She stared at it as well. Then it clicked. "Their faces."

"Whose faces?" It was a first: his voice carried something other than indifference. It was almost...eager.

"The Ri—they don't see it. They're so wrapped up in their victory that they don't realize their execution is about to unleash a terror on the land. And also the mass of people, because in contrast, they *do* see it."

"Yes," he said softly. "If the artist had painted different expressions on their faces, the entire meaning of the painting could change. So small, yet so important."

It could have been symbolic. It would depend on when the work was created, of course. She couldn't remember; art history wasn't a subject she had delved deeply into. If painted during the era directly after the despot's rule had ended, it might have been intended as literal—a memory of recent events, perhaps. But it wouldn't have been much later for it to take a more sinister, symbolic turn. The saviors of the masses in reality unleash a new horror: the war machine that came to be known as Setana, mercilessly swallowing land after foreign land on the backs of its people, perhaps?

It was fascinating; she reached up to touch the bottom of the painting before she realized what she was doing.

And then she felt Elidor's gaze on her. No, not her. On her arm.

Her sleeve had fallen back, revealing her self-inflicted wounds of the past weeks, many of which were healing, but a few of which were fresh.

She dropped her arm, flushing, but he grabbed it before she could tug her sleeve back down.

He turned her arm over to look at her forearm, and the new cuts from that afternoon started bleeding again as his grip pulled at the skin.

"You're—You're hurting me," she whispered.

He raised his eyes to meet hers but didn't let go.

For one tense moment, she was almost certain he didn't care. Her heart started pounding. The theory about him and Veryna luring unsuspecting girls here seemed more credible than ever. Perhaps that door didn't lead to his safe room. Perhaps it led to the chamber with all her other imaginings. And she had followed him into the most private room in his house.

He let go of her arm, and she cradled it close to her chest.

"You don't want those to get infected," he said. "I'll have my housekeeper send some ointment and bandages to your room."

She blinked. That was it? That was all he had to say?

He strode toward the cabinets on the other side of the room and threw open one of the doors.

All her fears were forgotten in an instant. There, on a shelf, sat a microscope.

Chapter Four

The microscope made her father's lovingly carved wooden version look like a child's plaything. Elidor's was made of burnished bronze, and the metalworking had attention to detail that was both pragmatic—such as the tiny clasps to hold a lens in place—and decorative.

The desire to both touch it and recoil from it warred within her. All at once, she was filled with an irrepressible longing born from warm memories that quickly turned to a hollow, heavy ache.

She wrapped her arms around her chest, trying to suppress the throbbing, and focused on the matter at hand. "I surmised you were well-off," she said to Elidor, "but I must have severely underestimated how much so if you own a microscope."

He removed the microscope from the cabinet and set it on his desk. "You've seen one before?"

She gave a tight nod. She didn't feel like explaining further. And he didn't ask her to. "All the better. It's on loan to me from the university."

The university had loaned him a microscope? How many were even in existence? "Da Veryna said you worked for the government."

Elidor removed a scrap of paper from one of the desk drawers. "You could say that."

"And...what services do you offer that warrant you getting to borrow a microscope?"

"I'm an analyst."

"An...analyst?"

He didn't respond.

"What do you analyze?" she pressed, unwilling to let it go now that he had given her a trickle of information.

"Trends in violent crime." He gestured to the microscope. "Do you know how to use this?"

There were people who studied trends in violence crime? She finally put her hand out to run a finger down the body of the device. "Yes," she said. "It's a little different than my..." She swallowed. *Just say it, Ivana. Will you choke on the words forever?* "My father's was. But it's not that complicated."

Elidor put the slip of paper he had been holding down on the desk. "I have reason to believe that this"—he tapped the paper—"might hold information critical to determining when a certain criminal might strike next."

She raised one eyebrow. "And this information will help you...analyze?"

He continued on as if she hadn't spoken. "But whoever wrote it managed to write in such small letters that I can't even read it with a magnifying glass." He pushed the microscope closer to her with one finger. "Hence the microscope."

Her other eyebrow went up. "Someone could write that small?"

He frowned. "You ask too many questions. Will you look at it or not?"

She shrugged. It was an odd request, but she didn't see the harm in agreeing.

So she finally took the paper, secured it in place with the clasps, and looked through the eyepiece.

The microscope had a knob on the side to adjust the magnification—a drastic improvement over her father's—and she twisted it until the letters came into focus.

She almost laughed when she saw what was on the paper. "I don't think the size of the letters is your problem," she said. "They're small, but not that small."

"What do you mean?"

"It's Xambrian, not Setanan. You must have assumed they were tiny, squished Setanan letters since you didn't recognize them."

Ivana looked up to see Elidor staring at her, his face unreadable.

And then she realized what she had said.

She scrambled away from the microscope. "That doesn't mean I know Xambrian!" she exclaimed, holding her hands out. *Damn!* "I recognize it, that's all. My mother—" But recognizing it was bad enough. Nothing she could say would make this better.

She backed toward the door, and once she reached it, she turned and tried it, but it was locked from the inside. When had he done that? She spun back around, her heart pounding. "You can't prove anything. I'll never admit—"

"Don't be naïve," he cut in. "Do you think the word of an orphaned Fereharian beggar girl would hold any weight compared to mine?" He put emphasis upon each word, as if to make sure she understood.

She understood.

Orphan. Fereharian. Beggar. Girl.

The words he chose piled upon her like shovelfuls of wet earth being heaved onto her grave.

He had played her. How was she still so gullible?

"Please," she whispered. "Why would the government care about me? I-I'm nothing. A nobody."

"Indeed, you are," he said. "But fortunately for you, I have no interest in your knowledge of heretical languages—"

She sank back against the door. "Then—?"

"—except inasmuch as I need you to translate this for me."

She swallowed. "I told you, I can't read it. I just—"

"You're lying. May I remind you that your alternatives are few?"

Few, indeed. What would she do, leave his house and freeze on the streets? Turn herself in, so she could be thrown in prison to rot—or be executed?

She stepped back toward the microscope, keeping one wary eye on him until she had to look back at the paper. Perhaps this was another trap.

It had been torn off a larger document. It took her a moment to work it out, but she managed it without too much difficulty. "It's incomplete," she said. "It reads, best as I can tell, '...drop at midnight, Yathyn's day. Come...' and then it's torn off. The next line is also incomplete, but it reads, '...40,000 setans, or she will die.'" She pulled back, disturbed. "That's it. Is this some sort of ransom note?"

"Excellent," he said, ignoring her question. He strode to the door and unlocked it. "You may go."

"That's it? That's all you needed from me?"

"Now that I know you have some unique skills, I may call on you again." He held the door open for her, his meaning clear.

She started through the door but glanced back at the microscope, the study, and then up at him.

His face was granite.

She suppressed a shiver. There was something dangerous about him. She didn't know if he had any intention of hurting her, but she had no doubt if he wanted to, there would be nothing she could do about it.

But because she had nowhere else to go, she returned to her tiny room in search of the blade that would help her sleep.

Elidor had lied to her.

Ivana was on the way back to her room after eating dinner alone the following evening when that thought occurred to her.

Of course, she *knew* that. He had deceived her about his ignorance of what was on the slip of paper to manipulate her into revealing knowledge about herself she should have kept hidden. But up until now, the significance of his falsehoods hadn't yet hit her. Where there was one lie, there could be more. He could have lied about where he'd obtained the microscope. About not intending to turn her in. About the silly painting!

Any or all of it could have been an outright lie.

Did he even work for the government or had that been a lie he had told Veryna?

Who *was* this man who had taken her in? And did she dare investigate further?

She stepped into her room. A bottle and a roll of clean, white bandages lay on the shelf under the washbasin, where she now stored her sister's necklace and her razor. Veryna must have brought the promised ointment; he hadn't lied about that at least.

But something was off.

The razor.

It wasn't there!

Her pulse quickened, and she scrambled to set aside the bottle and bandages so she could search the shelf. Looked underneath and behind it. And then under the cot, under the blanket, under the pillow—it was nowhere to be found.

Da Veryna. She must have seen the razor and thought, appropriately, that Ivana didn't need it.

Ivana sat back on her heels and rubbed her sweaty hands on her thighs. But she did need that blade. Temoth, she couldn't—

She closed her eyes and breathed in and out deeply, trying to calm herself. *Don't panic, don't panic.* She could find another blade. Surely, somewhere in the house...

She could sneak into the kitchen. There would be knives there. Veryna was gone, and Elidor was who-knew-where. No one would see her.

She didn't even think twice about leaving her room without a lamp. She had explored the house enough that she could navigate well enough by the moonlight streaming through the windows.

She padded down the dark hallways, through the dining room, and into the kitchen, where she rummaged around until she found what she was looking for.

She held up a small, slender knife. Likely for paring fruit, but it was sharp.

A shadow fell across the counter, and she spun around, an excuse on her lips—

But it wasn't from inside. Someone had blocked the moonlight coming through the kitchen window by walking near it outside. The person's figure was now retreating down the alley that the kitchen exited out to.

Elidor?

If so, this could be her first and possibly only chance to see where he went on his mysterious excursions. She grabbed a rag lying nearby, wrapped the blade of the knife, pocketed it...and then followed him.

This also had to be—next to the terrible mistake that had led her here—one of the stupidest things she had ever done.

She hadn't even thought to take her cloak and gloves—not that she would have had time to don them and still catch up to the figure—and it was still midwinter. Thankfully, she hadn't yet dressed for bed, and the wind was still.

The figure led her on a circuitous route through the city. Even the most familiar landscape—which, to her, Carradon was not—changed to unfamiliar terrain at night, and a few times she was afraid she had lost him, and therefore the way back to his house. Once, she had caught her foot on a loose brick, stumbled, and made quite the racket scrambling around the corner as he turned to look back.

She had huddled against the wall, certain Elidor would appear at any moment. But when she dared to poke her head around the corner, the figure's back was already disappearing around another turn, far down the street.

It didn't occur to her until she was well away from his house that he might have been going on a more extended trip. Had she intended to follow him for days with no cloak and no provisions?

Fortunately, this turned out to be a shorter journey. He stopped at a house on the edge of the city, where he was promptly admitted through the back door.

She couldn't follow him into the house, but she found a window low to the ground that looked into a partially-underground first floor. It had shutters, but one had a broken slat, and if she lay on the ground on her stomach and turned just right, she could see through the hole and into the room beyond.

A girl—Donian or Venetian by the dark brown hue of her skin—around Ivana's own age was tied to a chair and gagged, though the measures didn't seem to be necessary. Her clothing was in tatters and her head was bowed to her chest, and at first Ivana thought she was unconscious, but her head jerked up as feet appeared on the stairs beyond her.

An unfamiliar man, his skin tone similar to Elidor's, descended first, and then, in final confirmation that her chase hadn't been in vain—Elidor himself appeared.

It was Yathyn's day. Was this the girl the Xambrian note had spoken of?

Was he here to arrest the kidnappers and free the girl? Perhaps some sort of special investigator for the Watch?

Why had he been admitted so easily then?

She couldn't hear the conversation the two men had, but after a few exchanged words, Elidor set down the satchel he had been carrying and opened it. The other man looked in and then nodded, seeming satisfied.

Elidor was paying the ransom? Was this how the government intended to free the girl? To pay for her release?

The man picked up the satchel and turned to set it aside.

The next moment, Elidor had wound a long wire around his neck, shoved his foot against the man's back, and was pulling with a padded loop in each hand. The man collapsed to the floor, his neck partially severed, while Elidor stood over him wiping a cloth down the length of the wire.

Ivana stuffed a fist in her mouth to keep from vomiting, only morbid curiosity and shock driving her to continue watching. She grasped at rational thought, trying to process what she had seen. Apparently, the ransom was merely the means to get him in the house so he could kill the girl's captor. That stretched her investigator theory. A mercenary, a soldier, perhaps part of some secret arm of the Watch?

The girl had tears running down her face. Ivana couldn't hear her sobs, but she could see them reflected in her shaking shoulders. Elidor approached her, and relief strained every corner of the girl's face even as the tension drained out of Ivana's muscles. She could justify the murder in her mind if it meant saving this girl.

Elidor stabbed her in the chest with a dagger.

Ivana couldn't stop the half-gasp, half-whimper that escaped her lips, and she clamped them together, her eyes glued to the scene—wanting to look away but unable to—as the girl cried out through her gag, her relief turning to confusion and horror, and then she slumped forward against her bonds.

Ivana had stopped breathing. Her chest was burning, demanding that she breathe, but she couldn't, didn't until she couldn't take it any longer. She gasped, and then she began to shiver, from cold, fear, or both.

Without seeming at all perturbed by the bodies and blood, Elidor untied the girl's bonds and dragged her corpse toward the man. He rolled her so that she lay face-down in his blood and put the dagger near to her hand. He picked up the satchel, dumped out half the coins, and then dropped the satchel itself so that it landed on its side.

All of this, he did without dripping any blood on himself as far as Ivana could see.

He examined the cuff of his sleeve, as though he had suddenly noticed he'd lost a button.

He frowned, rolled up the sleeve, and then wrapped the cloak around himself and started up the stairs.

All at once, reality came rushing back to Ivana. She tore herself away from the window and fled back to Elidor's, her subconscious mind taking over, as she never once stopped to consider the way. She didn't stop until she was back safely in her room.

She sat on her cot, back against the wall, and drew her knees up to her chest. Had she been foolish to come back here? He hadn't seen her. He couldn't know. If she ran, he might guess and come after her. No, it was best to pretend nothing had happened.

But Temoth help her. She had been staying in the home of an assassin.

Irresponsible

"**I**'ve discovered something rather concerning, girls," Ivana's father said as they were finishing dinner.

He's found out about Cern, was Ivana's first thought. She laid her fork down and exchanged a look with Izel. Or maybe it was Tavil's bloody nose. Or—her stomach squirmed—*not the silt novels!*

Or had he somehow found out about the cider?

Burning skies, she had an awful lot of secrets lately.

She glanced at her mother. She seemed unconcerned, so it can't have been anything too serious.

Her father produced a crumpled piece of paper and smoothed it out on the table. "I found this trampled on the road today."

Both Ivana and Izel rose in their seats to see what it was.

It was a crudely drawn pamphlet advertising a...gathering...some of the local youth were planning. Ivana blew air out threw her mouth and sank back down. *Thank the gods.*

"Do you girls know about this?" His eyes were on Izel when he said it, of course. Out of the two of them, she was the one more likely to attend parties, and he knew it.

Izel shrugged. "Don't think so, Papa." She pulled off sounding nonchalant well, but one hand went to the pendant at her throat.

Her father exchanged a glance with their mother, and then he raised an eyebrow at Ivana. He would expect her to tell the truth.

Ivana sighed. "Might have heard some talk about it," she said. "But, Papa, surely you don't think either of us would go?" Actually, she had considered it. Briefly, before the incident with Cern. But that had been a silly notion; they would just find a way to make a laughingstock of her.

He frowned. "Good. I would hope you both have better sense than that. These youth think they're only having fun, but it'll be drunkenness and everything that follows, mark my words." He jabbed at the flier for emphasis. "Trouble." He glanced at Izel again, who was now eating her food as if it were an important research project.

Poor Izel. She always bore the brunt of their parents' scrutiny. Not that it was for no reason. If either of them were going to get into trouble, it would be Izel. At least, Ivana would have believed that until recently.

"They're looking for help at the tavern," Izel said, no doubt to deflect attention away from the subject of *trouble* as a whole.

"Are they," their father said, returning to sopping up the remnants of his meal with bread.

"I was wondering if maybe you might let us apply?"

Ivana raised an eyebrow at Izel. She *really* thought they were going to let—

"Actually, I think it might be a good idea," their mother put in, speaking for the first time during the exchange.

Ivana gaped at her mother. *What?*

Her father blinked. "Avira? What is this?"

Her mother wiped her mouth and laid her napkin on her empty plate. "I heard they were going to need some more help and was already thinking it might be good for Ana at least. Izel might be a bit young."

Izel slumped down in her chair and sent a disgusted look Ivana's way.

"Surely, she has better things to do—" her father began.

Her mother cut him off. "Let's face it, Galvyn. Neither of the girls is likely to marry into money, and we don't have a lot extra to offer. It can't hurt for her to start saving up a little."

Ivana's father grunted in response.

Her mother tried a different tactic. "Besides that, it would teach some responsibility. Hard work never hurt anyone. It'd give her some practice managing a little more money as well."

"Hmm," her father said, eyeing Ivana. "Ana, what do you think about this idea?"

Ivana sat up straighter. Was he actually considering this? "It would be nice to earn a little extra money," she said. And if she happened to see Handsome again, that would be a bonus.

Her father gave in. "I'll give my consent, then, to a trial period." He held up a finger. "But this can't interfere with your studies."

"Never, Papa," Ivana said.

And, because she was who she was...she meant it.

A week later, Ivana had a job.

Such as it was, anyway. The widow who owned the inn didn't want her at the bar to start, so her main duty was cleaning, both guest rooms and the dining area.

She was wiping down tables after the lunch crowd, lost in

thought about her father's latest discovery, and so she didn't know someone had snuck up on her until a warm voice interrupted her musings.

"I didn't know you worked here."

She jumped and dropped her rag. "Oh!" she cried, putting her hand to her chest, and she then dropped to her knees to fumble for the rag.

Handsome swooped down and retrieved it for her. She banged her head on the table as she came back up, and she took the rag with murmured thanks.

He nodded as though nothing had happened and then waited for a response to his comment.

She wanted to melt into the ground. "I... Well, I just started," she said. "Just a..." Her face was burning now. "A little extra money."

To her horror, he seated himself at the table she had been wiping. "Nothing wrong with that," he said. "Don't be ashamed."

She twisted the rag in her hands. "Dal," she said. "I, um, I didn't get to properly thank you for buying me a drink last week. Though it was a little stronger than I'm used to..."

He raised an eyebrow. "I thought you would appreciate not having to share with your younger friend."

How old did he think she was? "My sister, Dal." She didn't want to admit her age, but she ought to set the record straight. "Not that much younger than me."

"No? You can't be younger than seventeen."

"Just shy of sixteen, actually," she said. "And my sister's only a year and a half younger."

"You wouldn't know it," he said. She half-expected him to ogle her chest, then, but instead, he said, "You carry yourself more maturely."

She flushed again. "Um...th-thank you. I think." She dared to smile at him, and he returned it.

"Do you live here in town?" he asked.

"On Lord Kadmon's estate," she said. "My father is a tutor for his children."

He nodded, approval in his eyes. "Ah, and no doubt he's passed on an intellectual streak to you. I like that in a woman."

She swallowed, chest warming at the compliment.

"I don't think I have the pleasure of knowing your name, Da."

"An—" She broke off and drew herself up. "Ana" was a child's name. "Ivana. It's Ivana. And...you?"

"Airell. It's nice to finally make your acquaintance."

Airell? Airell as in Gan Gildas' eldest? A noble? And not just a noble, but part of the *Gan's* family? That was the highest appointment a noble could have. The only higher would be the Ri, who was ostensibly elected, not appointed.

He winced. "Ah," he said. "I see you recognize the name."

She straightened up and bowed, preparing to turn away. "My lord," she murmured. "I'm so sorry to have taken up—"

He held up a hand. "Please. Let's pretend..." He shook his head. "It would be nice to be merely Airell for once."

"Yes, my—"

"Please, no *my lords* between us. I'm not even four years your senior. Agreed?"

"I..."He was nicer than Lord Kadmon and his family. But why did he even care to talk to her? "Yes, Dal."

"Airell. Just Airell."

And why shouldn't he? she scolded herself. She had let the opinion of the *children* in town shape her view of herself for far too long. "Airell," she said.

"That's better."

The mistress of the inn swept by, and the look she gave Ivana was discretely annoyed.

"Ah," Airell said, standing. "I can see I'm about to get you in trouble." He bowed. "Good day, Ivana. I hope to see you again soon."

With a wink and a smile, he swept out the door.

Ivana lay on her pallet next to Izel, staring up into the darkness. She couldn't sleep. All she could think of was Lord Airell and his enchanting smile. A smile he had favored her with. *Her!*

Izel rolled over to face her. "All right," she said. "I can almost feel thoughts rolling off you. What's keeping you awake?"

Ivana turned her head to look toward Izel and then sat up. "I saw that nobleman again today," she said. "He came into the dining room and talked to me a bit more."

Izel sat up as well, alert. "Oh?"

"I-I think you may be right, Izel," Ivana admitted. "I think he might like me."

Izel was quiet for a minute. "Ana..."

"Do you know who he is? He's Gan Gildas' eldest, Lord Airell. Can you believe it? *Lord* Airell."

Izel was silent.

"What?" Ivana asked, a little annoyed. "You don't believe me? You're the one who said you thought he liked me first."

"I-I was partially jesting, Ana."

"Partially?"

"Well—I'm certain he *does* like you, after a fashion."

Ivana's throat tightened. "No," she said. "That's unfair. Is it so hard to believe that someone could like me for *me?* Am I so boring? Or perhaps you think the whole of who I am can be summed up in my breasts?"

"That's not what I meant, Ana, but he's a *noble*, for Rhianah's sake. There's only one reason someone like him would be interested in people like us."

"He's not like that," Ivana said. "He told me not to use any titles with him. He's so genuine, and he never looked at my chest, not once."

"That you saw," Izel said softly.

Ivana's ire rose. "I can't believe this. I would have thought *you* of all people—just last week you were dying to know about my encounter with Cern, and now—"

"Cern isn't one of *them*. Even I have better sense than that."

"I knew I shouldn't have discussed this with you. I couldn't expect *you* to understand."

"And what is that supposed to mean?" Izel snapped. "You think you're *oh*-so-mature since you *blossomed* before me? I thought you were more than your breasts!"

Ivana lay back down and turned her back to Izel. "I'm done with this conversation." She could sense Izel sitting up for a little while longer before she sighed and then also lay back down, silent.

A tempest raged in Ivana's chest. How dare she insinuate—she finally received some attention from a *real* man—

She was jealous, that was all.

And yet, Izel's words spoke to a tiny part of her, the tiny part that couldn't help but feel Izel was right.

That was what made her the angriest. Yathyn's scars, she wouldn't let Izel ruin this with sense. There was no harm in talking to him, and still plenty of time to back away if it turned out Izel was right.

With those thoughts to comfort her, she finally went to sleep.

Chapter Five

Something jerked Ivana out of her sleep far too soon. The paring knife she had fallen asleep holding rolled from her hand and clattered to the floor. She sat up and blinked, disoriented, and then she flicked her eyes around the room.

Elidor was standing in the doorway.

She bolted out of bed.

The grogginess of being woken after too little sleep and the pulse of energy that raced through her at the sight of Elidor combined to make her head swim. She reached out for the washbasin to steady herself.

He had found out. He had come to kill her. He had finally decided to make use of her in other ways. He—

He was looking at the freshest cuts on her forearm, which was streaked with dried blood. She had fallen asleep too tired, too weary, too upset to care about wiping it away.

A surge of indignation at his silent intrusiveness into her private life washed away the last vestiges of sleep. She shook her sleeve down to cover the cuts, bent to retrieve the knife, and set it with a snap on the washbasin, as if daring him to try to reclaim it. Everything else was gone. He wouldn't take away this as well.

She almost laughed out loud. And what would she do if he tried? She had witnessed this man murder two people without a bat of the eye.

Can't think about that. Can't let him see my fear. "Dal. May I help you?"

"You missed breakfast."

She blinked and squinted at the clock. "I...had a restless night. I must have slept later than usual."

"Then you'll eat now." He turned and walked away without explanation as to why he had awoken her, why he cared about her having missed breakfast, indeed, without even seeing if she would follow his command.

She gathered up the bedclothes in her fists. No reason to upset him, but neither was she going to jump to his whims without even washing up. No reason for him to think she was *trying* not to upset him.

She was going crazy.

Ivana entered the dining room a half hour later, after having washed her face and teeth, brushed her hair, and changed into clean clothes.

A spread of honey cakes, slices of cold ham left from the night before, and two ceramic carafes had been laid out on the table. As usual, a single place setting had been laid out. She started toward it and then jumped as the door to the dining room swung shut behind her.

Elidor stood there, waiting for her.

Something had changed.

But if he had found out about her little expedition the night before and was going to murder her for it, why the delay?

Elidor moved to his side of the table and sat down, his hands folded in front of him.

Was he going to just sit there and watch her eat? That was even creepier than usual. Still, she tried to act normal. She filled her plate and noted with some trepidation that Veryna was nowhere to be seen. "Where is Da Veryna?"

"I sent her home," Elidor said, his eyes not leaving her for an instant.

That didn't bode well.

"We have some things we need to discuss privately."

Her hand paused on its way to fill a glass with honey wine from one of the carafes. Perhaps now was a good time to flee. Why was she still sitting here?

And go where? Do what? Would she have a chance at a new life because she could grab some gloves and a cloak on the way out?

"Oh?" she managed to choke out. Her hand trembled, and honey wine sloshed over the edge of the carafe.

"You ought to be dead," he said.

The carafe slipped from her fingers, and the amber liquid spilled across the table and into her lap. "Oh!" she exclaimed. She rose to escape the flow and then looked around frantically for a rag to mop the mess up with.

Really? That was all she could think about? "I—I'm so sorry," she said. "I... Is there a towel? I'll clean it up—"

"Forget the spill," he snapped. "You can apologize for your clumsiness later." He advanced around the table toward her, and she backed toward the door. "Did you not hear me?"

"I-I heard you. I don't know what you mean. You rescued me, I know I should have starved on the streets..."

"Don't play games with me," he said. "I know you followed me last night, and I know what you saw."

He knew. He knew! How? And if he had known, why had he let her follow him? Why hadn't he sent her back or—

"I should have killed you then," he said. "Should still kill you now."

He had locked the dining room door. She didn't even have to try the handle to know that. She just knew. She had nowhere to go.

Was this it then? The months of struggle, to end here, in some twisted nightmare version of her life?

Perhaps it was better this way. What end did she see for herself after all? Some days, she was just so *tired*. "Then why haven't you?" she said, meeting his eyes.

For a moment, she thought he would. She even flinched back, certain he had a hidden dagger that was about to spill her blood as quickly as he had spilled the blood of those two last night.

But then something changed in him. Irritation flickered across his face. His chest rose in a slow, deliberate breath. He stepped back from her and turned away. When he faced her again, his countenance was more relaxed. "I think you could be of use to me."

Her? Of use to an assassin? How, she couldn't fathom, unless he had decided to make her his whore.

Or translator. Maybe he dealt with Xambrians a lot.

She was morbidly intrigued by that possibility.

"Please." He gestured to the table. "Sit down."

She skirted him warily and sat back down in a different

chair, one where the wine wouldn't drip into her lap.

"In your education," he said, moving on with complete ease, as if he hadn't just told her that he had considered murdering her, "did you study the apothecary arts?"

What was this about? "I wouldn't say I *studied* it, but I know my way around the tools and common ingredients."

"So you could make tonics, if you had the recipe and ingredients?"

"Well, simple ones, I suppose." She halted, remembering who she was speaking with. "What sort of...tonics...are we talking about?"

"You are perceptive. Very well. I can't always leave a bloody mess, after all, or even an obvious trace of physical violence. I can purchase most common poisons, of course, but there are a multitude of formulas that aren't made in advance and sold that might have use in specific circumstances. The ability to make precisely what I need, when I need it, at cost, without a trail, has advantages." He smiled, but it was a mimicry; it didn't reach his eyes.

She blinked rapidly. "What is *wrong* with you?" she burst out.

He raised an eyebrow, a normal gesture for him, which only increased her exasperation.

"You can't turn on and off being *normal* like changing your clothes and expect me not to notice."

The counterfeit smile faded. "I was merely trying to make you more comfortable."

"*More* comfortable."

"Yes."

"Dal, people aren't made comfortable by chatting about methods of murder over breakfast. Not even with a smile on your face. *Especially* not with a smile on your face!"

He pursed his lips. "Hmm."

She poured herself another cup of wine. Damn, she would need it. "And as to your question, I have never studied poisons in particular, and—"

He waved his hand, staving off any further objections. "But you say you have some basic knowledge, and you're obviously intelligent, therefore you are teachable." He stood up. "My own library continues to be at your disposal, but I will also see what more advanced resources I am able to gather for your further study. My housekeeper says you're bored, so the stimulation should—"

"Have you considered that perhaps I don't *want* to make poisons for you?" Ivana cut in.

He paused.

No, obviously he had not.

"What's to stop me from going directly to the authorities the moment you let me out of your sight?" she asked.

He laughed. It wasn't a warm, friendly sound. It was chilling. "I wouldn't advise that."

"And why not? You'll come after me?"

"Foolish girl. The authorities are the ones who employ me. All that would achieve is giving them a reason to order your own death."

"Wait, so you *do* work for the government?"

"After a fashion." He tilted his head. "Does this comfort you?"

"I don't know. Maybe it feels less...criminal."

Elidor sat down on the edge of the table. "What is the difference between a soldier and a mercenary?"

"Well...one is employed by the government, and the other hires their services out to the highest bidder."

"Mmm. And because the government tells the soldier to kill or pillage or destroy, that makes it...what would most people say...right? Surely, you don't have such great faith in our Ri."

"No," she said softly. "Certainly not." She had personal experience with how cruel and calloused their *noble* rulers could be.

"The innocent die because of political expediency, in war and intrigue. That girl may have been no threat to anyone but the power of some noble."

"You don't know why?"

"Does the sword know its master's mind?"

Ivana had no words to respond. How could he do that? How could he not care, not wonder, not *feel*?

"An assassin is a specialized type of mercenary. I work for the government, which makes me merely a specialized type of soldier." He held up his hand. "Don't, however, mistake that for justice. You are of little use to me paralyzed by fear or moral dilemma, so if it makes you more at ease, believe what you will." He stood up again. "Be prepared to start your new studies tomorrow."

Foolish

Ivana saw Airell frequently over the next three weeks. He was as gracious and charming as ever and, contrary to Izel's notions, never once stared at her breasts—though she might have caught him looking her over appreciatively once or twice.

Well, he was a man, after all. What could she expect?

He entered the inn as she was ending her shift one day. He gave her the smile she knew he reserved for her and slipped over to her side. "I have something for you," he whispered in her ear. "Can you get away?"

She flushed, her entire body tingling as his lips brushed her ear. "I'm almost done," she said. "I have to finish changing the linens in one of the guest rooms, and then—"

"Perfect," he said, then winked. He walked back out without another word.

She was mystified, but she shrugged and went to the closet to collect the linens.

She had just entered the room when she heard a rapping at the window. She pulled back the curtains and was astonished to see Airell outside, grinning at her. He held up a box and motioned to her to lift the window.

She giggled, glanced around, and did as he asked.

He clambered in and hastened to shut the door.

"Airell," she said, feeling somewhat giddy at the subterfuge. "What if someone catches us?"

"They won't," he said, and then he brushed her cheek with one finger. "Trust me."

She sucked in a breath. He had never touched her face before. Well, they had never been alone before, either, aside from the handful of times he had pulled her down a corridor to catch her unaware with a small trinket or flowers.

She swallowed and smiled at him, trying not to make it so obvious that she was unused to this sort of rendezvous—and trying to hide the way her heart was pounding.

He set the box on the bed. "Open it," he said, rubbing his hands together.

She lifted the lid gingerly and gasped. It was a dress—a dress precisely in the latest fashion she had seen in the clothier's window some weeks back. It was—

Well, it didn't seem so frivolous, coming from Airell. She picked it up out of the box and held it up. It was stunning.

And...

She laid the dress back down in the box and avoided his eyes. "I can't accept this."

He furrowed his brow. "Why ever not?"

"Airell, I know we're pretending that we're equals, but let's be honest for a moment. Where would I wear such a thing? I'm not likely to attend any fancy balls anytime soon." Not to mention, how could she accept such an expensive gift? What would her parents say?

He ran a hand over his face. "Well," he said. "Perhaps you're right. But..." He hesitated.

"What?"

"Could you try it on for me? This once?"

She looked down at the dress. What harm would it do to try it on? She would likely never have another chance to wear such a fine dress.

She flushed and picked it up again. "All right. Just this once. Then you must promise me you'll return it."

He nodded, and she stood and waited. "Would you, um..." She looked around. There wasn't anywhere for him to go. "Turn around?"

She couldn't believe she was even suggesting that she change while he was in the room. But he wouldn't look. He was a gentleman.

"Of course," he said, and he turned his back on her, pretending to examine one of the paintings on the wall.

She turned her back to him as well, to be on the safe side, and hurried to shed her plain, common dress and don the new one. She smoothed the fabric and turned around. "It's okay now."

He turned around, and for the first time, he looked at her, every part of her, openly and unashamedly, his eyes lingering on all the right places.

Wrong places. Wrong places, Ana! Burning skies, what had come over her? But she warmed with pleasure at his gaze, as though he were caressing her with his eyes, and didn't turn away.

He finally looked back up at her face. "Stunning."

"The dress?"

"No," he said, moving closer to her. He met her eyes. "You."

He reached toward her, and her pulse quickened noticeably—he was going to kiss her! But instead, he put his hands on her shoulders and turned her so she faced the only mirror in the room.

And he was right—agreeing with her own instincts about the style back when she had first seen it. It *did* look good on her. It accentuated her figure and drew attention in the right way to her chest—making her feel less like a top-heavy girl and more like a curvy woman.

"See?" he said, meeting her eyes in the mirror, his hands still on her shoulders.

She nodded. "You're right," she said. His presence directly behind her was rolling into her like waves against the shore.

"Are you sure you won't take it?"

"I-I can't. I'm sorry."

He hesitated again, opened his mouth, closed it, and then shook his head. "Very well. But I confess. I lied."

"Wh-what?"

"I can't return it. I had it altered for your measurements. But no matter. I'm sure someone in my household will appreciate it."

She blinked. "My measurements? How...How would you know that?"

He shrugged. "I guessed." He smiled. "I guessed right, apparently."

She finally turned around, but he didn't move, and they were closer than they had ever been before, her breasts brushing his chest.

He looked down at her, and then...

He kissed her.

A hundred thoughts exploded in her brain. That they shouldn't be doing this. That *she* shouldn't be doing this. That she hadn't intended on it getting this far. That she had never *thought* he would be interested in her enough to take it this far. That she had only known him for a month.

But the thought that she didn't want to think any of those things won, and she kissed him back.

And, *burning skies*, it was nothing like it had been with Cern. His lips were soft and gentle, not wet and sloppy; it was almost like he had done this before.

Maybe he has, the collective of other thoughts whispered.

She shoved them away. Who cared? He was here with *her* now.

Their kisses grew more heated. More heated than they had ever gone with Cern.

Oh gods...

She was delirious with pleasure, with giddiness, with nerves...

"Oh, Ivana," he whispered, finally leaving her lips to tease at her ear with his breath. "I-I have to confess. I've never felt like this about anyone before. And I want you so badly right now."

The shock of his words forced her to pull back from him. "Wh-What?"

He let go of her and ran a hand through his hair. "Too soon? I'm so sorry... I shouldn't have... Of course, I don't know how you feel about me."

She didn't want him to think she was a prude. Or that she didn't care for him. Or to go away and never come back.

"N-No," she said. "I just... I wasn't quite ready for... I'm not expecting... I don't know if I'm ready for th-that just yet."

"Of course," he said, still shaking his head. "I was wrong to suggest it. I'm so sorry."

She held out a hand as he stepped away, a part of her crying out for him to stop, to let go of her scruples and do whatever he wanted.

But it was too late.

He did lean forward and kiss her again, long, slow, and

sweet. "I'll see you later?"

She nodded, speechless, and he gathered up the box and climbed out the window again.

She sat down on the bed, hugging herself across her chest, realizing that she still wore the dress.

What had just happened?

Ivana didn't tell Izel about her meeting with Airell. Why should she? Izel didn't understand, and Ivana had simply stopped talking to her about it.

So they were silent as they lay on their pallet that night, Izel's chatter about the day's events long since fading into the regular breathing of deep sleep.

But Ivana was awake, still reeling over what had happened earlier. She still had the dress. She had rolled it up tight and shoved it into her bodice for the rest of the day. As little fabric as it had and as large as her bosom was, it wasn't even noticeable. She had then stowed it in her personal chest the moment she'd arrived home. She didn't know what she would do with it.

Had Izel been right? Had this all been a long ploy to seduce her? But he seemed so *genuine*, and why would he have stopped earlier if that were the case? He had respected her decision, regretted that he had asked in the first place.

No, he cared for her. Feelings like that could make people do strange things.

A soft rapping sounded at her window, and she sat up. She glanced at Izel, who was fast asleep, and crept over to the window.

She gasped. Airell stood there, a cock-eyed grin on his face and one finger to his lips.

She glanced back at Izel again, but she hadn't stirred. She

eased the window open, and before she could think, climbed out. She could hardly speak with him while in her room.

"Airell!" she whispered. "What are you doing here? How did you *find* me?"

He shrugged, seeming sheepish. "I asked around," he said. "Wasn't hard. As to what I'm doing here..." He paused. "I had to see you, Ivana. I couldn't get you out of my mind."

"You either?" she whispered back, feeling giddy again. But she tried to stave him off. "You can't be here. If my mother or father comes..."

"Do they usually disturb you in the middle of the night?" Airell asked. "Come with me. I have something else to show you, and I'll have you back long before sunrise."

She hesitated and looked back in the room. Her *parents* might not notice she was gone, but Izel, on the other hand...

This was foolish. She would get into *so* much trouble.

But instead of refusing, she held up a finger to indicate that he should wait and then crept back into her room to retrieve the dress.

Izel turned over and sighed in her sleep once while Ivana rummaged around, but she didn't wake.

Once she had climbed back out again, Ivana pressed the dress into his hand. "You forgot this," she said.

He beamed. "Hold on to it. Come on." He grabbed her hand, and together they snuck away, down the path toward the woods on Lord Kadmon's estate, but still within the walls.

She looked back toward the house before it disappeared out of view, almost expecting to see Izel's head popping out of the window, watching her go, but the house was still and quiet.

She pulled back as they entered the woods. "What of blood-bane?"

He waved his hand and tugged her forward. "There are no

bloodbane here."

She nodded, still nervous, but her nerves weren't related to bloodbane anyway.

Another set of boxes waited for them in a small clearing. So he had already been here?

"Open them," he said again as they reached the spot.

"Airell, not again."

He gestured. "Just open them. Then I'll explain."

She sighed and opened the top box. In it was a pair of shoes, finer than she had ever owned, would ever *need*.

"To go with the dress," he said, smiling.

"But—"

"Shh," he said. "Open the other box."

She shook her head and did as he asked. She stifled a gasp and reached out one trembling hand to lift a necklace from its velvet casing. It was beautiful. And so...expensive-looking. She set it back down. "Airell," she said firmly. "Enough of this. I am not—"

"I want you to go to the Harvest Ball with me this fall," he said, touching her cheek again.

She blinked. "What?"

"My father will be furious, of course, for not taking one of the noble-women he's been throwing at me, but..."

This was so far beyond the realm of possibility that she could hardly comprehend what he was saying. "I don't understand."

He took her hands in his and looked deep into her eyes. "I want to be with you, Ivana. Forever. I love you."

She swallowed and started to tremble. "But I'm-I'm—"

He pressed his lips to the back of one hand. "I don't care. I just need time to bring my family around to the idea. Can you give me that time?"

She swallowed and nodded. It barely registered that he

hadn't even waited to see how she would respond. And why should he? What sane woman would turn him down?

"Now," he said. "One more favor before I return you home."

She couldn't speak.

"Try it all on. I want to see how the shoes and necklace look. Ladies' fashion isn't really my area of expertise. I can exchange those if need be."

She didn't even protest this time. Her head was spinning so rapidly that she mutely waited for him to turn around again, and then she shed her clothes. She pulled the dress on and had barely pulled it up over her shoulders when his hands clasped her bare waist. He had tucked them beneath the fabric of the dress—which wasn't hard, considering that it had little in the way of a back.

Before she could speak, his lips were nuzzling her neck, and then her ear. "Ivana," he murmured. "It's just us."

His hands traveled up her waist and to her ribcage.

She gasped and turned around, shocked at his forwardness...but he kissed the protests forming on her lips away.

He finally pulled back to look at her, but his hands were warm against her back, tracing slow circles on her skin. "Have you thought about what I said earlier?"

She stared back at him, speechless once again. Her entire body was on fire, and her mind was foggy. She was having trouble thinking straight. But a thought pierced it all. *Burning skies*—Izel had been right. He had lured her here, and now he was going to take her, no matter what she said.

But he didn't kiss her again, seeming to sense her hesitation. "Of course," he said, starting to pull away, disappointment, even unhappiness, on his face. "If you'd rather not, I understand."

No. Izel was *wrong*. He loved her. He loved her, and he wanted her. They were going to be married.

She took his hand as he started to drop it. "No. I do want to."

He smiled, pleased again. "I was hoping you would say that."

Airell took the dress, shoes, and necklace for safekeeping. She had insisted. She couldn't keep such items in her house, even buried in her chest. She snuck back into her room, no one in her household knowing she had been gone. Izel still slept deeply, shifting once as she lay back down next to her, but not waking.

How was she supposed to fall asleep now, after such a night? He had swept away the last of her reservations with his smooth touch and gentle kisses, and before she had known it, she had given herself to him completely.

She couldn't shake the worry that she had fallen for some elaborate trap. And for what? But if all he had intended was to use her, surely he wouldn't have been so gentle, so understanding, so willing to please *her* in ways she thought only existed in silt novels.

Despite her initial feeling that she would never fall asleep, she did in fact fall asleep shortly thereafter, warring thoughts of ecstasy and shame tinting her dreams.

Chapter Six

The tinkle of a tiny bell announced Ivana's arrival in the apothecary a week after Elidor had set her to her new studies. He had given her money to purchase some basic supplies for her studies and future experiments.

Some herbs, of course, she would have to purchase from less "respectable" merchants, either because they were illegal or wouldn't normally be sold at a common apothecary.

She tried not to think about that. For now, she just needed the basics; Elidor had nothing by way of the supplies she needed.

Boden, the apothecary's apprentice, was there again, his back toward her while he pulled empty bottles off a shelf and replaced them with full ones from a box he held. He turned at the sound of the bell and flashed her a huge grin when he saw her.

"Ivana, was it?" He walked over to the counter to set his box down.

She nodded and handed him her list. "I need everything on this here."

He took a minute to read down through it, then looked back up at her, his eyebrow raised. "This is extensive. Planning on setting up a competing shop?" But his eyes danced as he said it, so he couldn't have been serious.

She repeated the script Elidor had given her. "I'm an apothecary's apprentice myself," she said. "Back home, in Ferehar. But I'm here in Carradon staying with a relative for a few months, and I can't neglect my studies while here."

She hoped she sounded convincing. Deception wasn't one of her strengths.

He tilted his head and studied her face. "So when you said you were looking for work..."

"Hoping to earn a little pocket money for staying in practice." She gave him a hesitant smile.

He returned the smile. "All right. Well, it'll take me a little bit to gather this together. You can come back if you're in a hurry, or..."

"I'm in no hurry," she said. Being in the apothecary was significantly more appealing than sitting in her tiny room staring at the wall. "You have everything?"

"For the most part," he said. "We might be out of turmeric. And dennil root..." He furrowed his brow. "We don't get requests for that one often. You're more likely to find it at one of the apothecaries closer to the university; we deal more with your run-of-the mill cough and fever here."

Ivana held up her hand. "If not, that's fine."

"I know Da Grania has it in her own supplies, but I don't know if she wants me selling out of that." He hesitated. "I'll see what I can do, anyway. If you don't want to walk all the way over there, that is."

"Yes, that would be fine," she said. "Thank you."

He rummaged around beneath the counter, pulled out a wooden box, and turned his back to her, one hand holding the list, the other trailing along bottles on the shelf behind him. He selected one, tapped out some of the powder within into a smaller container, and set it in the box. "So I've been dying of curiosity. Star-leaf as a pain killer?"

"Oh," she said, twisting her hands together. "It's a little something my—I mean, I discovered a while back. You can eat the leaves, but it has some pretty unpleasant side effects, especially in large doses. If you grind the leaves into a pulp, extract the juices, and dilute them into a tincture, the side effects aren't as pronounced while the benefits are nearly as effective."

He was quiet for a moment while he continued to gather the supplies on her list. Finally, he spoke again. "I don't think I've ever experimented with the leaves themselves. I mean, obviously the seeds..."

"You've experimented with the seeds?" she teased, recalling his reaction last time.

"No—well, yes." He held one hand out defensively. "But not in the way you're thinking!"

Something unexpected happened. She laughed.

And it felt...good.

He exchanged a smile with her. "You really do know about this, don't you?"

Her cheeks warmed. "It-It's not as much me as, well, it's sort of a family occupation, so I've had a lot of time to..." She trailed off.

"Your father or mother is an apothecary?"

She swallowed, any trace of her previous laughter gone as fast as it had appeared. "More like...scholars."

He raised his chin and studied her, his eyes serious now, as if he could tell that she wasn't telling him everything.

She cleared her throat, turned, and pretended to browse one of the racks behind her.

He respected her silence and returned to collecting her supplies. About ten minutes later, he spoke again. "All set. Everything but the turmeric and the dennil root." He held out her list. "If you want to try back in about a week, I know we'll have more turmeric, and I'll ask Da Grania about the dennil root and let you know when you return."

She nodded and moved to the counter. She took the list, pulled out the coin purse Elidor had given her, and then looked at him expectantly.

"Oh. Seven setans," he said. He hesitated, as if apologetic about the high price. "It was a long list."

"No problem." Elidor had given her three times that much. She counted out seven setans from the purse, and she slid them across the counter with a scrape.

And the memory of the last time she had counted out coins at an apothecary swept over her senses like a flash flood. The smells were suddenly overpowering, her vision wavered, and her lungs tightened as though for lack of air.

Boden's eyes flicked from the purse to her and back again. "You're welcome to open an account and pay monthly," he said. "If you think you'll be back a lot, that is."

She hardly registered what he was saying. "I might do that," she murmured, eager to leave.

"I don't know what kind of set up your relative has," he added, as though it were an afterthought. "But if you want more advanced tools, you're welcome to... I mean, I don't think Da Grania would mind if I showed you around a little."

He met her eyes and gave her a shy smile.

"Sure," she said out of reflex. She inclined her head, grabbed the box, and hurried out the door.

Ivana didn't check back at the apothecary for her missing ingredients for two weeks. She was irrationally afraid of being taken off-guard by her own weakness again. However, Elidor had been asking about her progress, and she was very rationally afraid of angering him.

But dennil root was an ingredient in a few of the recipes in one of the more advanced books Elidor had obtained for her.

So two weeks after her initial trip for supplies, she forced herself to return to see if Boden had managed to procure some dennil root for her.

Boden wasn't there, but a smartly-dressed, handsome man waited at the counter, looking bored. He glanced toward Ivana absently as she entered, and then he looked again. His eyes flicked over her several times and then rested on her chest, as if he were appraising the value of one of the alembics on the shelf. Then he lifted his eyes and winked at her.

She resisted the urge to fold her arms across her too-large bosom. Instead, she clutched at the fabric of her skirt with both fists and tried to ignore him. Why were so many men such asses? And such *overt* assess? At least Airell had had the courtesy to pretend to be a gentleman.

Then again, if he had been an obvious ass, she would never have—

She sucked air through her teeth. That only made her ten times more the fool.

The real question was: What was so wrong with her that she attracted their attention so easily?

A middle-aged woman entered the room from a door in the

back of the shop. She held a small bottle of amber liquid, and she held it out to the man, who turned his attention to her instead.

"One *thom* every morning for a week," the woman said.

The man jerked his head in acquiescence and pocketed the bottle.

"It could take up to three days to see improvement, so please tell your mother to be patient." The woman pursed her lips. "More than one *thom* will not speed along the process and may have ill effects, such as nausea, vomiting, or worse, depending on the dose."

"Right, right," the man said, turning away from the counter.

The woman's eyes narrowed on his back, and she shook her head.

The man paused by Ivana on the way out.

"Da," he said. "Have we met?"

"No," she said stiffly.

The man raised an eyebrow, shrugged, and brushed by without further comment.

Ivana closed her eyes and let out a long stream of air.

"May I help you?"

She opened her eyes. The woman had turned to her with a polite smile.

Ivana dropped her arms—and only then did she realize that she had at some point crossed them over herself in spite of her earlier attempt to keep them planted at her side. "Yes. I-I'm here to pick up some supplies that, um, Boden was looking into for me."

The woman's eyes swept over her, but it was in the manner of someone trying to determine if they had the right person. She reached under the counter and set a small glass bottle and a leather pouch on it. "Turmeric and dennil root?"

"Yes," Ivana said, surprised. "That's it."

The woman's smile spread. "You must be Ivana. Boden told me about you. I'm Grania, the owner of this shop."

Ivana curtsied. "Pleased to meet you, Da," she murmured, moving forward to take the ingredients and open her coin purse.

"Boden was impressed with your knowledge of our art," Grania said. "He said you're an apprentice yourself?"

"Yes, Da." And that wasn't *really* a lie, was it? She was an apprentice of the *art*, if not of a particular person.

"Very good. I'm happy to take from my personal supplies for another apprentice." She glanced at Ivana's coin purse, which Ivana still held open on the counter. "Three selmas, dear."

Ivana counted out the coins and set them on the counter gently, so as not to recreate the sound that had caused her distress last time.

At that moment, Boden himself walked through the back door. He appeared about to speak, but when he saw Ivana, his eyes lit up. "I was beginning to think I wouldn't see you back again," he said.

She didn't reply, not sure what to say.

"Da," Boden said, addressing Grania now, "did Dal Leam pick up the tonic for his mother's cough?"

Grania's mouth turned downward. "Yes. And I gave him very specific instructions regarding the dose and expected recovery. If he returns before three days complaining it isn't working or that his mother is vomiting, tell him he should have paid more attention when I was speaking and there will be no refunds." She sniffed.

One side of Boden's mouth curled up in a smile. "Should I say it just like that?"

Grania cast him a disparaging glance.

Footsteps thundered from the back of the shop. A moment later, a girl of about thirteen or fourteen flew in through the back door. "Have you seen Annan?" she asked, breathless.

Boden chuckled. "No, why? Have you lost him again?"

The girl muttered under her breath, and then she glanced toward Grania and Ivana in turn. She flushed and curtsied to Ivana. "Oh, I'm sorry. I didn't realize we had a customer."

"It's all right," Ivana said. The girl's bright eyes and carefree manner reminded her of her sister.

Her breath caught in her throat, and she firmly shoved that thought away. *Not now.*

"I'm sure he's around somewhere," Boden said.

Almost as if in answer to his statement, a shriek and a crash resounded through the still-open door. The girl's face grew stormy. "Annan!" she shouted, then marched back through.

Grania's lips pressed together. "Excuse me," she said, and she followed the girl.

"Sorry about that," Boden said. "Da Grania's children... Well, you've been lucky so far. They've been out both times you've been in before now."

"Are they a handful?"

"They're a riot," he said, grinning from ear to ear.

Her heavy heart couldn't help but lighten, and she smiled in return.

He glanced out the window of the shop. "Would you be interested in seeing Grania's workroom? I'm certain she won't mind." He hesitated, and then he forged forward. "Perhaps while we're there, you could show me your work on star-leaf?"

He was so sincere, so halting, she couldn't refuse.

***

Her quick trip to pick up a few supplies had turned into an all-afternoon event during which she had almost forgotten why she'd needed to purchase supplies at an apothecary in the first place. Indeed, almost forgotten why she was in Carradon in the first place.

The sun had almost set by the time she returned home. Elidor was waiting for her in the front room, and her memory was abruptly jogged.

"Where were you?" Elidor asked without preamble.

She held up the pouch and bottle. "Getting some ingredients the apothecary didn't have last time."

"You were gone almost all day."

"I..." For some reason, she didn't want to tell him what she had been doing. Was it any of his business if she had been out...forgetting?

So she just shrugged.

He pressed his lips together. "Is this the same apothecary you went to last time?"

"Well, yes... Hence, why I had to go back to get the ingredients they were out of."

He didn't seem to appreciate her cheek. "The next time you are in need of supplies, choose a different apothecary."

She blinked. "But—"

"There is no need for anyone to become overly familiar with you."

She met his expressionless eyes, and something in her rebelled. "I'm not the one who kills people for a living."

"You work for me now, and therefore by proxy you must observe the same caution."

"The same seclusion, you mean." She hadn't been aware of how bitter that notion was until she tasted it in her words just now. She had never been a social butterfly, not like her sister.

But the prospect of never having any company other than this cold, unfeeling man and his unobtrusive housekeeper was hardly pleasant.

He frowned. "Would you rather be back on the streets?"

"Do I even have that option anymore?" she shot back.

His eyes narrowed, and his non-reply was answer enough.

"So now I am a prisoner, then," she said softly.

"You were the one who followed me," he pointed out. He turned to leave the room, but then paused to throw over his shoulder. "Besides. Where else would you go?"

His words plunged her into a pool of ice-cold water.

Because they were true. She had nowhere else to go, no one she could tell. She was drowning in a world she had damned herself to by every foolish decision she had made that had dropped her at Elidor's feet, and every decision after.

What had begun as an almost-pleasant day ended as most did, for her.

In blood.

Naive

I vana sat on the edge of the bed and watched the reflection of Airell in the mirror as he buttoned his shirt and slipped his formal jacket over top of it.

She twisted the bed clothes in her hands. "Must you leave so soon?"

His eyes met hers in the mirror. "You know I have a dinner to be at tonight."

She did know. He had told her that already. But it was always something, some reason he couldn't stay, some reason he blew into town long enough for a dalliance with her and then had to leave again as quickly as he had come.

"Have you spoken to your father yet?" she asked.

He leaned over and gave her a quick kiss on the lips. "I'm working on it. We'll be together soon, love."

He gave her his cockeyed grin, the one that always melted her objections. And with that, he was gone.

She bit her lip, trying to stem the flow of tears before they began. She didn't want the owner of the house—a friend of his, he had said—to see her crying when she slipped out the back.

She didn't know what she had done wrong, but he was distant lately. What had begun as a breathless romance, three months later felt as suffocating as the day of the sky-fire, when one hardly dared to breathe until the all-clear had been given by the town militia.

Airell rarely made any effort to please her anymore, as he had at the beginning. Increasingly, rather than loved, she felt...used.

Yet still, every time they were together, he promised. A little longer. A little more set up before broaching the topic with his father. He loved her, after all.

She stood up and tugged on her own dress. Her parents thought she was still at work; she had to get home before they realized she wasn't. One of these days or nights, someone would realize, and then it would be over.

She couldn't decide whether that would be a relief or not.

But what would she do then? Would any honorable man want her, now?

No, she thought. Those were horrible thoughts to have. Airell would come through for her. She *knew* he would. He had promised, and he loved her.

Izel couldn't have been right. She *couldn't* have. Ivana must have done something wrong to cause him to withdraw, but she was afraid to ask him about it, lest he withdraw further.

The tears that she had held back pricked at her eyes. She took a deep, shuddering breath and drove them off in a flurry of activity.

Ivana sat by the window, worrying at the corner of the cushion on the chair. The corner seam had unraveled, and stuffing was trailing out.

Her monthly cycle was late.

A few days, she could brush off. A week even.

But it had now been two, almost three weeks.

She felt sure enough about it now that she was going to tell Airell that night. Certainly, once he knew she was with child, he would insist upon an immediate marriage to preserve both their reputations.

"Uh-oh. What are you thinking about?"

Ivana jerked her hand back from the cushion. She hadn't even heard Izel open the door to their room. "Nothing."

Izel closed the door to the room and plopped down on their pallet. "I know nothing, and that's not a nothing face."

Ivana looked out the window. It was none of her business.

"This is about Gan Gildas' son, isn't it?"

Ivana whirled to face her, shocked. "What?"

"Oh, come on, Ana. You think I haven't figured out about your little fling?"

Ivana worked her mouth for a moment. She wanted to deny it, and then to ask how she knew, and for how long, and a thousand other things, but only two words came out. "Mama... Papa?"

"They don't know."

Ivana sank back in the chair. "And you won't tell them, will you?"

Izel gave her a critical look. "How long are you going to let this go on, Ana?"

"Please, Izel. Promise me."

Izel pressed her lips together. "You know I'm not going to snitch on you. But—"

"We're going to be married, Izel."

"What?"

"It'll be all right. You'll see."

Izel's mouth dropped open. "Did he tell you that?"

Anger flared in Ivana's chest at the doubt in Izel's voice—mostly because it was an echo of her own doubts, the ones she kept trying to silence. "He didn't *tell* me that. He asked me, and I accepted, so now we're engaged."

Actually, that wasn't quite how it had happened, as she recalled. But it hardly mattered.

"If you think that man is going to marry you," Izel said, "you're only fooling yourself."

Ivana stood up. "Then you don't know anything," she said. "And you won't until you become a *woman.*"

Izel stared at her for a moment. Then she pressed her lips together, stood up abruptly, and stormed out of the room.

The words had hurt Izel, and at that moment, Ivana didn't care. Izel would see.

"Airell," Ivana said, trying to infuse her voice with a sense of urgency so that he would pay attention to her. "I have something I need to tell you."

It worked. He stopped unfastening his trousers and raised an eyebrow at her.

Her stomach churned. Why was she so nervous? This was a good thing, right? Yet it still took some effort to get the words out. "I think I may pregnant."

He stared at her for a moment, his face blank.

That wasn't the reaction she had hoped for. What was he thinking?

He didn't leave her wondering for long. He ran a hand through his hair and blew out a long stream of air. "Aw, damn."

Her stomach sank. No, definitely not the reaction she had hoped for. He wasn't happy. Well, they weren't married yet. It *wouldn't* look good. But she wasn't far enough along that they couldn't salvage the situation, if they hurried.

"All right," he said. "No need to worry. We can deal with it."

There. That was what she was waiting for.

He went to his jacket and dug his coin purse out of the inside pocket. He shook a handful of setans out of the purse and counted. Then, midway through, he shrugged, poured them back into the purse, and held it out to her.

She took it reflexively but held it tentatively, confused.

"I think there're about fifty setans in there," Airell said. "The apothecary in Eleuria can take care of it for you; ask for Patli." He nodded to the purse in her hand. "That should be plenty to cover the cost."

She was so confused that the fact that she was holding more setans in her hand than she ever had before in her life didn't even faze her. *Take care of it?* "I-I don't understand. A midwife?"

He looked at the ground for a moment, his jaw twitching, and then he looked up and met her eyes. "No, Ivana. *That.*" He flicked his hand at her abdomen. "Get rid of it."

Her stomach dropped to her feet. "Wh-What?"

"Look—I know that's not what you wanted to hear, but this is an inconvenience for me. My father hates bastards. It's not too late to fix the problem before it becomes a bigger one."

He couldn't be serious. He *couldn't* be! "But, Airell," she said, catching his arm. "If we marry quickly, no one will know. It won't matter."

"I'm not ready for that yet," he said. "Just *deal* with it."

"This is our *child* you're talking about!"

He shook her off his arm, and when he next met her eyes, there was no hint of the cockeyed smile he saved for her, no warmth, no concern. Instead, he fastened back up his trousers. "I need to go." And he picked up his jacket and left.

Ivana stared at the door through which he had left, momentarily immobilized.

She put her hand to her stomach. He wasn't going to marry her, not now, and she was beginning to doubt...

Tears stung her eyes. He didn't even *care*.

She couldn't hide this. This wasn't a clandestine meeting. This would be very, very apparent within months.

Deal with it.

She swallowed, and the hand that held the coin purse began to tremble. How had this all gone so terribly wrong?

Chapter Seven

The back door to the apothecary's shop slammed open, and Nessa, one of Da Grania's children, stood on the threshold, her hands on her hips. "Boden!"

Ivana stepped back in time to allow the girl to pass uninhibited as she marched through the aisle of the shop, clearly intent on finding Boden to give him a tongue-lashing for whatever wound, real or imagined, he had inflicted upon her.

Ivana had been here often enough in the past months that she was barely acknowledged.

In some ways, the apothecary herself, Da Grania, reminded Ivana of her father. She never dispensed an ingredient or tonic without accompanying it with a mini-lesson on its proper storage, use, and disposal. Her enthusiasm for her work infused every interaction Ivana had had with her. That was why, despite Elidor's directive that she not return, Ivana found herself visiting this shop more often than she ought to. In fact, at times, she found her feet dragging her into the shop even when she didn't need anything—just to ask questions.

What Elidor didn't know wouldn't hurt him.

Boden had told her that Da Grania was almost never without an apprentice, and Ivana could believe it. She was obviously the sort of person who would enjoy the opportunity to pass on her knowledge.

Boden, like his mentor, was eager to share his knowledge, and Ivana was eager to learn. She spent many long afternoons during Elidor's absences in the apothecary with Boden, bent over a box of new ingredients or grinding herbs for no particular reason other than that it was good practice—and she didn't mind the more pleasant company.

In another life, she might have been in Boden's place somewhere.

A pang at the knowledge that all of that was lost to her now went through her.

Still. She found herself, with her new studies, for the first time since everything had gone wrong, occasionally enjoying herself.

It almost made spending the bulk of each day in Elidor's study either researching or experimenting with poisons worth it.

It almost made returning to her dark, lonely room bearable.

Almost.

Nessa had disappeared through the front door, but a few moments later, Boden himself entered through the back.

He ducked his head when he saw Ivana. "Sorry," he said, though Ivana wasn't sure what for. "I'll be back in a moment, but you're welcome to wait in the back. Don't tell Nessa I came this way?"

Ivana shrugged and nodded, and Boden followed Nessa out

the front.

Her eyes followed him until he was no longer in sight. Boden was only a year older than Ivana. Unfailingly polite. A bit bashful. Hardworking, but with a sense of humor.

It had occurred to her on more than one occasion that he was the sort of young man that her parents would have been pleased to encourage as a suitor—and that she might not have minded.

But none of that was possible anymore.

She drifted into the back room to wait for Boden. This room, ostensibly for storage, had its own outside door, the door the family used to enter their apartment above the shop. A long wooden table littered with an assortment of bottles and piles of herbs was evidence that the workroom, off to her right, had spilled into the "storage" room as well.

Da Grania herself was the next to march through the room, this time coming from the shop entrance. Annan, her youngest by a wide gap, was on her hip. She threw open the back door and yelled something indistinguishable out into the tiny yard where they kept chickens.

Ivana didn't know what Grania heard in response, but she whirled around, her eyes searching the room. They passed over Ivana twice, as if she were hoping to find someone else— probably one of her other two children—and then settled on her after all.

"Would you mind keeping an eye on Annan for a moment, dear?" she asked.

"Ah, I suppose," Ivana said, a bit taken aback by the request. "I mean, of course, Da."

Grania set the child down on his feet. "Thank you, dear. I won't be but a minute." She whisked out the back door.

Ivana settled onto the floor to wait. Annan eyed her for a

moment and then pointed to the door.

"Um...she'll be right back," Ivana said, guessing at what he wanted.

He pursed his lips, studying her face.

She offered him a tentative smile.

His lower lip protracted for a moment.

Please don't cry, please don't cry, please don't cry...

And then he burst out into a full, beaming smile and held his hands out to her. "Uh!"

"Oh. Sure."

He settled down onto one of her legs, took one of her hands, and began chattering happily in his nonsensical language. "Ungh?" he asked, pointing to a stool in the corner.

"The stool?"

"Na. Ungh mo?" He pointed to a stairway that led up to the family's apartment.

"Er...I don't think I should go up there."

"Mo. Ungh mo?" This time he pointed to the back door.

"I'm sure your mother will take you up there when she gets back."

He giggled, face beaming, and then stood up and toddled toward the stairs anyway.

"Oh...no..." she said, rising. "Really. Wait..."

He shrieked and sped up. Ivana caught him as he was starting to scramble up the stairs, and he giggled hysterically again. He then looked at her directly in the eyes and patted her face gently. "Na."

It didn't seem to require a verbal response this time. So Ivana patted his head. In return, he laid his head on her shoulder.

Ivana was unprepared for the wave of emotion that swept over her. She leaned against the wall, feeling unsteady. Tears pricked her eyes.

With her new studies keeping her busier, she could almost forget. Now, she wanted to push the child away, flee, drown herself, anything, *anything* to smother the despair.

The back door opened again. "It seems he's found a new friend," Grania said, taking the child from Ivana just in time.

"Mo," Annan said to his mother.

"Yes," she said, kissing him on the head. "I know."

Ivana didn't know what or how she knew, but she was grateful not to be alone any longer and yet at the same time craved escape.

"Thank you, dear," Grania said. "Are you waiting for Boden?"

"Yes, Da, but I..." Ivana swallowed. "Actually, I-I think I'll just come back tomorrow."

Grania raised her eyebrow. "Are you well?"

"Oh, yes, Da. Thank you."

Grania studied her for a moment. "Homesick, perhaps?"

Ivana gave her a forced smile. "Something like that."

"I recognize the look." Grania put Annan down, who darted toward the stairs again, and leaned against the work table. "I suffered three miscarriages and a stillbirth between Annan and my next oldest."

Ivana blinked. So that was why there was such a gap. But what relevance did this have?

"That's almost ten years of heartache. It was my work that saved me, kept me going, even as I experimented with herb after herb, trying to figure out the problem." She nodded to Annan, who, in fact, had not climbed the stairs but was sitting on the bottom stair and swinging his little legs into it with a repetitive *thunk, thunk.* "And now I have this little one." She patted Ivana's hand. "You'll make it through, dear."

Would she?

"Yes. Thank you, Da." Ivana turned and left the shop before her emotions overran her. Not even a hundred feet down the road, however, footsteps slapped the ground behind her, and someone called out her name.

She turned, surprised, and found Boden sprinting after her.

He stopped when he reached her and leaned over his knees, catching his breath.

She waited.

Finally, he straightened, flushing. "I'm sorry I took so long," he said. "I wanted to catch you. I-I've been meaning to talk to you about something."

Her stomach squirmed. *Oh, no.*

"I..." He ran a hand through his hair, then swallowed, twice. "Well, I guess there's nothing to do but come out and say it. I think—well, you're so interested in the apothecary I thought maybe..."

Don't do it, Boden. Please. Let it lie.

He gave a short laugh. "This isn't coming out the way I anticipated. Let me start over." He ran his hands over his shirt, smoothing imagined wrinkles. "I-I've taken a liking to you, Ivana. And, I was wondering if, perhaps, you might consider...me. I mean, we could explore..." He trailed off, his face darkening even further.

His verbal stumbling would have been sweet, perhaps even endearing, if the situation had been different. Instead, Ivana could only stare, her mind paralyzed by the sudden onslaught of a thousand thoughts.

Her stomach clenched. She knew this might happen. She would have been a fool not to notice how much Boden liked it when she came around.

She was a fool for continuing to do it. She should have listened to Elidor.

But all she had wanted was to feel normal again, that just one thing was right in the world.

Now, her fantasy had been ruined. She had to face reality. The world she had dabbled in the past couple months, the people whose company she had enjoyed—life with them, life as they lived it was unattainable for her as anything other than a sad imitation of what life might have been.

He was still waiting for a response, and as her silence stretched on, his brow furrowed in either, she supposed, anxiety or confusion.

"I-I don't know what to say," she said at last. And it was the truth. In another time, another place, other circumstances...she might have gladly accepted his offer. She might have even dared to hope for it. But now? What he was asking...it was impossible, for more reasons than he could ever know. How did she explain that? How could she make him understand that it wasn't him?

The furrow reached its deepest point, and then his eyes widened. "Oh!" He held out a hand, as if to ward away an unspoken objection. "You're from Ferehar. I wasn't even thinking. I'm so sorry. I'm happy to write your parents, first, if you feel that's necessary?" He chuckled nervously and looked at her hopefully.

"No," she said quickly. "I mean..." She bit her lip. "That's not it."

His face fell. "Oh. Well, I suppose that's better than an outright rejection?" Before she could reply, he went on. "Of course, you should have some time to think it over. I'm so sorry. Let me know one way or the other?"

"I-I will," Ivana said, and then she turned and fled before the hard lump that had been growing in her throat dissolved and her tears betrayed her.

* * *

Later that night, Ivana rolled a glass vial between her fingers while Elidor brought a cage holding a single rat into his study.

Elidor set the rat's food dish, filled with scraps, in front of Ivana and gestured to her. "Let's see it then."

He had returned later that afternoon after being away for almost three weeks and had made it clear that by the time he returned, he expected Ivana to be ready with an actual poison to test.

What he would have done had she not been prepared Ivana didn't know, but it didn't matter because the tiny vial held just that.

She hadn't known how he had intended to test it until he'd brought the cage into the room.

"You want me to poison the rat?" she asked.

"Obviously."

Ivana stifled a sigh. He didn't understand that the reason she had asked had nothing to do with misunderstanding his intent. He usually didn't. The more she came to know him—if it could be called that—the more she noticed peculiarities such as these. Half of his cruelty was merely his severe personality combined with a certain obliviousness.

The rat snuffled about in the cage, looking for its missing food dish.

It was a rat. Just a rat. Never mind its intended usage. Ivana uncorked the vial and tapped a drop onto the scraps.

Elidor whisked the dish away and placed it back into the cage.

Together, they waited and watched while the rat scarfed down its dinner, unaware that it had eaten its own demise.

The lull gave space in Ivana's mind for her previous thoughts to encroach again. She didn't want to go back to the apothecary, ever.

Grania had been kind to her, and her misplaced advice repeated in Ivana's mind. She didn't understand. She didn't know what Ivana had been through. And while it was true that work kept Ivana's mind off her troubles, they were always there waiting for her when her work was done.

Reminding her of how life would never be the same again, how she could never have anything of what she would have once dreamed.

Boden?

Part of her wanted to accept the young man's interest. To dare to see what would happen. It could be the chance at the new life she longed for—the life that had previously seemed so out of reach. But she doubted Elidor would approve. He hadn't even wanted her going back to the same apothecary. She was in far too deep.

If Boden knew, if Grania and her husband knew, the things she had done, the mistakes she had made, they would surely reject her out of hand. They were kind people, but Ivana couldn't confess to them the details of her past and trust they wouldn't care.

No. She had learned that no one was *that* kind.

The pain that could almost be forgotten while at the apothecary, and that had lessened to a dull ache while working with the poison, returned in full force. Ivana could almost hear words in the throbbing—words whispering about what she had lost, what she had given up, what she could never have, all because she had been a fool.

She had let herself be seduced by Airell when she should have known better, and she had lost everything because of it.

She had run north, instead of south, wanting to escape Ferehar as soon as possible, and had nearly died crossing the mountains at the brink of northern winter.

She had naively thought someone might hire her to do something useful, and were it not for Elidor, she would have starved or frozen to death on the streets or been forced to seek refuge in the workhouses and ended up a little more than a slave.

She had followed Elidor, allowing her curiosity to overcome the wiser path to let well enough alone.

In every instance, she had followed the whims of her heart, and in every instance, it had led her wrong.

To her horror, the tears that had been threatening all afternoon and evening started to fall.

Elidor didn't notice at first. He was too busy watching the rat. It had lain down on the floor of its cage and stopped moving. Dead.

She wished she could feel that way. It would be so much better to feel dead than to feel this never-ending cycle of regret, guilt, agony—to be lifted out of her tormented existence for a moment only to feel it even more keenly when she was plunged back in.

Elidor opened the cage door and poked at the rat. "Excellent." He turned to face her, blinked, and frowned. "What are you sniveling about?"

Damn it all. She didn't want to speak. It was like the pain had latched on to the wave of tears and intended on riding it to the end. If she let words come out of her mouth, it would be like tearing down the only dam she had left holding back the full force of it.

"Are you upset over the *rat?*" he asked, his tone not incredulous, as some people's might have been, but reproachful. He had already come to that conclusion based on the evidence in front of him, and he thought her daft for it.

"No," she said. "I don't care about the stupid rat!" As she had feared, speaking made it worse. She curled over onto herself, feeling like the girl who had first curled up into a ball in Elidor's tiny guest room four months ago. She had fooled herself into thinking she was managing the pain with her blade, but it had never gone away, and she just wanted it to go away.

"Then stop this nonsense. You have more work to do. You've successfully created a simple crafted poison; now try something more complicated." He glanced at a book of formulas lying to the side. "There was an intriguing recipe in there for a tonic that mimics the symptoms of blood fever. That could be useful."

The mention of blood fever, at that moment, in her current emotional state, was too much. The memory lodged in her throat until she felt as though she were choking.

Elidor was staring at her as though she were simple.

"My mother—blood fever," she managed to gasp out. She made no attempt to explain further. Elidor wouldn't understand or care. She was as certain of that as she was that the rat was dead.

His lips thinned and he shifted, annoyance flashing across his eyes.

No, he definitely didn't care.

The thought was so powerful that it stopped her torrent of tears. He didn't *care*!

How? "You don't care about any of the people you kill, do you?" she whispered.

"Does the sword care about the lives it takes?"

She managed a strangled laugh. "You're not a piece of metal, Elidor. You're a person."

"What is the point of this?"

"How?"

His eyes flashed with irritation again, but she didn't care.

"How, what?"

"How do you not care? How do you not *feel*?"

He snorted. "By feel, you mean driven about by foolish notions and urges like you and other pathetic creatures?"

Pathetic? Yes. That about summed it up. "Something like that."

"I was born with such superior abilities."

She wilted. She had hoped he had learned some trick he could teach her to simply cut off the emotions that tormented her.

Still, she pressed further. "Can you teach me?"

"I can't teach something I never learned." He stroked the dead rat absently. "However, I suppose..." He eyed her. "As with anything, one could learn by practice. Others of my profession are less emotionally volatile than the average person." He stopped with his hand on the rat. "But I know of only one way to teach you to be like me, and that is to teach you to *be* me."

And then the meaning of his words crystallized in her mind. "You mean...you would take me on as an apprentice?"

"I didn't say I would. While it's true that the government occasionally desires us to forge new swords, that has never been an interest of mine." Still, despite his words, something glimmered in his eyes. Was it a spark of interest?

The hope and desperation grew. It was crazy. But it might work. How did she convince him? "Look—I don't know why you took me in. I don't know why you've kept me here this long. I don't know why you didn't kill me when you said you should have. But surely I can do more for you than make poisons. Perhaps someone with a different perspective might help in other ways. Perhaps—"

He held up his hand, and she fell silent.

And the silence stretched on while it seemed he was studying every aspect of her face.

"Very well," he said at last. "But you should know that if I agree to this, I *must* inform my masters in order to secure the proper training for you. There is no turning back from that point. If they agree, you will be known as my apprentice, and you will not be able to work on your own until I say you are ready. If you try, they will order me to kill you." He raised a finger. "And if they do not agree, they will also order me to kill you."

She swallowed, wavering. Was this what she really wanted?

The answer came immediately. No. What she wanted was her old life back. But that could never happen, so in lieu of that, this might be her only option for building a new life.

Every decision she had thought was right had led her astray.

Perhaps it was time to make the wrong decision.

"I understand." She set her jaw and drew herself ramrod straight. "I'll do anything." Anything to make the pain stop. Anything.

He smiled. Not one of his performance smiles. But the smile that she had learned was genuine to him. It was mirthless and cold, but a smile nonetheless. "We shall see."

Chapter Eight

The next morning, Ivana sat at the dining room table penning a note to Boden. She felt remarkably calm about her decision to become Elidor's apprentice.

Perhaps it was that it was still a bit surreal. Perhaps it was that she didn't *want* to think about it more than she needed to.

All she needed to know—better, to desperately hope—was that when her training was complete, she would no longer be the girl who curled in upon herself night after night, trying to drive away the pain, who let her own blood to control it, who distracted herself with fantasy to ignore it.

She would be something else entirely, but she would, at least, be the master of her own mind and emotions again, as Elidor was.

She tapped her pen against the table and sighed. This was a coward's way, but she couldn't go back to the apothecary to decline Boden's overtures in person. There had never been hope of

Elidor allowing such a relationship.

Not that she was worthy of it. Boden deserved a woman untainted and whole. Not one who couldn't control herself, who could barely function, who crumbled at the merest mention of her lost family. Certainly not one who bled herself each night in an attempt to quell her own pain.

Her reasons, on paper, were twisted half-truths in an attempt to soften the blow, and she didn't want to face his questions—or even his disappointment.

"Your new training will begin today," Elidor's voice said from behind her.

She jumped and put a hand to her chest. She hadn't even heard him approach. "Your masters have agreed?" She tried to surreptitiously slide the paper under her elbow. It wouldn't be the first time she had sat at the table writing, and she hoped he would ignore it.

"Obviously, or you would already be dead. Now, your first lessons... What is that?"

She cursed herself. Her attempts to be surreptitious had only resulted in him taking note of her movement. "Um...just a note."

"A note," he repeated flatly. "To whom?"

She felt like a schoolgirl caught being inattentive. Except she had no doubt the consequences would be worse than a sharp rap on the knuckles and her note read for the whole class to hear.

No, lying would not serve her. All he had to do was take the note and read it. "To the apothecary's apprentice."

He pressed his lips together, and she hurried on before he could speak. "He made it clear he was interested in pursuing a courtship, and I needed to decline. Of course."

Elidor, as she had expected, held his hand out for the note, and she reluctantly gave it over.

He flicked his eyes over the paper. "Is this the same apothecary that I specifically instructed you *not* to visit again?"

He was not merely scolding her. His eyes were hard and his voice was cold. If he could channel the elements, like she had heard some Banebringers could do, she imagined she would be able to feel the chill wafting off him like a block of ice.

Now that she was officially under his tutelage, would he punish her physically for her disobedience?

That thought, too, remarkably engendered little more than a cringe. Nothing physical could match the darkness that had swallowed her, a darkness of her own making. She already punished herself daily for her mistakes; what was one more lash?

Frankly, she wasn't sure what had come over her this morning. She found herself raising her chin, looking him in the eye, and quipping, "Yes, Dal. But I'm afraid they had the best ingredients."

Peculiar mood notwithstanding, she quailed under his sharp gaze.

"This is not a profession with which one plays games," he said. "What I said then is doubly important now. You will not defy me again, in this or anything else."

She pressed her lips together. "No, Dal."

He laid the paper back down on the table. "Send your note. It will suffice to explain your foolishness."

Was that it? She hardly dared ask, with such luck, but she did need to know. "Where should I obtain my supplies from now on?"

But he didn't seem bothered by the question, perhaps because it was practical. "Do you have enough right now?"

She had more than enough. She had bought things she didn't need just for an excuse to visit the apothecary. But no more. A pang of regret hit her, and she pressed it away. She couldn't allow such feelings to master her anymore. "Yes."

"Good. Advise me when you need more, and I will answer that question." He didn't wait for a response to continue. "As I was saying, your first lessons will be in basic combat, which I have delegated to one of our trainers. I hardly have the time to waste on a neophyte."

Ivana picked up the paper tentatively, folded it twice, and held a bar of wax over a candle flame. "Fighting? I thought your type of work was best done through stealth and trickery."

"Indeed," Elidor replied, "but what will you do should you get caught?"

"Run?"

"And what will you do if someone has seen your face and shouldn't have? What if you encounter resistance? Leaving someone merely maimed is not an option. How will you know where to place the knife for maximum effectiveness? How long and where to grip the throat for suffocation? How—"

Ivana held up her hand, starting to feel sick. "I understand your point." She caught a drop of wax on her letter and sealed it. "Should you be discussing these things so freely with Da Veryna about?"

"I turned her back when she arrived early this morning. She is no longer in my employ."

Ivana blinked. "What? Just like that? No warning, no nothing?"

"Her presence is a liability with your new station."

"She's worked for you for five years!"

"What relevance does that have?"

"It's just not—" *Polite.* Ivana tried a different tactic. "Who will keep the house for you?"

"You will. It is time I received some return on my generosity."

The thought of taking over housekeeping duties was not appealing, but Ivana could hardly protest. The truth was, as often as he was gone, she would mostly be looking after herself.

"The kitchen is open to you. You may go to the market and prepare meals for yourself whenever you wish; I will inform you in advance when I will be present as well. You will also keep our rooms clean and handle the laundry. I trust your mother taught you the basics of all these things?"

"I am capable of doing the work," she said stiffly. "However, do I need to remind you that I am still totally dependent on your charity? I have no additional money with which to buy food."

His eyes flashed. "I'll give you a monthly allowance to cover your necessities. Do you have any more uninvited observations, or may I continue?"

His unkind comments and tone used to hurt her; now, her reaction to them ranged from her own irritation to incredulity. If nothing else, living with Elidor had toughened her skin.

Today, she dared to provoke him when he was already irritated. "Yes. How long will it take for me to master elementary skills?"

"That depends on the degree of your ineptness. At a point I deem appropriate, I will take over your combat training. Then, we will introduce 'stealth and trickery,' as you call it, into your schedule. You will also continue to improve your apothecary skills. Is there anything else you must know at this moment?"

"When do I begin?"

"This morning. Change into something appropriate."

With that, he left—with no guidance as to what "appropriate" might entail. She guessed it wasn't a frilly dress and dancing shoes, if indeed she had even owned them.

Da Veryna had bought her several changes of clothes shortly after Ivana had arrived, one set of which was a pair of trousers, a plain shirt, and boots. She donned these, feeling not at all prepared for whatever the day might bring.

Elidor took her to a large field littered with groups of men, some running, some doing other exercises, some sparring, and most being yelled at by stern older men.

It was awfully busy for their purposes.

"Where are we?" she whispered to Elidor as they paused at the edge of the field. It was early, both in the morning and in the spring season, and the words came out of her mouth in wisps of steam.

"The training grounds for the Cadmyrian army."

She blinked. "Should I be training so openly?"

"Who is the master?"

"I was just—"

"Sometimes the best disguise is the one you flaunt," Elidor said. "Llyr is fully capable of maintaining the needed discretion. Now, silence." A man—presumably the aforementioned Llyr— older than Ivana, but younger than Elidor, had spotted them and was now sauntering in their direction. Despite the cool morning air, his shirt was already soaked with sweat.

He didn't grasp Elidor's arm in a friendly greeting, but a smile plucked at the corners of his mouth. "Dal," he said. "You're having me waste my time with a girl?"

"If I thought it was a waste of time, I wouldn't be here," Elidor said, which was the closest he had ever come to complimenting her. "You have her every morning until I deem her skills adequate. The sooner, the better. Don't waste *my* time."

The man inclined his head, and Elidor turned to leave without so much as a nod or grunt toward Ivana. In seconds, she found herself alone and face-to-face with a strange man, who was now looking her up and down with far more scrutiny than made her comfortable. But she stood her ground, resisting the urge to shrink away from him or try to hide her body with her arms, as she had from the irksome man in the apothecary. She had decided to train under Elidor, and she would do whatever it took.

"In my opinion, you're far too sweet for this sort of thing," he said, finally meeting her eyes. "But Elidor wouldn't have taken you on at a whim, so I suppose we'll see what comes of it."

Too sweet? He could tell that by sizing up her body?

Oh. That was *exactly* what he meant. She bit her lip, her face burning.

"First point of order," he said. "Next time, bind those melons of yours." He looked pointedly at her chest. "They'll only get in the way."

She locked her jaw. She never liked comments on her appearance. But he was right. She hadn't thought of it.

Still, his distasteful attention was reminiscent of the immature boys in her hometown, right down to his choice of words. Her initial discomfiture churned itself up into indignation— the ire of the naïve girl who had once defended her sister's honor; the righteous fury that had been stripped away by her own shame.

And for the first time in a long time, she felt more alive, more aware, less surreal, and more herself, or whatever was left of her.

He cracked his knuckles. "Now," he continued. "You ever hit someone?"

"Once." She folded her arms across her chest. "A *boy* who commented one too many times on my melons." Actually, it had been the comment about her sister's that had snapped her, but no need to get into that.

He grinned. "Good. Give me everything you've got."

She didn't need to be told twice. She lashed her fist out, as she had once before, but instead of connecting with his face, it connected with his palm. The next thing she knew, he had grabbed her entire arm and hurled her to the ground.

Her back hit the packed dirt, and the force of the impact stunned her. She lay staring up at the sky, lungs struggling for air.

He crouched next to her, balanced on the balls of his feet. "Gonna have to do better than that, sweetheart."

She finally drew in the needed breath, sat up, and shoved him over. He tipped backward for an instant, off-balance. "Then why don't you stop fooling around and actually train me, smartass?"

He brushed himself off and stood up. "Feisty. I like that in a woman." He winked. "My name's Llyr. You would be...?"

"Ivana," she muttered.

And she hated him. With every fiber of her being. He was the representation of every immature, irritating male in her life who had made her so self-conscious about herself that she had fallen for the first man who had made her feel comfortable in her own skin.

That was a sudden self-revelation. Was that what had happened? Was that why she had given in to Airell so easily? Because of her own insecurities?

So much more the foolish mistake.

No more. She would meet Llyr's challenge, and she would win.

Imprudent

I vana held her cloak tightly around her and squinted into the blowing rain. She was glad that she had an excuse to wear the oiled cloak today. While as of yet, no one else had noticed her growing abdomen, *she* could see it when she looked at herself in the mirror unclothed, and she was self-conscious about it.

She clutched the cloak even harder. She had told her parents she was at the inn today, working a double-shift because someone was ill. Then, wanting to give herself plenty of time to make the trip to Eleuria, do whatever it took, and get home before anyone noticed, she had spent a bit of the money Airell had given her to hire a carriage.

She'd told the driver to drop her off here, outside an inn, ashamed to reveal where she was going. So she caught the attention of a man hurrying down the street.

"Excuse me," she said. "I'm looking for the apothecary?"

The man raised his head long enough to point down the street. "You're almost there," he said. "On the corner of the next intersection." He hastened away, no doubt eager to get out of the rain.

She swallowed and continued on until the building he referred to came into view. Sure enough, the apothecary's sign hung outside, dancing with the wind.

She smoothed her hair and pushed open the door.

A tiny bell tinkled, and a kindly-looking middle-aged woman looked up from behind the counter, where she was looking through a shallow box of vials. Her creamy tan skin wasn't nearly dark enough to be a native Fereharian; more likely she was from one of the three central regions.

She gave Ivana a warm smile. "Good morning, dear," she said, then glanced through the store window. "Though I don't know if it could rightly be called good, yes?"

Ivana looked around the shop. It wasn't the first time she had been in an apothecary. Her own town, Tian, had a modest one she frequented, fetching ingredients for her father and his experiments.

But Eleuria was much larger than Tian, and the apothecary was more impressive to match. Shelves and shelves held meticulously labeled ingredients in bottles and bundles and vials—some she had never even heard of. She was so fascinated, she almost forgot why she was here.

She turned back to the woman. "I-I'm looking for Da Patli," she said.

"Then you've found her," the woman said. "What can I do for you? An order of medicine?" She winked. "A love potion perhaps?"

Ivana stared at her. She wasn't in the mood for jests, and certainly not jests about love.

The woman's smile faded, and she studied Ivana for a moment. "I see," she said. "A different sort of customer then. Come with me."

Ivana didn't know how the woman knew why she was there,

but she didn't have time to explain before she was forced to follow her behind the curtain into the back of the store.

A girl around Ivana's age was there, poring over a ledger.

"Are the boys still out?" Patli asked her.

"Yes, Mama," the girl said.

"Good. Mind the front for a bit and see that I'm not disturbed."

The girl bobbed and then disappeared back through the curtain.

Patli browsed another set of shelves, still meticulously labeled, but instead stacked with small and medium boxes and crates. She selected one that had been shoved to the back, opened it, and then put the lid back on and tucked it under one arm. "Follow me," she told Ivana.

Again, Ivana obeyed. The woman led her up a narrow flight of stairs, and they emerged into a small kitchen—no doubt part of Patli's living area.

Patli gestured to a chair at the kitchen table.

Conscious that her cloak was dripping all over the floor, Ivana slipped it off and hung it on a coatrack next to the top of the stair, and then she sat, feeling increasingly uncomfortable by the moment.

Patli set the box down on the table. "You're with child?

Ivana flushed. "Yes, Da. I-I was told y-you could..." She couldn't even finish the sentence.

"You were told correctly," the woman said briskly, her kind demeanor gone. "Does the father know you're here?"

She could barely squeak the words out of her throat. "He's the one who sent me."

Patli's mouth turned downward. "Of course he is," she muttered. "Well. How far along are you?" Her eyes slid over Ivana, as if to make a judgment for herself.

"I think no more than five months."

"You have payment?"

Ivana put the purse she had been clutching in one hand on the table.

Patli took it and shook the coins out of the purse. One eyebrow rose. "Let me guess: Gan Gildas' eldest?"

Ivana's mouth went dry. She nodded. "How—?"

"He's the only one of them who is *so* wealthy he doesn't even care that he gave you triple what I ask." She turned away to start pulling ingredients out of the box.

"Only one of *them*, Da?"

"Damn nobles."

Ivana didn't want to hear this. She had hoped, even up until this moment, even when Airell hadn't returned since the day she had told him about the pregnancy, that he hadn't been what Izel had warned her about, that he hadn't been what she had feared, near the end.

Yet she couldn't help it, like pressing on a new bruise to see if it still hurt. "I'm not the first to come to you bearing his seed, I take it."

Patli was at the stove now, heating water, and she turned around to regard Ivana. Pity entered her eyes, interrupting her now-brusque manner. "Poor soul," she said. "Is that a revelation to you?"

That moment was the first time Ivana knew what it was to hate herself.

It shouldn't have been a revelation. She should have seen, should have known. She *had*, on some level. She just hadn't wanted to believe it.

She should have known better.

Patli sighed and turned back to the stove. She tapped a bit of powder from a vial into the now-boiling water.

"Forgive me, Da," Ivana said, "but you don't seem keen to provide this...service."

Patli jerked her head. "I do this because at one point, it put food in my stomach and the stomach of my children. If it weren't for irresponsible nobles, me and mine would be living on the streets right now, if not dead."

Ivana hesitated. "Your husband?"

She snorted. "Good-for-nothing man who dragged me to this backwater region seeking riches and then left me alone with three little ones when he didn't find them."

Ivana blinked. That was terrible. She could never imagine her own father doing such a thing. "But does the shop not provide—"

"Too late for that now," Patli said. "I'm one of only a handful of apothecaries in all of Setana who knows anything about seeing this done, at least safely. If I refused, the nobles would see me out of business as soon as the coins were back in their greedy hands. They don't like bastards. Not good for anyone."

Ivana rubbed her forearms. She had never thought of herself as living a privileged life, but it struck her deeply that such things had never affected her. They lived comfortably off her father's income educating Lord Kadmon's children. She had never known what it was to be hungry, or to fear lack of shelter or warmth over the winter.

"Sometimes," the apothecary said softly, as if to herself, "one does what one must do to survive." She finally turned back, holding a steaming mug. "Now," she said. "Before we continue, you need to know what you're getting yourself into. We'll need a few hours. I trust you have that?"

Ivana nodded. She was glad she'd splurged on the carriage.

"This isn't going to be pleasant. Expect heavy bleeding, pain, weakness, and when all is said and done, a terrible headache.

But it will cause you to miscarry."

Ivana's stomach churned. "Is—is it safe?"

A not-quite-smile twisted Patli's lips. "For the mother."

The word, a word Ivana had associated with warmth and care, now ran cold into her gut.

Mother. She hadn't yet thought of herself in that way, yet that was what she would be if this continued. And yet the father would be no father. How was that fair? How was that right? And yet...

"Hopefully," Patli continued, "you will be wiser going forward, yes?"

Ivana's throat closed at the reminder of her folly. He had beguiled and seduced her, and she—*she!*—had fallen for it, allowed herself to be used, against every shred of common sense, done everything, *everything* he had asked.

An unbidden rush of air escaped her lips, and something fierce began to burn within her.

No. Not this time. She wouldn't let him have the satisfaction, would take his blood money and use it to raise the child he so despised.

She stood up so abruptly, the chair nearly toppled over. "No."

Patli raised an eyebrow.

She breathed in deeply, wanting the words to come out confident, bold, but found that her voice quivered nonetheless. "I-I'm sorry I've wasted your time, Da, but I..." She choked on her words for a moment and then spit them out. "I can't do this."

Patli studied her. "You realize that you won't get a setan more from Gan Gildas' treasury?"

Her resolve wavered. "I..." But she could force no other words past the lump in her throat.

Patli nodded, and then she slid aside a number of the coins still lying on the table. "I'm sorry to say, I still have to take my payment. The herb that makes this work so well is rare and quite illegal, as it grows outside Setana. I pay a high price to have it imported under the noses of the Conclave." She gestured to the abandoned mug. "I can't get it back now."

Ivana bit her lip. "I understand," she whispered.

Patli swept the remaining coins back into the purse. "Lucky for you, Lord Airell's carelessness and arrogance has its benefits as well." She gave the purse, still heavy, back to Ivana.

A bribe. Payment to dispose of a bastard, and payment to silence the mother.

To make her fade away.

The flame that had spurred her to this decision sputtered as self-loathing rose in hot tears behind her eyes.

She bowed to Patli and hastened to leave. She didn't want the apothecary to see her cry.

She would reserve that for the lonely carriage ride home.

The two hours of thinking about how she was going to tell her parents and deep breathing to calm herself were wasted.

Izel was waiting for her at the end of the path leading to their huddle of homes, and she was pacing.

Ivana wasn't given to swearing, but she did then, even if only in her head. That could only mean that her parents had found out she wasn't working at the inn today.

Her carefully crafted lead-ins to telling her parents would be worth nothing now.

She resumed the deep breathing, hoping she could at least appear outwardly calm as she approached Izel.

Izel's face melted from worried to relief to glee. "Ana! You are in *so* much trouble."

Ivana hadn't even told Izel that she had lied about her

planned whereabouts that day; in retrospect, perhaps she should have. Izel had safeguarded the secret of Ivana's romance all this time; why would this have been different?

Only she knew why.

Ivana didn't trust herself to speak. She didn't want to waste whatever composure she had stored up on Izel. So she merely glanced at her and walked by.

Izel dogged her footsteps. "Was this another secret meeting with—?"

"Hush," Ivana said, though it hardly mattered now.

"I didn't say anything, if that's what you think." When Ivana didn't respond, Izel offered an explanation anyway. "Mama and I were in town this afternoon buying cloth for new dresses, and she decided to stop by the inn to see how you were doing."

It had been inevitable that something like that would happen eventually. She had been lucky until then.

Perhaps it would have been better had she been found out sooner. Then she wouldn't be in this state.

In retrospect, she had been a fool.

The purse in her pocket was like a lump of lead smacking against her thigh, reminding her of the disgrace she was about to bring upon herself and her entire family.

Had she made the right decision? She was short on good decisions lately; it was as though she didn't even know her own mind, which she used to prize.

So much for a sound mind. She was a stupid girl, a stupid, foolish girl.

Tears pricked at her eyes again, and she blinked them back.

Not again, not yet. She had to hold it together a little longer.

Both her mother and father were waiting for her as she walked in the door. Her father turned around from near his lab equipment, and her mother rose from the couch, the shirt she had been mending falling off her lap onto the floor. Izel slipped by and loitered near the door of their room—no doubt in case she needed to make a hasty exit.

Her mother rushed to hug her. "Ana! Where have you been? We've been so worried!" She pulled back, and the words tumbled out of her. "Why did you lie about working today? Whatever could you have been thinking? Whatever could you have been *doing*? We were so *worried!*" She took in a sharp breath, and her tone changed. "You had better have a good explanation. Your father had to miss a tutoring session to go look for you!" She swung her head to pin Izel with a glare.

Izel tugged on her pendant and sank a little deeper into the doorframe of their room.

No doubt she had been interrogated thoroughly and hadn't even given her parents her best guess, which would have been a good one.

Her father said nothing, but his eyes reflected the worst thing Ivana could have seen there—disappointment. Not at the lost session. At the insensibility of his sensible daughter.

Oh, if only he knew.

He would know. There was no way around it now.

Her stomach tightened again. She tried to speak, but the words wouldn't come out. How could they? No rehearsals could prepare her for this. She didn't even know where to begin.

Best to get it over with.

"I'm with child," she said softly, but loud enough for them to hear. The last thing she wanted to do was repeat the words.

The silence in the room mimicked the suffocating weight of her shame. Then at last, her father blinked and shook his head.

Ivana could almost hear his internal monologue. *No, he would say. Not my daughter.*

"Were you forced?" he asked instead, always the pragmatist.

She shook her head, and he closed his eyes.

Not my sensible, intelligent daughter.

I'm so sorry, Papa! she wanted to cry out in response, but her tongue stuck fast.

Her mother sank back down onto the couch, treading on the forgotten shirt on the way, her hand to her mouth.

Izel's eyes widened in shock and then—oh, how terrible it was to watch—there was the loss. As much as she harassed Ivana, Izel had always looked up to her, despite Airell.

But this.

This was too much, even for Izel, her equal parts carefree and careless sister.

This was the lowest of shame.

Ivana wished someone would speak. Wished everyone would stop staring at her.

Her father pressed his lips together, shook himself, and strode over to his writing desk, purpose in his steps. He opened a drawer, lifted out a sheet of white pressed paper, the best kind, reserved for correspondence with the university or nobles. "How far along?" he asked.

"I-I think around five months."

He grimaced. "Well, there will be no avoiding a scandal," he said. "But it will fade, soon enough. I'll send an entreaty to the boy's parents and insist upon an immediate marriage. No boy is going to seed my daughter and not share the consequences."

Her mother still sat, silent, hand over her mouth, tears shimmering in her eyes.

Her father sat, picked up his pen, and held it at the ready over the inkwell. "Well, what is the boy's name, Ivana? Come.

Let's get this over with."

Ivana met Izel's eyes. Why did it all seem so clear in hindsight? What had she been thinking? How could she have ever thought he loved her? How had she ever been so foolish as to think he would *marry* her, a commoner—a commoner in good standing, yes, but still a commoner, a nobody.

She wanted to sink into the floor, to cover her horrible, seductive body, the heat of shame pricking every part of her.

"Ivana?"

"Airell," she said. "It's—It was Lord Airell, Gan Gildas' eldest."

The room went dead silent. The tapping of her father's pen against the side of the inkwell, the soft rustle of her mother worrying at a handful of her skirt—gone.

Ivana didn't dare look at him.

"You realize that you won't get a setan more from Gan Gildas' treasury?"

Her normally levelheaded, calm father simply couldn't take it anymore. She jumped as the sound of his pen snapping against the desk broke the silence. His chair scraped back against the floor. "Gan Gildas' eldest? *Gan* Gildas' eldest? Surely, you jest. *Tell* me you jest!" He didn't wait for a response. He knew she wouldn't jest about that. "How could you *be* so utterly foolish? How could you have so little *sense?*"

She cast her eyes down. "I'm sorry, Papa," she whispered, the tears she had been holding back finally spilling over.

He didn't seem to notice. Instead, he strode from one end of the room and back. "It's one thing to have a dalliance with the stable-boy. At least then there would be a good chance of marriage. But a *lord?* What were you *thinking?* Why, Ana, *why?* Of all the imprudent, thoughtless—"

Her mother finally collected herself. "Galvyn," she said firmly. She stood up, paced to Ivana, and put one hand on her shoulder. "This isn't helping."

Her father brought himself up short and turned to face both of them.

Once he stopped talking, Ivana drew out the pouch of coins and held it out. "He gave me the money to get rid of the child." When he didn't take it, she walked over and put it on his desk, trembling, trying to radiate strength, and failing. "I went—I went to the apothecary. Today. That's where I was." More tears spilled over. "But I couldn't do it." Doubt seeped into her. *Why? Why hadn't she just done it?* "I-I... Did I make the wrong decision?"

Uncertainty, confusion, fear—they conspired together to suffocate her.

It was like the year of the sky-fire when she had been seven years old, and Izel not yet six, and a tear had formed behind the walls of Lord Kadmon's estate. She could still remember the sound of the bloodbane's enraged shrieks at finding itself trapped, the rending of wood as it spent its fury on structures nearby, the shouts of Lord Kadmon's guards as they bravely tried to corner it and herd it through the gate, so it could flee into the countryside beyond the walls...their screams as they died.

It had taken them five guards' lives and three days to manage it. Three days of hiding, listening, praying it wouldn't come in their direction.

And she had been but a child. She felt like that child now, confused, scared, suffocated...just wanting her father and mother to tell her it would turn out okay.

Her father looked down at her face and deflated. He hesitated, then drew her into his arms in a rough embrace. "I'll do everything in my power to make this right," he promised, and then he kissed the top of her head.

He didn't answer her question, one way or the other, and

Ivana could do nothing else but weep.

Chapter Nine

For the first time, it was Ivana staring smugly down at Llyr, instead of the other way around.

Granted, she had cheated.

Llyr groaned and rolled to the side, clutching at his crotch. "Ground rules. Unfair move. Doesn't count."

"And the point of all this is for me to learn *fair* combat?" she replied. The situations she would be using these skills in would be anything but fair.

He opened one eye to look at her, and then he sat up and draped his arms over his knees. His eyes flicked to her face, her clenched fists, her tense posture. "What's wrong, sweetheart? Did I offend you?"

"Stop calling me that!" The urge to kick him again—in the face, in his groin, anywhere she could connect and cause him more pain—was so strong he must have seen it, because he flinched back.

He studied her for a moment and then stood up. For a moment, she thought she might get an apology out of him, but no such luck. "I think training is done for the day," he said instead.

"What? What about weapons?" They typically started with hand-to-hand and then for the past month or so, had ended with knife fighting.

"You think I'm putting anything resembling a weapon in your hand right now, as angry as you are?"

She blinked and stepped back from him. His constant crude remarks about her appearance and suggestive comments about things they could do outside training made her angry, yes, but he was right.

She wasn't certain what she might do if he put a blade in her hand and he made one more crass remark.

What was happening to her?

She hadn't wanted to turn into a monster. She wanted to not *feel* at all. Was trading despair for rage helpful?

She swiped at a drop of sweat threatening to drip into her eyes and noted with dissatisfaction that her hand trembled.

Fine, she thought stubbornly. She was tired and hot and didn't feel like training anymore today anyway. Spring was drawing to a close, and for the first time this year, she could feel the near-summer sun beating down on her mercilessly.

She turned away from Llyr, meaning to set off toward Elidor's home, but instead spotted the man himself headed her way. He occasionally stopped by to watch her train—to mark her progress, she presumed—so his presence wasn't a surprise.

She met him at the edge of the field.

"Where are you going?" he asked.

"Llyr told me I was too angry to keep practicing," she said. She didn't care what Elidor thought of that.

"Did he? Interesting." He waved his hand in the vague direction of his house. "Go home then. I'll meet you there."

Ivana had expected him to be more irritated at her proclamation. To say something about how she was wasting time and money.

She dutifully started in the direction of Elidor's house, but not before throwing a glance back toward Elidor. He was conversing with Llyr intently.

Perhaps this was the end of it. She couldn't succeed as a scribe, a tutor, a daughter, a sister. What made her think she would succeed as a heartless killer?

Misery quickened her steps. Several months of training with Llyr had done nothing to abate the despair that crept in at night. The sharp edge of her knife still waited to give her relief.

Ivana stood in front of Elidor's desk, feeling like a misbehaving student about to be scolded by the school master. It had been a while since she had allowed such a juvenile emotion to grip her, which in turn made her sulk more.

Elidor watched her in silence for what must have been fifteen minutes. She didn't know what he was hoping to find by studying her face for so long. She wanted to break the standoff, but she refused to be the first to speak. Some of her mood was simple stubborn petulance.

Finally, Elidor spoke. "Llyr tells me that you delivered an unfair blow today."

She grunted. "It seems to me that's the best kind for my purposes."

He nodded, and for the first time, there was *approval* in his eyes. "Correct. There are no rules when it comes to the type of fights we might engage in, other than to not leave yourself in a compromising position." He rapped the top of his desk with his knuckles. "Still. You let your anger control you, instead of the other way around. You must *always* be the one with the control."

She gritted her teeth. "I'm sorry, Dal. But he makes me uncomfortable. Can we find some other trainer?"

"Uncomfortable?"

"He's always..." She waved her hand in the air. "Making rude comments and such."

"And that's why you became angry?"

The condescension in his voice annoyed her. "Don't lecture me. I *know* you get angry, or at least irritated. I can see it in your eyes sometimes. If you feel nothing else, at least you feel that."

"I do. And it can be useful, but only if you are the one controlling it. If it controls you, you may do something rash in a moment when you need your head."

"All right, *master*," she said. "What would you suggest I do?"

"Fortunately, Llyr has informed me that you have passed your evaluation period. I have permission to continue your training at my discretion, and so you no longer need to train with Llyr."

Elidor's first statement intruded on her relief at the second. "I *passed?*"

He gave her a grim smile. "Indeed. Did you think our masters would simply accept at my word a new apprentice? Your combat training served dual purposes: to prepare you for more advanced study, and so that our masters could evaluate for themselves whether you are capable of this job."

"*Llyr* is one of your—our—masters?" she asked incredulously. Burning skies, she hoped not.

"He reports to them," Elidor said.

She exhaled through her nose. "And what if I had failed?"

"You would not have lived to know it."

Ivana swallowed. She had expected that answer, but it still

sent a shiver down her spine. She had jumped into this hole with eyes open, and she couldn't go back. "So what are the next steps?"

"Now that you have satisfied my masters, I am in full charge of the direction of your training. We will begin to focus more on skills specific to our profession—'stealth and trickery,' I believe you once called it. You will continue to practice the hand-to-hand and dagger skills you have already learned. You will continue studying the apothecary arts. And"—he held up a finger—"I wish you to renew your study of foreign languages."

She blinked. That had been unexpected. "But why?"

"Not all of our targets are Setanan," he said. "I could see the usefulness of being able to understand the languages of the surrounding countries. And since you already have a foundation, there is no reason not to build on it."

"Is this...*sanctioned?*"

"Absolutely not," he said. "And you will not mention it to anyone, least of all our handler, when you finally meet him."

"Of course," she murmured, lowering her eyes. "But what will I use to study?"

"I will see to obtaining the necessary resources."

She nodded, hardly daring to look up, lest Elidor see the excitement reflected in her eyes. She didn't think he would approve.

"I have one final course of training that you will begin immediately," Elidor continued.

She did look up then. His tone...

He stood up and clasped his hands behind his back. "You have one advantage over me. You are a woman."

She furrowed her brow. That was an advantage?

"I would estimate ninety percent of targets are men. Of those, half—if not more—would be easily manipulated into doing or saying exactly as you please, if only you have the right tools. I—at least in most cases—do not. You, on the other hand..." He turned to look at her, and then, for the first time since she had met him, his eyes swept over her in an appraising manner.

Oh. Oh! She felt herself flushing. "I-I..."

"Stop stuttering."

She pressed her lips together and forced herself to meet his eyes. "You mean to say, I can trick men into thinking I'll sleep with them, so as to put them in a position where I can do what I need to do." She still tried not to think about the result. It was all hypothetical right now.

He gave a cold smile. "Oh, no. You *will* sleep with men to put them in a position to either use them or kill them. Overcome by base urges and thus prone to irrational and foolish decisions, and likely alone...often you will find this to be a perfect setting to do your work."

Ivana's rage, despair, petulance, and even anticipation—anything she had felt in the past several hours—were washed away by his words, leaving in their place a disbelieving numbness. "What?"

"Was I unclear? You will learn to use your body as part of your arsenal of tools."

"You're serious!"

"I," he said, nostrils flaring, "*do not jest.*"

He was irritated again, but she didn't care. She was trying to wrap her mind around his suggestion. No, his demand.

She couldn't do that. She just...she couldn't. It was the one thing she couldn't do. "I can't. I-I won't."

His eyes glittered dangerously, though his speech was measured. "This is the most logical direction for your training. You will not defy me."

"You don't understand," she said.

"You would hold to your purity over your life?"

She clenched her teeth. "I'm not—I'm not pure."

"Then I don't see the difficulty."

Of course he didn't. Even if she tried to explain it to him, she doubted he would.

"On the contrary, this seems to me to be the perfect solution to your earlier problem. If you wish to control an aspect of yourself, then you must become numb to that which provokes you."

Numb. That was what she had wanted, wasn't it?

She cast her eyes to the ground, her palms sweaty. "What is it you want me to do?" she whispered.

"This is not something I can train you in. For the next few months, one Da Lavena, the proprietor of a local consort house and informant for our masters, will instruct you in this matter. I have already made the arrangements."

That could not mean what she thought it meant. It couldn't. "Consort house?"

"In common parlance, a high-class brothel."

It did. "You...you want me to train to be a *whore*?"

Elidor glanced absently at his calendar and continued on as though she hadn't spoken. "Since the sky-fire is in three days, you will begin one week from today. This will give time for preparation and any cleanup needed after the sky-fire. Obviously, if cleanup turns out to be extensive this time, we can be flexible." He frowned, as if the possibility that a roving monster might interrupt his plans was merely an annoyance.

But she had barely heard him. Who cared about the sky-fire? Bloodbane be damned—he wanted her to train to be a *whore*? Her mind was spinning, her stomach clenched tight in revulsion.

"From what you've told me, this should be nothing new to you."

Apparently, he *had* heard her.

And it stung. It shouldn't have, coming from Elidor, but it did all the same. It pierced her chest and wormed its way into her already broken heart, making her relive the taunts, the whispers, the looks, all in one moment. *Whore. Whore. Whore.*

She wanted nothing more than to desperately escape back to her room and her blade.

For months? How would she survive such humiliation?

This was not playing with herbs in a back room. This was not sparring with blunted blades. This was not poring over books or learning how to pick a lock.

This was not hypothetical.

"Unless, of course, you wish to pursue your other option?" he asked.

She swallowed. Death. She had committed to this, knowing she couldn't back out. And she *had* said she would do anything, hadn't she? She had thought that meant slitting people's throats, not seducing men.

She almost laughed at the craziness of what she was feeling. *You think you can kill someone, but you can't sleep with another man? Remember why you did this in the first place.*

She gritted her teeth. She *could* do this. She could look it in the face and laugh, and if in the end, it numbed her to everything she was feeling right now...

She bowed her head. "I am at your service."

Chapter Ten

The door off the back of Elidor's study did indeed lead down to his safe room, which doubled as his wine cellar, apparently—a luxury she hadn't even realized he had.

Ivana dropped the last of the supplies they might need in a corner of the room and shook out her arms, glad to be done. Elidor had told her to haul anything they might need to the safe room and then disappeared. He had given her no further parameters. She didn't know if it was supposed to be some sort of test, to see if she had enough foresight to gather supplies not only for the night, but for any potential lengthier stay, or if he was just lazy.

Either way, he conveniently appeared now that all the hard work was over, carrying a single satchel.

She said nothing while he surveyed the pile.

Enough food and water for up to a week. Sleeping rolls and blankets. Books, paper, writing utensils. Lanterns and oil to keep them burning. Two large covered chamber pots. And a moveable screen.

His gaze lingered on the last, and he turned to her with one eyebrow raised.

"For privacy," she said, lifting her chin. The gods knew it was bad enough to be cooped up for a single night with other people and nowhere else to go. What if they had to stay longer?

One never knew how bad it would be any given year. The tears in the veil between worlds that appeared during the annual sky-fire—the tears that also let hundreds or even thousands of bloodbane through—manifested at random, and the monsters that came through them could be anything from mostly benign bloodsprites to horrific beasts that didn't even have a name.

Therefore, cleanup from the sky-fire could likewise mean anything from repairing minor damage to days of the Watch having to hunt down and fight bloodbane that were rampaging around the city. Meanwhile, citizens were trapped in their homes, or safe rooms, if they had enough means to build one.

Despite his scrutiny, Elidor ended up making no comment on the screen or any of the other supplies. He merely set his satchel down on one of the many crates in the room and then returned to the safe room door. Ivana supposed he was satisfied with her preparations.

He put his hand on the handle. "The first fire is crossing the sky. If there's anything else you need..."

She shook her head.

He gripped the handle, leaned back, and put all his weight into forcing the heavy metal door to move. It groaned, but once it had moved an inch, it swung the rest of the way with relative ease.

It shut with a resounding clang.

Elidor slammed the metal bar down across the door as an extra precaution—causing a secondary clang.

Ivana had been prepared for the first clang; she jumped at the second and chuckled to tame her nerves. "I guess no one's ever sneaking into your wine cellar to steal some wine."

He flicked his eyes to her and then settled down onto one of the crates to begin unpacking his satchel.

Right. He didn't jest.

She sighed and sat down cross-legged on another wooden crate in the corner. She nestled her back against the corner and picked up one of the books. This was going to be a long night.

A few hours later, Ivana was still reading the same book.

At least, she was trying to read the book. It was plenty bright enough—she had placed several lanterns around the room—it was just...quiet.

Too quiet, given that she wasn't alone.

She lifted her eyes for what seemed like the hundredth time since Elidor had shut the safe room door and studied the man who sat across the room from her.

He had made a makeshift desk by laying a thin, flat piece of wood on top of a crate, and he sat hunched over on the crate adjoining it, poring over a sheaf of papers and occasionally making notations on what looked like a ledger.

He hadn't spoken a word to her since the door had shut.

He seemed absorbed in his work.

She knew better.

She had caught him watching her at least four times since she had started reading. Well, not *her* precisely. Her hands. Usually when she was turning a page.

It was difficult to read a book without exposing one's hands, and it was becoming a little disconcerting.

He glanced at her hands for a fifth time; he wasn't trying to hide it very hard. She gave up.

She laid a bookmark in the page she was on, closed and set aside the book, and waited.

It took a moment, but he finally lifted his eyes to meet her own.

He regarded her for a moment, dark eyes glimmering with unreadable thoughts. And then he turned back to his work.

She exhaled. She didn't know if she could take this much longer, and the gods forbid that they might have to stay longer than the night because of rogue bloodbane.

She stood up and stretched. She had to do *something* to keep her mind off her impending training in four days, and the pile of blankets she had dragged in to sleep on didn't seem inviting at present. "Would you believe I've never spent a sky-fire in a safe room?"

"Of course you haven't."

That gave her pause. It wasn't the answer she'd been expecting. It wasn't the *expected* answer, which should have been polite surprise or further inquiry.

"What is that supposed to mean?" she asked.

He made a mark on a paper. "If you had come from stock able to afford a safe room as a child, I would not have found you a half-starved wretch on the streets."

She wasn't sure whether she ought to feel affronted or abashed. Since she was sure to be plenty abashed in the days to come, she chose affronted. "And I suppose *you* come from a long line of well-to-do assassins?"

"I was raised in an orphanage. I haven't the faintest idea who my parents are—or were."

She blinked. She hadn't expected him to respond to her sarcastic reply, except perhaps with derision. Certainly not with an *actual* answer. "I-I didn't know. I'm sorry."

"Why?" he snapped. "My parentage and background is of no consequence to me. Neither will yours be to you, if you learn your lessons well." He flipped over a page. "And don't stutter. It shows hesitancy. There is no room for self-doubt in this profession."

Ivana choked back a laugh. No room for self-doubt? She had practically perfected the art of self-doubt. That didn't seem to bode well for her work in "this profession."

She sank back down to the crate, pulled her knees up to her chest, and wrapped her arms around them. Was it even possible for her to become what Elidor was? It had been over a year and a half since her father had died, and she felt no closer to finding peace than she had on that day. Perhaps this whole endeavor was crazy.

If so, it was too late to turn back now. She would learn indifference like Elidor, or she would die trying. Either option was acceptable.

And yet... "You make it sound so easy," she said, more to herself than him.

His pen hovered above the paper, and though he didn't look at her directly, his head tilted. For a moment, she dared to hope for some sympathy. A friendly squeeze of the shoulder, assuring her not to worry, how one day she too could care as little as he about the wreck she had made of her life.

But an edge of something beyond merely *cold* now crept into his voice. "Dozens of times in as many years I have spent this evening, and occasionally a few beyond, in pleasant solitude."

She should have known better. "If you enjoy your solitude so much, why in Yathyn's name did you agree to take me on as your apprentice?"

"A mistake I could easily correct."

She swallowed and laid her head back against the stone wall behind her. There wasn't a back door to his safe room, was there? The only exit was the entrance, the heavy metal door that was now shut and sealed against any bloodbane that would come through tears created that night.

She wasn't even sure she'd be able to open it without his help.

Elidor was still looking down at his work.

He hadn't changed his cold, clipped tone when he had made the not-so-subtle threat. She studied him again. He was so normal-looking in his loose tan shirt and brown trousers, hunched over his ledger like any businessman. One would hardly believe that he could trade that pen for a dagger in an instant.

A dagger he no doubt had with him, though she didn't see it.

She ran one hand absently along the top of the crate next to her. Why *had* he agreed to take her on? He certainly had no fondness for her. He obviously had no need or desire for company. He had made no indication that he wanted a free whore—were that the case he could have now taken the opportunity to "train" her himself, rather than delegating the task to someone else. Did he feel some connection or obligation to her, because—as she had discovered—they were both orphans?

But he didn't seem the type to put weight on such commonalities.

She couldn't come up with any logical explanation, which was, perhaps, the most disconcerting part of it all.

A sudden and sharp pain shot through her hand. She jerked her hand back in surprise and spread it wide in front of her. A clean slice ran across her palm. Though it was shallow, blood was already oozing out of the length of the cut.

What in the abyss? She squeezed her hand shut and then leaned over to look at the crate. The metal closure on the crate had one sharp, jagged bit sticking out, and in her distraction, she had run her hand across it.

She opened her hand again, tentatively. It could be worse. The gods knew she had dealt worse damage to herself in the past months.

Somehow, this was different. It stung, and she hadn't wanted it there.

She bit her lip. Elidor said nothing. He probably hadn't even noticed, and she was sure he would be annoyed by her making a mess, asking for aid—anything related to another disturbance to his peace.

She hesitantly lifted her eyes to him.

She was wrong.

He was already watching her—or, her hand.

"Um," she said. "Do you have a rag or something? I'm not sure what I did... This box..." She was mumbling, and he, by all accounts, wasn't listening. "Never mind." She slid off the crate. "I'll use one of my blankets. I'll-I'll work on getting the stain out later." She went to the pile of blankets, bent down, and picked one up with her uninjured hand.

And as she straightened and turned, she was startled to find him standing directly behind her.

Without a word, he grasped her wrist and turned the hand over. He pressed his thumb into the bottom of her palm, right below the cut. She flinched back as the pressure forced more blood out of the wound—but it also forced her to keep her hand open.

It trickled down the side of her hand and dripped onto the floor.

"Did you... Did you have a rag then?" she whispered.

He wrenched his eyes away from her palm and met her own, and she was almost certain that he knew exactly what he was doing.

He lifted his free hand, in which he held a clean cloth, and pressed it into her palm. "This profession also does not tolerate carelessness."

He let go of her wrist and stalked back to his place on the crate.

She wavered for a moment at the release of his grip, then stood, frozen to the floor, staring at him as he went back to his ledger as though nothing had happened.

She wrapped the cloth around her hand as best she could, tied it sloppily at one end, and then moved back to her crate and picked up her book.

She opened it and pretended to read, but instead she watched Elidor.

He didn't look at her hands again.

Disgraced

Ivana's father used his pristine sheet of paper to write a letter to Gan Gildas the same night she had told her parents, demanding an annual stipend for the care of the child. Gan Gildas could certainly afford it.

Ivana knew that far too personally.

Weeks went by without a response. Her state could no longer be hidden, and she was fired from her job at the tavern. The town talked, and Ivana rarely left the house because of it. She couldn't bear the scrutiny, the looks that told her what everyone thought of her, though most wouldn't say it to her face.

Whore.

Izel kept her informed about what was being said, but Ivana didn't need the confirmation from her sister. She could see it in their eyes; she could hear the whispers when her back was turned. She saw it and heard it so often that she began to believe it.

Whore. Whore. Whore.

The only thing worse would have been becoming a Banebringer.

Her father, despite his initial reaction, became her staunch ally and would stare down anyone who dared to look at her askance if they were together, including Lord Kadmon himself. Despite the well-known fact that Kadmon had sired a few of his own bastards in his day, his father's noble employer might once have dared to suggest that it was a bit of a blemish on his household to have a man in his employ with a known whoring daughter—at which point her father dared him to find such an accomplished scholar to replace him at the price he paid.

Kadmon had backed down; his reputation for cowardice and greed served their family well in that case.

Her mother busied herself with sewing clothes for the baby and fussing over Ivana anytime she even hinted at feeling ill or tired.

And Izel...

Well, they didn't speak much anymore. The entire affair had breached their relationship. Ivana didn't know if Izel felt guilty for keeping Ivana's secret or if she thought Ivana's whoring would rub off on her, or both.

Whatever the case, it was that relationship that Ivana missed the most.

There were days when Ivana could almost pretend that this was a happy occasion. That she were married and visiting her parents during her last months of pregnancy.

She sat on the couch on one of those days, marveling at the strange feeling of tiny kicks and punches coming from inside her own body while her mother knitted, when the front door slammed open.

Her father marched in. "Gan Gildas is here," he said.

Her mother rose, panic on her face. "What? Here? At our house?"

"No," her father said. "At Kadmon's estate, on business." He went into their bedroom, and when he had come out, he had changed his tunic for formal wear. A ceremonial dueling sword hung awkwardly at his hip.

"Galvyn," her mother said, eying the sword, "what do you aim to do?"

"Nothing drastic, I assure you. I'll give him the benefit of the doubt. Perhaps my message never got to him." Her father sounded doubtful. "So I aim to deliver it personally."

"Perhaps if you tried again—"

Her father spun. "The man is deliberately ignoring me. He's hoping I'll go away. Well, I won't. He'll answer me, one way or the other, and then we'll at least know what we have to work with."

Ivana's mother bit her lip. "We can manage without the money," she said. "Is it worth all of this?"

Her father slammed his hand down on his workbench. "It's the principle of the matter, Avira! If he were truly noble, he would live up to the namesake and do what is *right*."

Ivana's mother inclined her head.

Her father strode toward the door. "Ivana, come with me."

Ivana's head jerked up. "What? Me? Why?"

"A man's word may not be enough to move him; a woman with child may be," he said.

She didn't want to go out there. She didn't want to see Airell's father, or anyone else. But she rose obediently.

Her father was her ally, but her mother seemed to understand the impact of the situation on Ivana's psyche in a way her father didn't. She glanced at Ivana. "Is that really necessary? It's turned so cold. She should stay in."

"She's pregnant, not an invalid," her father said.

Her mother sighed, and Ivana gave her a small smile for the

effort.

Ivana wrapped herself in her winter cloak—it did little to hide her growing abdomen—and followed her father out into the cold.

Ivana was out of breath by the time they reached the gate to Kadmon's estate house proper. It was easy to underestimate how tiring it could be carrying such a load on a long, brisk walk.

"Dal Galvyn," the guard at the gate said with a nod as they approached. He glanced once at Ivana and then averted his eyes, as though he had seen something shameful he shouldn't have.

She ducked her head, her face burning.

"Did the Gan arrange a special session?" the guard asked, consulting a list and frowning. "You aren't normally here at this time."

Her father seemed to grow larger. "Attie," he said. "I'm here to speak with Gan Gildas."

The guard's eyes grew wide. "I-I'm sorry, Dal, but I don't have such an appointment on the list."

"I don't have an appointment. I'm content to wait until he finishes his business with Kadmon."

The guard glanced back at the guardhouse and then shifted from foot to foot. "Ah. Then you'll have to wait here, Dal."

Her father frowned. "Very well," he said. "Could my daughter wait inside the guard-house, at least?"

The guard hesitated and then shrugged. He didn't look at Ivana again.

Ivana's throat tightened. *Don't draw attention to me, please,* she wanted to say. She wanted to shrink and disappear into the ground. "I'll be fine, Papa," she whispered, hovering at his elbow. It wasn't *that* cold.

"No doubt," he said. "But your mother will have my head if she finds out I let you loiter in the cold."

Were there other guards in the guardhouse? She didn't want to bear their scrutiny.

Fortunately, she didn't have to face the vexing situation because at that moment, Gan Gildas' carriage pulled up to the front of Kadmon's house. The man himself appeared through the front door, shaking Lord Kadmon's hand vigorously while a footman hopped down and opened the carriage door.

She couldn't help but wonder what deal they had just made.

Another guard appeared from the guardhouse as the carriage approached, and together the two guards pulled open the gates to let the carriage pass.

"Stand aside, please, Dal," the guard her father had been speaking with said.

Ivana moved back, and her father moved out of the way so they could open the gates.

He did not, however, stand aside.

The moment the carriage passed through the gates, he strode to the middle of the road and stood there, forcing the carriage driver to stop.

The horrified guard moved to remove him, but Gan Gildas' head poked out of the carriage to address the driver. "Why are we stopped?"

"Dal, you must move," the driver said.

The guard drew his sword. "Dal Galvyn," he said, his earlier hesitancy gone, "I demand you stand aside. Now."

"Papa!" Ivana cried, her heart pounding.

"Gan Gildas!" her father called. "I insist you meet with me since you've ignored my messages."

Messages? He had written multiple letters? That was news to

her.

Gan Gildas held up his hand to stay the guard and scowled at her father. "What is it, man? You think I have time to deal with every man who thinks they have a grievance against me? Come, speak up! I haven't got all day."

That didn't bode well. "Papa," she said in a low voice. "Please. Can we go?"

Gildas flicked his eyes toward her. They roved over her entire body. Then—then—as if her state were a distasteful jest, he *rolled his eyes.*

Her throat tightened. They weren't going to get anything out of this man. They should leave. But her father ignored her plea.

"Very well, my lord," her father said. "I had hoped to handle this discreetly, but I shall come straight to the point. Your son, Lord Airell, sired a bastard on my daughter." He gestured to Ivana, who wanted to melt into the ground.

Both guards' eyes widened. The talk of who the father was had been the second-most common rumor, after the rumors of her whoring ways. Her father had insisted the family keep quiet. He wanted to deal with it in as honorable way as possible and give Gildas a chance to do the right thing.

"I insist upon a stipend for care of the child. That is all, my lord, and a fair request given the circumstances."

They were attracting additional onlookers—those who had been going about their business on Kadmon's outer estate.

Gildas snorted.

"Fair, indeed," he said, smiling to the growing crowd as if this were some grand jest, "if what you claim is even true. Do you think every man claiming my son sired a bastard on his daughter ought to get a share of my treasury? For all I know, you set her on him just for that purpose."

Her father's jaw jumped, and he opened his mouth, but

Gildas cut him off. "Good day to you." He made to duck back in his carriage, but her father took the opportunity to speak again.

"I will accept an upfront lump sum," he said, "if an annual stipend would be a hardship for you."

Ivana wished the wind would whisk her away somewhere, anywhere else. She could hear the whispers. Why, oh why, couldn't her father just let it go?

Gildas' smile froze on his face. Her father's words were respectful, but no one in their right mind believed that Gildas could not afford some small annual sum to help with the care of a child. He was one of the wealthiest nobles in Ferehar. There was some talk that he was posturing to be the next Ri.

No, no one could miss the sarcasm in her father's voice, least of all Gan Gildas.

Gildas exited his carriage and strode to meet her father. He was a large man—not fat, but tall and well-built. Even her father, who was not a small man himself, could not match him in size. Gildas dwarfed him in every possible way. "*You* will accept?" He sneered. "You are Kadmon's tutor, are you not?"

So he *had* received the messages. That was the only way he could have known that. Gildas had never met her father before.

He didn't wait for her father to reply. "Well, let me give you a lesson, man. You do not tell me what you will accept. *I* will tell you." He glanced around the crowd. "And I do not accept your claims." His gaze fell on Ivana, and she shrank back. "Next time, rather than demanding another man's money, keep your whoring daughter under control."

Ivana felt rather than saw her father's anger grow. "Perhaps, rather, you should keep your 'whoring' son under control, Gildas."

Gildas' eyes glinted, a murmur ran through the crowd, and the cold finally seeped through Ivana's skin.

"You dare to address me as an equal?" Gildas spat. "Insolent, ungrateful man. I will be sure to inform Lord Kadmon of this incident."

Ivana felt sick. Her father couldn't lose her position over this. He couldn't! What would they do? She found herself shivering in fear. "Please, Papa," she tried again. "Let's just go."

Then, to her utmost horror, her father drew his sword. His pitiful ceremonial sword, worn when Lord Kadmon wanted to put him on display at some banquet or ball. It was sharp, to be sure, but her father was a scholar, not a swordsman. "Coward," he said through his teeth. "You can't even accept enough responsibility for your son's misdemeanor to dip into your own overflowing coffers for a token gesture." He held his sword up. "You are dishonorable and don't deserve to be called 'noble.'"

Ivana gasped. "Papa! No!" she cried out. What was he *doing*?

Gildas snorted again and drew his own sword. "Know that you have forced me to this," he said, pitching his voice so that everyone could hear him. He paced back several steps and held his sword up in front of him by way of salute.

Her father didn't even have the chance to defend. No heroic clash of steel upon steel filled the air, no dance of dueling feet—a single stab from Gildas, which her father tried, and failed, to meet with his own sword.

"Papa!" Ivana screamed. She broke out of the crowd and ran to her father's side, who had collapsed to his knees, doubled-over. "Papa, Papa," she cried, trying to get him to respond. He looked up at her dully. "I...didn't really think he would..." He crumpled to the side.

"No," she whispered. "No, no, no!" She flung herself over him, heedless of the blood flowing from the wound in his chest. "Please, Papa!"

Gildas still stood over them. Ivana looked up at him. His

dripping sword dangled carelessly from his hand, as though he did this every day. Tears of grief and rage blurred her vision. "Monster," she whispered.

Gildas leaned down next to her ear. "The next time you want to play the whore, girl," he said, for her benefit, "at least ask for payment *first.*"

He straightened up and waved to the guards. "Get them out of my path. I've wasted too much time here already."

Guards dragged her, kicking and screaming, out of the middle of the road, then dragged her father's body.

They left them there at the side of the road. "Help him!" she screamed at the retreating guards. She turned to the crowd, which was fast dispersing. "Someone, please, help him!" But it was too late. The blood had slowed, and her father's eyes had gone blank.

She clung to his still-warm body, denial and disbelief choking her as the carriage moved away, leaving them in a cloud of dust.

Why did he have to be so brave, so stupid? For what? For *what?* For the principle of the matter? What use were principles when one was dead?

This was her fault.

That terrible knowledge sank down over her like the dirt that would bury her own father's corpse.

Every tear that dripped off her face was a silent accusation. Her fault. Her fault.

Her fault.

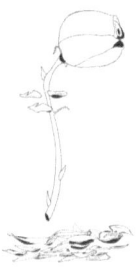

Chapter Eleven

The sharp *tap-tap-tap* of heeled shoes against the hardwood floor of Elidor's dining room slowly encircled Ivana, around and around. She was torn between following the woman who was inspecting her with her eyes and looking away in embarrassment.

The former won; whether it was a spark of defiance or curiosity, she didn't know, but she studied her all the same.

With the creamy brown skin of the central three regions, Da Lavena was solidly Setanan, like Elidor. Her hair was chestnut brown, thick and luxurious despite the strands of grey interwoven throughout. Her eyes weren't as hard as Ivana had imagined, but neither were they sympathetic. They were professional. Shrewd. And encased in a thick line of eye makeup.

She didn't seem bothered by Ivana's scrutiny; indeed, the few times her eyes flicked to meet Ivana's own, she seemed almost amused by it.

Elidor stood nearby, his hands behind his back. "Well?" he finally said, a note of impatience in his voice. "Can you work with her?"

"Dal," she said, "I can *work* with almost anything." She tilted her head and circled Ivana once again. "The real question is, will she work with me?"

Ivana swallowed. She could tell. She could see the fear, the hesitation, the shame in Ivana's eyes.

Elidor waved his hand in irritation. "She will work with you. But am I correct? Will this sort of training be of benefit? I do not wish to waste her time."

Lavena stopped in front of Ivana. Her eyes swept over Ivana's body once more, then settled on Ivana's eyes. "She could fit in among my ladies easily enough."

Was it supposed to be a compliment that she wouldn't stand out among whores? Then again, she already knew that. Bile rose in Ivana's throat and then settled back down in her stomach as bitterness.

"I don't need her trained for entertainment," Elidor said. "I need her trained as a weapon."

Lavena's lips pursed. "Is there a difference?" She turned to face Elidor. "Yes. She will do. But I will only train her if certain conditions are agreed to. First, I require unrestricted access to her. If I say she needs to come with me, she comes with me, no matter the time or day."

Elidor jerked his head in acquiescence.

"Second, in addition to my fee for this service, you—or your masters—will pay any costs associated with her training. I am not ultimately to be her mistress; I will not invest my own money in her."

"Such as?" he asked.

"Clothes, makeup, and the like," Lavena answered. "And certainly tanthalia, at some point, until she no longer needs it."

Ivana recoiled. Tanthalia? She would never bear a child again. It would rob her womb of anything capable of sustaining life—permanently.

It was like another piece of herself being stripped away. This time, it would be literally.

And did she have grand plans to marry and start a family now? Why did it matter?

It shouldn't. This was what she wanted, after all. She needed it not to matter.

"Very well," Elidor said. "You may begin immediately." He left the room, without so much as a glance at Ivana.

Once again, Lavena turned to face her. To Ivana's surprise, her eyes had softened with the departure of Elidor. "I am not a cruel mistress," she said. "This is merely a means to an end for all of us—a means to make our way in this world. Let me tell you what to expect." She gestured toward one of the chairs at the dining room table, and Ivana sat. Lavena continued to pace back and forth in front of her. "Today, during our first session, we will merely have a frank conversation. I need to know what foundation we will be working with. In subsequent sessions, I will take you through my normal training for new hires.

"Contrary to what you may assume, most of the initial training focuses on transaction rather than technique: how to extract the greatest fee from the client." Lavena stopped her pacing for a moment to glance Ivana's way. "I believe you will find this—the art of manipulation—to be the most useful for your goals. Technique is not unimportant, but learning to *be* what you are expected to be, *do* what you are expected to do, and *say* what you are expected to say, so as to put the client at ease, will serve your purposes in particular."

Ivana almost snorted. *Be what I am expected to be.* She already knew how to do that. But the way Da Lavena described it, it almost sounded like it was her whores who were the ones who were in control—unbeknownst to their clients.

"We will also spend a brief amount of time on safety. Those who frequent *my* house know my guidelines for treatment of my girls, and therefore this is not usually a problem. However, we welcome new clients, and every once in a while we run into a rotten one. I train all of my girls to be able to extract themselves from situations that they sense are turning sour. You will be no exception, and once again, you may find this useful in applications beyond this training."

In spite of her own misgivings, Ivana was beginning to understand how this training might serve her—and Elidor's—purposes.

"Then, yes," Lavena continued, "we will spend some time on technique, especially in areas where you may be lacking experience. Rather quickly, we will move to practice, because as with most things, that is where the real learning will occur. I will select appropriate clients for you, and as far as they know, you are a new worker." The *tap-tap* of her shoes stopped again, and she gave Ivana a sharp glance. "And you *will* obey my rules and treat the training seriously, or it will end, no matter how well I am being paid for it. I will not have the reputation of my establishment sullied."

Ivana lowered her eyes. If Lavena terminated her training early, Ivana was certain there would be consequences. "Yes, Da," she murmured, then hesitated.

"You have a question?"

"Do many of your new, ah, workers, already come to you with significant experience?"

"Some, but not all. Don't concern yourself with your level of experience. I've trained everyone from the sexual neophyte to the one who thought she knew it all—frankly, the worst kind. You will get there."

Ivana said nothing. She had enough experience to last her a lifetime.

"On that matter, let us begin." Lavena found another chair, pulled it over to face Ivana's, and then sat. "This is not the time for false modesty or prudishness." Lavena paused and her eyes caught and held Ivana's. "Leave nothing out."

Unwanted

"...the bleeding..."

The words Ivana could make out from the other room as she drifted in and out of a half-conscious state were not encouraging. She was so tired. She was too tired to even cry out in pain with the contractions anymore. The pain seemed to go on, and on. Hours and hours...

A wet cloth was placed on her head, and she roused herself enough to see her mother's haggard, anxious face above her. "Ana? Stay with us, sweetie. The midwife says we're almost there."

"I can't do this anymore," she whispered.

"Shh. Yes, you can." She offered her a smile. "I did it, twice, and so can you."

But something was different. Something was wrong. The baby was coming too early. Even she knew that. Barely a month had passed since her father—

She turned her face away as unbidden tears rose. She couldn't think about that right now. She had to prepare herself for yet more pain. She had to be rational. Though everything within her screamed otherwise, she knew enough to know that the chances of the babe surviving for long were slim this early, unless she had miscalculated.

She clung to that hope.

Her mother left her side to hold another hushed conference with the midwife, and Ivana focused on their faces.

Yes, something was definitely wrong, and not only with the early birth.

She wanted to vomit, but she couldn't even manage the strength to empty retch. There was nothing left in her stomach by now. They had finally made her lie down for a bit because she was too weak to continue crouching.

She was dizzy. Maybe she was going to die. It happened sometimes. Childbirth could be dangerous. Why, just last year, the baker's wife in town had died while giving birth to their third daughter.

"Am I going to die?" she whispered. Was she afraid or relieved at the idea? A just reward, it seemed, in her pain-hazed state.

The midwife and her mother exchanged glances. After paying for a proper burial for her father and a month of rent to Kadmon to stay in their house, they had used some of what was left of Airell's blood money to pay for a midwife to attend her when she started having problems a week ago. Pain when there shouldn't have been. Bleeding.

There wasn't much left of the money. What would they do when it was gone? They had enough savings for maybe another month of living expenses.

The pain intensified again.

With her mother on one side and her poor sister on the other to help her stay upright, Ivana finally delivered the child into the midwife's hands.

Even though she was exhausted and dizzy, all she could think about was seeing the baby as her mother and sister had helped her back into the bed.

It wasn't crying. Why wasn't it crying? Weren't babies supposed to cry after they were born? "Where is he?" she asked, frantic.

"She," the midwife said, and she handed her the babe wrapped in a blanket. Tears were in the midwife's eyes. "I'm sorry, child. I had hoped... But it's clear that it was too soon. I'll be surprised if she lives out the hour. If you could have lasted another two or three weeks, there might have been some hope." She shook her head. "We need to deal with your situation right now."

She didn't even ask what her situation was. She just looked down at the tiny body in her arms. If she could have lasted another few weeks. If only she could have... If only *she*... Her fault again, somehow, perhaps something she'd done.

What was worse, it had all been for naught. She could have taken the apothecary's damn medicine, saved her reputation, saved her father.

Her thoughts were becoming sluggish and scattered. Possibly, she might have even saved herself.

Why hadn't she just taken it? To retaliate against a man who didn't even care? The principle of the matter?

She was too much like her father.

She touched the cheek of the child—purple, wrinkled, and covered in a white film, but *her* daughter—and then her miniscule hand, which had escaped the blanket. A wave of grief washed over her, and then another wave of dizziness before... She lost consciousness.

***

A week passed. Ivana sat on the couch, staring off into space, numb. Her mother had insisted she get out of bed. The danger to herself had passed, and now she needed to move around.

They had taken away her daughter, who had died several hours after Ivana had delivered her, and buried her next to her father the next day. She could have taken the apothecary's poison and none of this would have happened.

After everything, it hadn't even mattered.

Her mother handed her a steaming mug, urging her to drink. Ivana didn't know how her mother did it. How did she go on, as if everything were normal?

But she saw the grief and exhaustion and pain in her mother's eyes.

It was the only way she could cope. And Ivana had driven her to this shell of a life.

A knock sounded on the door, and Izel, who had withdrawn even further from Ivana, rose to answer it.

A messenger handed Izel a sealed letter, then hurried away, no doubt eager to get back inside somewhere warm.

Izel closed the door and handed the note to their mother wordlessly.

She took it, looked at the seal, and then opened it. Her eyes roved over the message, once, twice, and then a third time, and then she set the note down on the table with a trembling hand.

"What is it, Mama?" Izel asked.

"Lord Kadmon," she said, her voice tight, "offers his condolences. He also informs us that he has found a new tutor for his children and thus we will regrettably need to find new living accommodations within the week."

They had known they wouldn't be able to stay there forever—but so soon?

They would lose their father and husband, a child, and now the only home Ivana and Izel had ever known within the course of a month.

They were monsters, the nobles, demonspawn, every last one of them, each in their own way. How had Ivana ever aspired to be a part of their ranks?

"Well," her mother said, breaking the silence. "No matter. I used to scribe, and I can do it again. We'll find something comfortable in town until we can get back on our feet, yes?" She clapped her hands, as though this were a merry jaunt through the woods. "If we only have a week, we'd best start packing."

Chapter Twelve

I vana had never set foot in a brothel in her life. She had never deliberately passed by one. To her knowledge, she had never even spoken to a whore.

Yet here she lay, surrounded by them.

She had come to learn that Lavena's "consort house" was superior in quality to a common brothel in the slums. They serviced only the upper-class and nobility—or those who could pay like them—and her women received a flat percentage of the profits for each appointment in addition to any personal tips a client might leave.

It all amounted to the same thing, as far as Ivana was concerned.

Consorts. Ha.

She was curled up in a ball on her bed in the large room the women shared, facing the wall with her back to the rest of the room and trying to pretend she didn't hear their quiet snickers or feel their eyes on her.

After three weeks of discussion and instruction, Da Lavena had finally brought her here and introduced her to the four women who were in her employ. The creative story was that Ivana was a new worker at a colleague's house who was having trouble acclimating; Lavena had therefore offered to train her and then send her back.

The others seemed to accept the story. Perhaps this wasn't the first time this had *actually* happened, or perhaps they didn't care.

Either way, none of them seemed pleased to have her there.

She wasn't particularly pleased to be there, either, but it was preferable to death, she supposed.

She tried to tell herself that she didn't care what a group of whores thought about her, but in reality the situation reminded her far too much of the way many of the other girls about her age had treated her on Lord Kadmon's estate, or in her hometown. The barely polite greetings. The sniggers when she wasn't looking. She was too smart, too quiet, too proper, too good, and, later, too ample in the chest—all of which combined to produce the general opinion that she was too stuck-up.

Ivana wished Lavena hadn't felt the need to have her *stay* at the brothel. Not only did she not have access to her blade, but she preferred the solitude of her own small, dark room to the whispers and glances of these women.

Perhaps she was already more like Elidor than she thought.

"They'll warm up eventually," a voice said.

Ivana turned over and sat up. One of the women—a dark-skinned Venetian—was sitting on her own bed, the closest to Ivana's.

"Your pardon?" Ivana asked, startled.

The woman flipped her thick braid over her shoulder.

"They're just jealous. They're always like this with new workers."

Ivana couldn't help but give a short laugh. "Jealous? Of me?"

The woman chuckled. "Sure. They don't know yet how the clientele might react, especially since we don't have any other Fereharians among us. You're unknown. You could steal some of their regulars, deliberately or not."

Ivana blinked. "But why..." That remark had spawned so many follow-up questions, she didn't even know how to finish.

The woman flashed her a brief smile. "The better you know a client, the easier it is to know what they want, and thus get better paid."

"I-I see." *Don't stutter.* Ivana flipped her own hair over her shoulder and tried to feign more confidence. *"You're* talking to me."

"I've been around for ages. My clients aren't going anywhere." She shrugged. "And I know what it's like to be new." She paused. "My name's Cozama. So what's your story?"

Ivana stared at her.

"You know." Cozama shrugged. "You didn't grow up aiming to be a whore, did you?"

Ivana had never thought of it that way. "I was orphaned," she said. "And had nowhere else to go." Close enough to the truth.

Cozama nodded. "Happens that way a lot." She jerked her head toward a pale-skinned Fuilynian woman. "Fianna over there was raised by her grandmother, and she sends the money home so her grandma can afford her rent and medicine, and probably her lupque. The woman talking to her, Maeveen, she, well, she came from a real bad place.

"Then there's Mabina. She was orphaned real young. Worst kind of pimp dragged her out of a workhouse when she was eight and put her to work."

Ivana shuddered. *Eight? Burning skies.*

Cozama nodded. "Lavena rescued her a few years back."

Rescued? Ivana hadn't spoken, but the look on her face must have spoken for her.

"Look, first thing you have to learn, working here: you're lucky. You're real lucky. Most of us know the other options. Lavena treats us right. She makes sure the clients are respectable. She doesn't tolerate abuse. She runs them through all the tests for disease before they lay a finger on us." She paused. "It's not always like that, maybe not even usually like that. Ask Mabina. She'll tell you." Cozama winced. "Don't ask Maeveen. She doesn't like to talk about it."

Ivana swallowed. "And you?"

"I've got a daughter at home; she lives with my sister. Bastard who got her on me left after I had her, and we didn't have much as it was." Cozama made a face, as if she had talked about eating her least favorite food. "Good riddance. Anyway, I send the money home like Fianna. I'm lucky. I don't know what would have happened if I hadn't had a sister to help."

"Why not live with your sister?" Ivana asked before she could stop herself.

Cozama gave her a side glance. "You had it nice before you were orphaned, didn't you?"

Ivana's face burned. "I guess I did."

"Point is, no one here cares who you are or where you're from. They want to know if you're a threat to our group." Cozama looked her up and down. "I don't think you are."

"I'm no threat," Ivana said softly. "I don't even want to be here."

"That's what Lavena said. Had trouble?"

"I thought I could do it."

Cozama leaned forward. "Women like us, we're doing what we can to survive. Some of us, we didn't have an option, some of us, it's a better option than something else." She waved her hand at the only window in the room. "You can take your chances out there or in a workhouse, but you'll probably end up in worse straights." Her braid had snaked back over her shoulder, and she tossed it back again. "You remember that. You tell yourself that—over, and over. You're doing what you gotta do, and we've got it pretty good. There isn't anything more to it than that."

She leaned back. "Anyway, Lavena's the best," Cozama said. "If anyone can get you through the first couple months, she can. After that, it gets easier. I'm sure you'll be able to handle it back at your house by then."

Ivana nodded, and Cozama threw a glance at the clock. "It's that time of night," she said. "Several of us have regular appointments." She winked at Ivana, rose, and left the room.

The other three women in the room eyed Ivana, and she gave them a tentative smile.

None smiled back, so she turned over on her bed and faced the wall again.

Cozama was right. The other women did eventually accept her. First one, and then another, and then finally all of them loosened up. Maeveen, the one who had "had it bad," was quieter than the rest. But even she warmed up, in her way.

They talked more freely around her. They stopped casting her side glances. They did her hair and makeup, offered tips and encouragement as she continued her lessons with Lavena, and gossiped about things their clients had said or done while she was around and Lavena wasn't. Occasionally, this last warranted some snickering, but only at the clients' expense.

And the most uncomfortable thing she had had to do so far

was discreetly—though with the permission of the client—observe a few of the *interactions* some of the other women had with their clients—those who stayed at the house for their appointments—and discuss her impressions with Lavena afterward.

She had a feeling her turn was coming soon.

Three weeks after she had moved in to the brothel, Lavena handed her a pouch of tanthalia and sent her back to Elidor's with instructions to take an increasing daily dose until the tanthalia was gone and the bleeding had stopped. Then, she was to report back.

Tanthalia, when used infrequently and in small doses, could safely prevent pregnancy if taken directly after intimacy. When used frequently and in small doses, it would, given enough time, damage the womb beyond recovery. The line between "frequent" and "infrequent" was blurry and different for every woman, so it was a risky herb to take if one wanted to remain fertile.

Of course, when taken every day in large doses in a compressed period, it would destroy the womb within weeks. When Ivana returned to Lavena, she would never be in danger of becoming pregnant again.

Ivana had known this was coming, but she didn't know how she felt about it. On some days, motherhood seemed such an unattainable objective that it hardly mattered. On others, she remembered that she had once wanted a husband and a family, and she remembered why she was doing this in the first place.

She also didn't know if it was a relief to be back at Elidor's or not. On the one hand, she had never experienced such companionship before as she had with that small group of women, and it was a bitter irony that she had found it among a group of whores. Their own little family. They looked out for each other.

They took care of each other. Ivana was still an outsider, but they accepted her—far more than the "respectable" girls back home ever had. She didn't know if it was like that at all brothels, but at Lavena's, anyway, the women were a close-knit group.

Indeed, because of this, her first reaction had been to protest when Lavena had indicated she would stay at Elidor's while taking the herb. But Lavena had insisted she would be more comfortable "at home" for what was to come.

On the other hand, once she was back at Elidor's, he put her back to studying more interesting topics, like lock picking or learning the language of the Yunqi, the so-called heretics far to the east of Setana. Elidor said it was more likely that she would have Xambrian clients than Yunqin, due to the fact that a mountain pass separated Xambria and Setana and a vast, dense forest populated by bloodspiders separated Setana and Yunqi—but it was the next most common foreign language in their part of the world, aside from technically forbidden regional languages, like Fereharian or Donian.

She didn't know where Elidor had obtained a book on Yunqi, but she supposed he could find anything through his less-than-legal sources.

It kept her mind off what would come next with Lavena's training—at least until two weeks after she was back at Elidor's when the cramps started.

Once again, she found herself curled into a tight ball on her cot in her tiny room at Elidor's—but this time, it was due to physical pain.

Lavena had warned her that there would be cramps and bleeding, but Ivana had never felt anything so horrendous in her life. Even childbirth didn't compare.

Her entire abdomen was in a vise, and unlike contractions, the pain was relentless.

She hadn't left her room the morning the pain had started, and about an hour into it, Elidor showed up at her door.

"You weren't sent home to sleep," he said.

"I'm ill," she said into her pillow. "Actually, I feel like I'm dying."

"That would be unfortunate, after all of the resources I've expended on you."

She had no patience for him and his rude manner today, but she made the effort to roll over and glare at him. "You haven't the faintest idea"—she gasped—"what this feels like. It's worse than childbirth."

He frowned. "You didn't tell me you have a child. That is a liability that—"

"I don't have a child," she snapped. "She..." She grimaced. "She died shortly after she was born."

"Good," he replied, then turned. "Lavena told me this might happen, near the end. You may have the day to recover." He left without another word.

Her physical pain drowned out the sting of his insensitivity—the only positive she had gained so far. "You're so generous," she muttered, and then she curled back up to wait for this misery to end.

Chapter Thirteen

"You know, it's hard for a Fereharian to look pale, and yet you've managed it," Cozama said.

Ivana didn't respond. She was sitting on the same bed she had first talked to Cozama on, and her stomach was queasy.

Cozama had unofficially taken her under her wing. Ivana didn't know if the woman felt sorry for her or if she always did that with new workers. But of all the women, she had been the most supportive, the most encouraging. Almost a friend.

A wave of sickness not having to do with her impending *appointment* that night washed over her. Did life enjoy mocking her? First Boden and the apothecary, and now this group of women she would never be a part of.

Not that she wanted to remain *here*.

Why couldn't she have the apothecary, Boden, these friends...all somewhere else, in some other context?

And why did she still care so much? The whole point of this was to stop caring.

She closed her eyes. "I can't do this."

"You must," Cozama said. "Lavena isn't cruel, but she won't have you embarrassing her—or tarnishing the reputation of the house."

"I'm not ready. You can go in my stead."

"I can't. Lavena already told the client that you were Fereharian and this was your first appointment." Cozama pulled her braid back. "She'll have assigned you someone understanding. He won't hold nerves against you."

How did she explain that she didn't give a damn about what the client thought?

Cozama reached out and dragged a nearby floor-length mirror to the beds and then turned it to face Ivana. "Look at yourself, hun. Go on, do it."

Ivana raised her eyes reluctantly to the mirror. Her hair was curled and pinned up, aside from some locks left down to brush the side of her neck. Her face was painted: cheeks rouged, lips full and dark red, eyes shadowed in blue cream. And the dress— oh, the dress. It looked remarkably like the one Airell had bought her, though it hardly needed altering to make it more indecent.

She could not think of her father, her mother, her sister. So instead, she wondered: What would Boden think if he could see her now? "I look like a whore," she whispered.

Cozama nodded. "Exactly."

Ivana looked back at Cozama. "What is this supposed to prove?"

"That you *look* the part," Cozama said. "You've been training for what, now, six weeks? Two months? You know what to say. You know what to do." She pushed the mirror out of the way and leaned forward. "You know how to play this role, Ivana. But at the end of the night, that's all it is. A role. It doesn't affect who you'll be once you wash that gunk off and put on something more comfortable."

And who am I? she desperately wanted to ask. She looked into the eyes of this kind woman and felt the urge to divulge it all. Instead, she drew in a deep breath. "So, what, look this in the face and laugh?"

Cozama chuckled. "Sure. As long as you're not laughing at the client." She winked. "They don't tend to like that."

That finally elicited a smile from Ivana.

The door opened, and Lavena popped her head into the room. "Ivana? He's downstairs. Come. Now."

Cozama squeezed her hand and then Ivana went to join Lavena at the door.

She looked back at Cozama, who pounded her chest once.

I must gain control of this, she thought as she descended the stairs. *I can control this.*

A well-dressed middle-aged—and balding—Setanan man stood waiting at the counter downstairs.

She didn't know what she had expected. Airell?

Somehow, the stark differences between them made it easier.

He took her hand and kissed the back of it. "My dear, you look lovely."

She met his eyes and gave him a charming smile. "Thank you, Dal."

He offered her his arm, and she accepted it gracefully.

"I thought we might start with a private dinner," he said as he guided her out of the consort house's front door. "And then take a tour of my wine cellar. I currently have twenty-three vintages." Pride swelled in his voice, and she took note of it.

I will control this.

"Perhaps we could open one tonight?"

And I will excel at it.

"That would be lovely," she said. "I'm partial to sweet reds, though they're so hard to find." She moved in closer to him and lowered her voice. "I don't suppose you have anything...exotic?"

He beamed down at her. "Oh, yes. I take great pleasure in collecting as wide a variety as I can." He gave her a meaningful look, which she took to mean, whether legal or not.

She could see why Lavena was excellently positioned to be an informant for the government.

Ivana murmured a trite compliment that would stroke the man's ego, and he launched into a detailed discourse on bouquets and fermentation. Midway through, he halted, as though he realized he had forgotten something important.

"Ivana, is it?" he asked.

Not tonight. "Yes, Dal."

Two months later, when Lavena finally sent her back to Elidor's for good, Ivana bought a jewelry box with some of the money she had earned at Lavena's, laid her sister's necklace in it, and shoved it as far under her bed as she could.

Far enough that by the time she stumbled on it again, she had high hopes that the Ivana who cared would no longer exist.

Chapter Fourteen

"No," Elidor snapped, his dagger pointed toward Ivana's chest. "You are still too hesitant. If I had actually been a threat, you would already be dead."

Ivana sheathed her own dagger with a snap. "If you had been a threat, I would *surely* be dead because your decades of experience trump my, what, less than a year?"

Elidor lowered his blade and glared at her. "That," he said, "is beside the point."

"In fact, it is very much within the point," Ivana said, folding her arms across her chest. "If I were attempting to assassinate you, I would not succeed by engaging in a face-to-face confrontation."

Elidor grunted, which was likely as much as she would get by way of a concession to her point. "But this is not as much about training you to fight your targets head on as it is about training you to react *confidently* and *without hesitation*. Which you cannot seem to do!"

Ivana sighed. She was tired. Since she had returned from her temporary stay at the brothel three months back, Elidor had been relentless. In addition to Lavena still occasionally calling on her to handle a particular client in order to teach her some nuance or other of manipulation, Elidor had her making him poisons, studying languages, continuing her combat training with him, and—the last was new—planning her course of action in response to hypothetical jobs or scenarios that Elidor invented.

The challenge with the last was whether she could produce a plan that Elidor would approve of and then field any supplemental questions that he had to his satisfaction.

The former had happened, once or twice, but even if he didn't find an obvious flaw in her initial plan, he usually managed to invent a follow-up scenario that could stump her.

It was almost entertaining—like a puzzle to be solved—as long as she didn't ruminate over much on the intended outcome of the *non*-hypothetical puzzles these were preparing her for.

But it all amounted to the same result: she was exhausted, mentally and physically. The only positive was that she hardly had time to feel emotionally exhausted. The knife hidden in her room saw less and less use as she fell into bed each night utterly drained.

Still, less use was not the same as no use.

"Again," he said, jerking his head toward her sheathed dagger.

Ivana drew her dagger back out. There was no use in arguing with him. He was deaf to all complaints of any and all physical ailments, whether it be fatigue, hunger, thirst, or illness. The fastest way to get him to let her go was to comply.

As tired as she was, it was no surprise that she lasted less than a minute. The skirmish ended when he managed to slap the flat of his blade against her wrist bone, causing her to drop her dagger in pain and surprise.

"Dead," he said, shaking his head.

She ignored him, instead examining her wrist, which throbbed. A bruise had already appeared, and a thin line of red was blossoming on the skin right above it. "You cut me."

They had started with blunt blades, but when Elidor had not been satisfied with her progress, he had switched to his normal dagger in the hopes that a sharp blade would provide better motivation. There had been no mishaps until today.

She would receive no apology from him, so she didn't wait for it. She bent and picked up her dagger.

When she straightened, she caught him looking away from her—or more accurately, her wrist.

An idea sprouted in her mind. She ambled in his direction, ostensibly toward the door. "Lavena says that my training with her is coming to an end."

"And what do you think?"

"I don't care one way or the other." She was surprised to find that it was true. Five months, how many men? She had lost track.

It didn't even matter anymore.

"Good. Then your training with her is done. I have more than enough to fill that time with."

"I'm sure." She stopped next to him. "Also, if I was attempting to assassinate you, I would not do it when I was already beyond exhausted." She held up her arm so that he could see the cut his dagger had made. "You can see the results yourself."

He didn't reply. His eyes were on her arm.

She moved behind him, as if to leave, and then she spun and

dug the point of her blunted blade against his lower back, pushing on his kidney. "If I were attempting to assassinate you," she said, "and had no other option, I would do it like this."

He whirled around to face her, and for a moment she was certain he was going to backhand her.

He didn't. Instead, he met her eyes.

She smiled sweetly. "We all have our weaknesses, don't we?"

His jaw jumped once. And then, finally, *finally*...

"Well done," he said. "You may go."

She nodded and moved to leave.

"And you may have the rest of the week free from other duties."

She turned, shocked.

"Except." He held up a finger. "One week hence I will leave for a job." He gave her one of his mirthless smiles. "You will spend that time planning our execution of the assignment, and you will accompany me."

Over one week later Ivana crouched in the empty stall of an inn's stable.

In the stall kitty-corner to her, a stableboy grumbled about the early hour. Ivana concentrated on slow, even breathing, to calm her pounding heart. All the stableboy had to do was walk away from where he was preparing the target's horse, and he would see her.

There wasn't supposed to be a groom here yet. This wasn't starting well.

"Don't know why it's always me," the stableboy grumbled. "Damn messenger can get his own tack. 'Adie'll get your horse ready, Dal, no matter the hour.' Sure he will." The stableboy spat into the straw and turned his back on the stall where Ivana was hiding. He flexed his fingers, blew into them once, and then crouched down to tighten the girth on the saddle.

The saddlebags still lay in the middle of the stable walkway.

Now was her chance.

Ivana gritted her teeth, imagined what form Elidor's ire might take if she messed this up, and slid out of her stall. With one eye still on the stableboy, she pulled the canteen out of the saddlebag and dumped a vial of white powder into it. She then put the canteen back and slipped back into her hiding spot.

Ivana breathed out.

Just in time. The stableboy turned, picked up the saddle bags, and fastened them to the saddle.

When he crouched yet again to check the girth, she slipped out of the stable and made her way to the edge of the woods outside the inn's courtyard, settling down in the trees to wait.

The sky had not yet begun to lighten, though it would soon. Here, fifteen miles out from Carradon, the chances of encountering a roving bloodbane were slim during the day. But only a messenger with the most urgent of messages would dare to ride long distances while still dark.

Their target probably didn't have the most urgent of messages, but it was urgent enough—or he was being paid enough—that he was leaving while stars could still be seen in the sky.

She looked up at those stars. The Eagle was clearly visible at this time of year. It was one of the more important constellations of her ancestors—native Fereharians—though truth be told, she didn't know why. The Setanans called it Temoth's Dice, so she assumed whatever symbolism it had once held, the Conclave disapproved.

Whatever the name, she hoped Temoth's Dice rolled in her favor tonight.

The hard thud of horseshoes against packed dirt drew her attention back to the courtyard. The same stableboy was leading the horse out into the middle of the courtyard. He stopped, one hand holding the reins, the other shoved in his pocket, his chin tucked into his upturned collar, and waited.

At least she was wrapped in more appropriate clothing given the time of year.

It was hard to believe that a little over a year ago, she had instead been huddled against a cold city wall with that scrap of cloth she had called a cloak. Now, her cloak was thick, her hands gloved, and her feet warm in fur-lined boots.

Finally, after what seemed like far too long, the messenger himself strode out of the inn, right as the stableboy was in the middle of a yawn.

The messenger spoke one sharp word to the lad, who handed him the reins of the horse and dutifully provided his own knee as a stepstool for the messenger to mount.

The boy sagged once the messenger had prompted his horse forward, and then the boy scurried inside.

Ivana wouldn't be relieved until the messenger drank from that canteen.

She shivered, and it had nothing to do with the cold. It wasn't poison, she reasoned. Only a sedative. No *actual* assassination for her tonight; no, tonight she was only an accomplice.

Only? What kind of person reasons that she's *only* an accomplice to murder?

Elidor's sources had told him this particular messenger always began his journeys, whatever the weather, with a slow ride and a swig of hard liquor to get himself going for the day.

The messenger passed her position in the woods and then, true to form, he reached back, flipped open the flap to one of his bags, took out the canteen, and took a nice, long draw.

He wiped his mouth and returned the canteen to the saddle-bag, none the wiser.

Ivana rose to a crouch and followed him to the side and behind within the shadow of the trees, out of eyesight.

A quarter-mile later, the messenger continued on, humming to himself as the road gently descended and the village disappeared from sight. He drank more of the liquor, which was fine. It wouldn't be enough to make a difference to the timing.

After another quarter-mile, he had reached the bottom of the hill, and he blinked a few times and rubbed at one eye with the hand not holding the reins.

Come on. A half-mile, at a walk—that's all it should have needed!

But the horse continued to clop steadily down the road.

They were between the town he had left and the next village along the road. Not a soul was in sight. A large swath of woods ran along the opposite side of the road. Perfectly positioned for about another half-mile, when the woods would thin out, dawn would start to touch the sky, and farmland would come back into sight, right over the next hill.

She gnashed her teeth. *Work!* Elidor would have her head, possibly literally. She had planned this job, and everything came down to precise timing. She had even tested the damn sedative on herself, modifying it for her increased mass over the rats.

And she was two-thirds of this man's weight. She bit her lip, cursing herself for failing to take his additional mass into account. A stupid mistake.

At almost the mile mark, where the road was already ascending the next hill—the top of which would bring him in view of the next village—the horse finally stopped.

Ivana held her breath.

The messenger frowned. He slid off his horse and almost collapsed onto the ground.

He fumbled with the flap on his saddlebag, drew out the canteen, unscrewed the cap, and sniffed at it.

He wouldn't smell anything other than the alcohol, Ivana was sure of that much.

His mind would be foggy at this point—later than it should have been, but since he hadn't moved farther along the road, it was good enough. He clutched the saddle for support, blinking rapidly. He was probably trying to sluggishly put pieces together.

That was when, apparently, the picture finally formed.

His eyes widened, and, cursing, he tried to hoist himself back up on the horse. He slapped its side, and the horse jerked forward, the man still hanging half off its side, unable to muster the strength to pull himself up.

An arrow thudded into his back.

He lost his grip, tumbled to the ground, and the horse, still startled, cantered up the hill.

She ignored the horse. It had already slowed, as if realizing it had left its rider behind. As long as it didn't prematurely warn anyone, it didn't matter.

The man, on the other hand, lay where he had fallen, either dead or unconscious. The sky had started to grey. Where in the abyss was Elidor?

Almost in answer, Elidor appeared at the edge of the woods. Without comment, he helped her drag the man as far into the woods as they dared, given the timing.

It was still dark under the dense foliage. Even so, Ivana averted her eyes after Elidor pulled out his dagger first and then a wicked-looking serrated knife.

She didn't want to know how he was going to make it look

like the messenger had been attacked and killed by a bloodbane.

After a few minutes of noisy tearing and rending that she tried to ignore, Elidor spoke. "Time to go."

Less than a day later, Ivana sat across from Elidor in his study. His eyes studied her as they often did before he was about to lecture or question her.

He had a glass of wine. He had offered her nothing, so she had clenched her hands in her lap to keep from fidgeting.

When Elidor had told her beforehand to relate the plan she had come up with, he had given no feedback—which was unlike his normal tests. He had merely instructed her curtly to do whatever she needed to do to prepare.

It seemed she was to be drilled now.

"Your impressions of the job," he said at last.

"Well... He's dead, isn't he?"

Elidor stared at her. Apparently, that was *not* the answer he had been looking for.

"And I'm pretty sure no one will realize it was, um, intentional."

"'Pretty sure' isn't good enough."

She exhaled. "Fine. I'm confident."

He nodded. "I agree. However, you cut the timing close."

She bit her lip. "I might have...miscalculated the strength of the sedative."

"Might have?"

She gritted her teeth. "I failed to take into account the messenger's greater mass, so it took a little longer to fully set in."

"Why," he said, "did you choose to use such a roundabout way of accosting the man? Since you knew his trajectory, surely it would have been easier to waylay him along his path."

That, she knew the answer to—and she wasn't sure whether he did, too, and was just probing her, or whether he truly didn't know. "Easier for you, perhaps," she said. "But you told me to plan this as though I were the one who had to handle every detail. If it had been my responsibility to carry out the actual assassination, overpowering a man of greater stature than myself on horseback would have been even riskier." He opened his mouth, and she held up a finger to stave off the objection she knew he would have. "And I am worthless with a bow at present. If I had missed or hit the wrong spot, he would have been alerted and on his way to the next town before I could recover."

He grunted. "Why a sedative? You trained for months with Da Lavena. You could have played a wounded or helpless girl alongside the road to lure him off the horse and into the woods."

She hesitated. "I felt that was too risky, not knowing his character. What if he had failed to stop?" Actually, she hadn't wanted to look a victim in the eyes and do something that would lead to their death. But she didn't think Elidor would approve of that reasoning. "I felt it better to rely on the precision of my measurements."

"The measurements you calculated incorrectly, you mean?"

She flushed. "It won't happen again."

"Indeed, it will not. Mistakes can be fatal in this profession, girl."

"I understand that," she murmured. She hesitated. "So, did I succeed?"

Elidor was silent for a moment. "You overcomplicated the job," he said. "Sometimes the simplest solution is best." He raised an eyebrow at her. "However, as you noted: he's dead. Questions?"

She was going to ask if he had a backup plan, in case things went wrong, but something else came out instead. "Why did the government want a simple messenger dead?"

"As I've told you before, they don't disclose their motives to me, and there is no point in dwelling on it."

"Aren't you ever even curious?"

"No."

She sighed. "How did you do it?"

"Do what?"

"Just...rip that man's body apart like that." Her stomach felt queasy even thinking about the brief glimpse she had seen.

"With a sharp knife," he said.

That hadn't been what she'd meant, and he knew it.

"But now that you mention it, a hands-on lesson or two in human anatomy might be useful. I will see about obtaining a cadaver from the university."

She opened her mouth to protest, but he jerked his head. "Dismissed."

Great. Just great.

Alone

I vana's mother drove them on. Despite her own pain, she kept their family from complete despair. She found a small apartment in town that they could afford on the trifling income that she brought in hiring herself out as a scribe.

Small was generous. The apartment had two rooms: one larger room that sufficed as their shared bedroom, living area, and kitchen, and a small space barely large enough to hold the chamber pot and washbasin.

Ivana tried to find work to help, but no one would hire her or even Izel, as though whoring were a disease that might rub off on their own children. Thankfully, that didn't seem to extend to their mother.

Their mother tried to encourage them, saying that things would get better once the winter was over. For now, they had to spend a good bit of her income on wood for the woodstove to keep their apartment warm. Both Ivana and Izel offered to chop wood themselves, but their mother wouldn't have it. She couldn't take the time from work herself to chop wood, and she wouldn't have either of the girls out in the woods alone, lest bloodbane or other more intelligent predators fall upon them.

Once spring came, she insisted that money could go to other things to improve their situation. She would also have more work once the winter passed; perhaps they could then scrape together the money to go to her relatives in northern Ferehar—she had already sent a letter after all. If not, Cohoxta, the capital of Ferehar, was closer and therefore less expensive of a trip, and she would be sure to find more work there.

Her mother was being optimistic. They had yet to receive a reply to her mother's letter, and they had no way of knowing if it had even reached its destination. If it had, how would her relatives send help from so far away? They were hardly wealthy.

As it was, they had had to use the rest of Airell's coins and sell most of their possessions to secure the apartment, since the landlord had demanded three months advance payment—which was just as well, since they no longer had room for most of their things anyway.

The last items of any value that they still owned were her father's microscope, which Ivana and her mother, in particular, were loath to part with, and the small chest her father had kept his notes and ramblings in. At last, they mutually made the decision that they had to try and sell those items as well.

The chest was a fine cedar chest lined with velvet, as her mother remembered. It would fetch a good price, but it was locked. Her mother didn't know where the key had gone, and none of them had dared to force the lock, lest they ruin the chest and decrease its value. Ivana would first have to take it to a locksmith to see if it could be picked without damaging the chest itself. It was a hassle, but doable.

Selling the microscope would be the more difficult task.

Unfortunately, while a microscope might bring in a large sum with the right buyer, those buyers were few. It would be useless to everyone else.

But Ivana had just the person in mind, and it just so happened there was a locksmith in the same town.

Her mother insisted that Ivana take some of their precious coins to buy a carriage ride to Eleuria, and truth be told, Ivana was relieved. The idea of walking the eight miles to Eleuria and back, some of which, with short winter days, would have to have been while dark, chilled her even more than the cold would have. The most vicious bloodbane weren't common in this area, as there were too many small villages and towns about, but that didn't mean the threat was non-existent—especially at night.

The carriage ride to Eleuria and the walk to the apothecary were eerily familiar. She couldn't help but wonder how things would have turned out if she would have taken the poison. Her father would be alive, and life would have gone on. She might have even still had the chance at a decent marriage, if no one had found out about her affair with Airell.

But she had no one to blame but herself.

The tinkling of the tiny bell alerted the girl at the front; the same one Ivana had seen before. She took one look at Ivana, then called to the back. "Mama!"

The older woman named Patli appeared shortly thereafter. She saw Ivana, blinked, and then dismissed her daughter. "My dear," she said, once her daughter was gone. "I never thought I'd see you again." Her eyes swept over her, but she didn't inquire after the child, for which Ivana was grateful. That pain, among others, was still too raw. "What can I do for you today?"

Ivana lifted the microscope out of the bag she had carried it and the chest in. Then she set it on the counter and removed the protective cloths she had wrapped it in.

A pang went through her as she touched the surface of the apparatus, memories of all of the times she and her father had looked through it, marveling at what the naked eye couldn't see.

Patli stared at it, her mouth slightly open. She held out one hand to touch it and then looked up at Ivana. "Is this a microscope?"

Ivana gave a tight nod. "My father made it." She didn't elaborate. "I... I find myself in need of some extra money, and I was hoping you might be interested in purchasing it—or know someone who would be."

Patli ran her hand over the side of it. "I haven't seen one of these since..." She shook her head and examined it more thoroughly, turning the dials and then looking through the scope. "Marvelous," she said. "Your father is quite the scholar."

Ivana said nothing. She didn't trust herself to speak right now. She wanted the apothecary to take it, so she could be done with it.

Finally, the woman shook her head. "As much as I would love this device, I know I can't give you even close to what it's worth," she said. "You would have better luck taking it to one of the cities, especially if you could get to Carradon or Marakyn."

The capitals of Cadmyr and Donia, respectively, both of which had universities. Neither of which was a remote possibility. Either journey would take months, and would take her through vast expanses of uninhabited land—the places bloodbane liked to haunt the most. They could never afford to pay their share of a guarded caravan, or they would have already tried. "I'll take whatever you can give me," Ivana said. "If you want to pass it on at a higher price when you have the opportunity, I understand."

The woman sucked her lower lip in, studied the microscope, and then finally nodded. "Very well. If you're certain you don't want to try for a higher bidder... I'll return in a moment."

True to her word, she returned with a purse. "Frankly, it's worth twenty times this amount, but I don't have that much in capital." She slid the purse across the counter. "I hope this will help anyway."

Ivana took the purse without counting it. It hardly mattered. It was what it was. She took one last look at the microscope and then started to turn away.

A thought struck her, and she hesitated, glancing down at the bag. "There is something you could do for me. Not money. If you feel you owe me more."

She slid her father's chest out of the bag and lifted it onto the counter. It was as long as her arm, but only as deep as her hand and as wide as two of her father's journals—easy to stash in a narrow space.

"Could you keep this for me? It's just some personal things. Mementos. I was going to sell the chest, but I think if you could keep it, perhaps I could come back for it sometime, once I'm a little better established. I-I hate to see it all go."

The woman flicked her eyes over the chest. "Easy enough," she said. "It's a deal." She gave Ivana the warm smile she had given her when Ivana had first walked through her door. "The best of luck to you, dear."

Ivana nodded and left the shop.

She was going to need a whole lot more than luck.

Ivana was surprised to find her mother home when she arrived back at the apartment. She usually worked late into the evening. Instead, she found her curled up on their pallet under a mound of blankets. Izel wasn't there.

Ivana knelt at her mother's side and put a hand to her head. She felt like she might have a bit of a fever. "Mama?"

Her mother stirred. "Ana. Did you get the things sold?"

"Yes, Mama." She didn't tell her about the chest. There was no point now. She took out the purse and held it out to her mother.

"Help me up," her mother said.

Ivana moved to help her mother sit up. Her mother took the purse, dumped it out, and then counted soundlessly.

She sighed when she was done. "Well. It'll buy us some more time, anyway, once our three months are up." She laid her head back against the wall, her eyes closed.

"What's wrong?" Ivana asked.

"A bit of a headache, that's all. Nothing to worry about."

At that moment, Izel walked in, carrying a sack of what passed for their food supplies. Ivana rose to meet her. "What happened?"

"She came home early this afternoon," Izel replied. "Said she didn't feel well, and needed to rest."

"She came home because she had a bit of a headache?"

"I know. It doesn't seem normal, does it?" The two looked at each other, and in that moment, everything that had happened in the past months was set aside in their mutual concern for their mother.

"We'll keep an eye on her," Ivana said.

Izel nodded.

"What are you two muttering about over there?" their mother called. "The gods know you have enough burdens for your age without worrying about me. I'll be fine in the morning."

But she wasn't.

Her fever worsened over the course of the week and didn't go away. After another week, she started complaining of abdominal pains, and then one day, she didn't even try to get up.

She wouldn't eat, wouldn't drink. She just lay there.

Ivana and Izel agreed to spend some of the coins they had from the sale of the microscope on a doctor, as they were helpless to do anything themselves.

The doctor checked their mother over thoroughly and then gestured to the girls. They huddled in one corner of the room. "She doesn't have the rash," the doctor said without preamble, "but I'd say she's caught blood fever." He packed up his bag.

Ivana blinked. Blood fever? But that afflicted the poor and...and...

What are we? "Isn't there anything you can do?" she asked.

"No," the doctor said. "Nothing to do but keep her comfortable and hydrated and wait it out. She'll get worse, and then likely she'll get better within another week or so."

"Likely?"

The doctor gave them both a kind but firm look. "I don't believe in mincing words. We'll hope for the best, but you'd best prepare for the worst." With that, he left.

They both stared at their ill mother.

"Ana," Izel said. "I'm scared."

Chapter Fifteen

A shadow fell over Ivana's book and the sheet of paper she was practicing the Xambrian script on. "Yes?" she asked without looking up. She had learned that Elidor liked to be dramatic like that. Sneak up on her without announcing his presence. Almost as if to see if he could startle her.

It wasn't as easy as it used to be.

"It's time," he said.

Ivana's pen froze mid-word. "I thought you said it would be at the end of this week?"

"Sometimes things change. The target is moving on before we anticipated, and our instructions are that he must be eliminated before he leaves the city."

The dot of ink that had begun as the top of a letter was growing into a spreading stain across the paper.

This was it then. Five months after Elidor had started taking her with him on jobs, tonight it would be Ivana, her blade, and a man marked for death.

Ivana laid the pen down and turned to face Elidor. "The sky-fire is tonight."

"Indeed. My informant tells me the target intends to use it as a cover for slipping away. All the more reason to hurry." He held up his arm, and from his hand dangled her sheathed dagger on its belt and her cloak.

Great. Of all the nights for her final test. Not an interpreter. Not a body-hider. Not a trap-setter.

Not an accomplice.

Elidor would be nearby to observe—and ensure she didn't fail to complete the job.

She inhaled through her mouth and then exhaled through her nose, trying to calm her racing heart. She stood and took the proffered items.

"Then let's go."

The streets were already deserted at dusk, even though the sky-fire never started until after midnight. People were no doubt already preparing to closet themselves up in their safe rooms, if they had them, and if not, to huddle together in the darkest corners of their homes, hoping and praying that none of them would be changed into a Banebringer on this, the single night of the year when new Banebringers were created by the heretic gods.

Hoping and praying that if someone else nearby was changed, or a tear opened, the summoned bloodbane would think the house unoccupied.

Ivana had never been sure whether bloodbane were intelligent enough to know the difference, but since detailed information on bloodbane and their Banebringer summoners was difficult to come by, she supposed people thought it was better to be overcautious.

Certainly, there was no reason to make oneself a target.

By walking alone down a deserted street on the most feared night of the year, perhaps?

As Elidor said, all the more reason she should get this over with quickly.

Their information said that the target was staying in a house that was outside the walls, but the sprawl of urban life couldn't be contained by stone. Either way, it would be more than a two hour's trek to the other side of the city, given that she would have to avoid the city's main thoroughfares. Though the streets looked deserted, Watchmen were scattered strategically around the city.

The paths less traveled were not empty, despite the date. She could feel the periodic pair of eyes on her as she wound her way through back alleys in the dark, gauging her as a target for robbery.

Ivana wasn't concerned; she was vigilant. She heard the skitter of a rat she had startled, the soft brush of a footpad's tunic down the alley she had just passed, a dog barking in the far distance. Anyone who tried to surprise her would have a nasty surprise in return.

By the time she had closed in on the target's location, the sun had fully set. She crouched in a tangle of overgrowth, listening to the sounds drifting out of the open window beside her.

Strangely, there was laughter. She could distinguish three or four voices, and none of them seemed overly concerned about the sky-fire drawing closer.

Then again, if Elidor's information was correct, the target was preparing to leave, not hide.

Still, she hadn't expected so many people to be around. He

was supposed to be alone. This increased the complexity of this allegedly easy job.

Nearby, in and out. No long-term setup, no games—a test to see if, in the end, she could actually do it.

She fingered the sheath of the dagger at her thigh. If she couldn't do this, if she froze, if she lost her nerve—it would be the end of this long experiment. There were no second chances. Even if she escaped, Elidor was somewhere nearby, hiding in the dark and watching her every move. Waiting for her to fail.

Failure was not an option.

What was the target *doing*?

The clink of plates and cups shortly thereafter told the story plainly enough. A meal before he left. She amused herself by trying to listen to the conversation. They were speaking quietly, so she only heard bits and pieces as one person or another became a little too fervent in their opinions:

"...the anti-Sedationists and their damn..."

"The Conclave will never cede..."

"...stupid argument!"

Ugh. Politics.

She had to confirm that the target was among those inside.

She opened the satchel at her waist—the only item she carried other than the dagger at her thigh and knife in her boot—and selected a strange-looking object from among those few she had brought with her for this job.

It was a long tube with mirrors positioned at an angle at both ends, which were bent. She had obtained the curious device from a festival in the city a couple months ago. Someone had made dozens of them to sell, purporting to allow the owner to see over the heads of the crowd.

Of course, Ivana had seen other applications for the tool.

Now, she raised one end of it over the edge of the windowsill until she could see inside the room. As she had guessed, four people sat at a table, eating. Her target was Fereharian, and only one Fereharian was in the room. She studied him for a moment. He fit the rest of the description as well, down to the scars of a slave's brand on one ear.

She lowered the device and slid it back into her satchel. He was definitely here. Now to get him away from the others. Should she wait him out and catch him a little ways down the road? But *she* didn't want to be wandering too far away from the city at night, let alone this night.

Her dilemma was solved when the back door opened a few minutes later.

Ivana shrank deeper into the overgrowth.

It was him. He had a pot full of leavings from dinner and was headed directly toward the compost pile.

She glanced back toward the open window. The three left were still talking. No one else was around. A quick flick of the dagger, just like she had been taught...

She would be long gone by the time they wondered what was taking him so long.

He had his back to her as he emptied the pot, humming to himself, and didn't show any sign he heard her as she slunk around him to find a better position.

This was it. The moment she had feared and anticipated, the moment Elidor was scrutinizing from wherever he hid. There was no more spying, no more gathering information, no more planning.

Her heart pounded erratically, and her hand was sweaty as she loosened the dagger from its sheath.

It's his life or yours.

And before she could think more about what she was about to do, she attacked.

Her dagger struck true. She muffled his cry of pain with her arm, which she had wrapped around his face at the same moment she'd stabbed him, and then he collapsed.

He lay motionless, eyes open, and she checked his pulse. Dead.

She felt numb as she stared down at him. Who was he? Why did the government want him dead?

How had she become someone who could do this?

She turned away. Nothing mattered now except getting away from here as fast as possible.

And when she turned, she faced the abyss.

Literally.

Black flames licked out from a split in the air, directly in front of her face.

She stumbled back, shocked and horrified, and then glanced up at the sky. The sky-fire hadn't started yet! How could...?

She tripped over the body and caught herself in a pool of his blood. Blood that, when she rose back to her feet, glistened silver on her hand.

Rhianah, he was a Banebringer!

She turned to run. She had only seen bloodbane a handful of times before, and even once was too many.

But it was too late. A half-dozen black shapes burst forth from the tear, screeching as they came. Most of them flew harmlessly past, but one headed directly at her face. She caught it before it could claw at her face, and for a few terrifying moments, she grappled with what looked, at first glance, like an overlarge bat: a bat with white, pupil-less eyes, claws at the ends of its wings, and dozens of tiny, needle-like teeth in its mouth, which was open and screaming at her. She tried to grab one of its wings to hurl it away from her, and it grabbed at her cloak with its claws, swung around, and sank its teeth into her shoulder. She bit her tongue to keep from crying out—she could not be caught.

But it was too late for that. The bloodbane's cry had alerted the three remaining people in the house, and they burst out of the door. They stood, gaping for a moment, taking in the scene, and then all started yelling at once.

"Temoth, they found him!"

"The bloodbat! Kill it!"

"Grab her—don't let her get away!"

Her head spun. The bloodbat had attached itself to her shoulder by its teeth and obviously had no intention of letting go. The pain was overwhelming. The shouting of the men, the certainty that one way or another, this was it for her...

And then, in a blur, Elidor burst out of the darkness.

The scene around her turned to carnage before Ivana had finished staggering out of his way, all three men as dead as their companion.

Elidor whirled on her, his eyes flaring with rage.

She dropped to her knees, the treacherous bloodbat still hanging by its teeth from her flesh, and waited for his dagger to strike her down as well.

Instead, Elidor ripped the beast off her shoulder, and it took a chunk of her flesh with it, finally tearing a cry of pain from her throat. Elidor hurled it with tremendous force to the ground, scraps of her skin still between its teeth, and shoved his dagger into its chest with all his weight behind it.

Even then, the bat thrashed and screamed, refusing to give up, trying to sink its teeth into Elidor's hand—anything it could grab hold of. Elidor held firm, pushing the dagger down, further, and further, until finally the beast lay still.

"Get up," he hissed.

"But—"

He lifted her to her feet by her hurt arm, and she bit her tongue again. "And get home—now!"

A fleck of fire streaked across the night sky, like a burning claw mark against a tapestry of black. The sky-fire was beginning.

The sky was so bright with fire by now that at times it felt like daylight. Ivana was running across a densely populated city during the height of the sky-fire.

She didn't know if she would make it. In the major cities of Setana, there were always *some* Banebringers created—and some random tears as well.

Some years, the damage was minimal. Most years, there was enough property damage to keep workers busy for weeks. A handful of years, there had been pure carnage.

It was one of the risks of living in a city.

She didn't bother with the alleys. No one in their right mind was out now, not even the opportunists. She just wanted to get back to Elidor's as fast as she could.

Her shoulder was on fire, she had a stitch in her side, and her frantic pace was fast draining her of any energy.

Then a more sinister sound rose above that of her feet slapping against the pavement—the sound of a hundred rats scampering down a road that would soon intersect with the one she was on.

It was an ominous, unnatural sound, and surely didn't portend anything good.

She wasn't going to make it.

She caught her bearings and searched frantically for an alternative destination.

Her breath caught in her throat. Was she close to...? Yes, she was.

She couldn't go there.

The scratching was getting closer.

She had no choice. She darted down a different side road instead, stopping only to discard the sheath with her dagger and her cloak in a dumpster.

She didn't even stop when she reached her destination. She let the door halt her momentum instead as she slammed into it, then banged on it with both fists. "Help! Someone!" she shouted, praying to whatever god would listen that she would be heard by someone other than a god.

If they were in a safe room, no one would ever hear her. Did they have a safe room? She didn't remember ever seeing one, but...

The door was flung open, and Boden stood there, gaping at her.

Chapter Sixteen

Unlike Elidor's converted wine cellar, Da Grania's root cellar was just a root cellar.

The wooden door wouldn't stop a determined bloodbane, but it kept her family out of the way and hidden.

Ivana sat on the ground in one corner, her arms wrapped around her knees, while Grania knelt next to her, tending to her shoulder.

Ivana winced as she pressed a wet compress against the wound, but the initial sting wore off quickly, and then the constant burning cooled.

"We'll keep that there for a little while," Grania said, securing the compress to her arm with a bandage, "and then I'll do what I can to stitch it back together until you can see a proper doctor."

"Thank you," Ivana whispered. She felt lightheaded with pain and exhaustion.

Grania patted her uninjured shoulder, rose, and went back to her family.

It had been over a year since she had seen Da Grania and her family, who were playing a game by lamplight. The youngest, Annan, whom Ivana remembered as an incoherent almost-toddler, was now quite verbal, though at present he only peered out at her from between his mother's legs, oblivious to the danger that might be roaming the streets.

Oblivious to the danger that sat in this very room.

She flashed the boy a smile because it felt wrong not to, then looked away.

I shouldn't be here.

A pair of legs appeared, and then Boden, crouched in front of her. He held out a steaming cup. "Tea?"

"Thank you," she said again, taking the cup.

Boden moved away, returned with a blanket that he arranged gently over her shoulders, and then settled down next to her.

Boden hadn't spoken much, what with the flurry of activity that had surrounded her arrival. After he had ushered her into the root cellar, Grania, upon seeing the extent of her injury, had dared to dart out and collect what she needed to tend to it while Ivana waited and Grania's husband tried to keep the eyes of their curious children from seeing the mangled flesh.

Even then, after things had settled, Boden had seemed hesitant.

No wonder, since their last interaction had been a letter Ivana had sent declining his overtures.

If only he knew that since that letter, she had lain with so many men that the very idea of overtures toward her ought to now appall him.

"Bloodbat?" he asked.

"Yes." No one had asked what had happened. On a night like tonight, no one needed to.

He nodded. "I've seen their bites before. They're vicious." He fiddled with the ties on his shirt. "What in the abyss were you doing outside, though, and so far away from home?"

To her knowledge, he didn't know where she lived. But she obviously hadn't run *there* for refuge.

Why indeed?

I shouldn't be here.

She managed a weak smile. "You're going to think I'm superbly foolish."

"Anything that could have brought you out of the safety of your home tonight must have been important."

"I suppose that's a matter of perspective. We have a mouser that I've..." She looked at her hands and gave a little chuckle, feigning everything but the flush itself. "Well, I've grown fond of it. She decided today would be a grand time to go for a jaunt across the city. I was trying to find her before the sky-fire started." She shook her head. "Like I said. Foolish."

He didn't laugh at her. "Did you find your cat?"

She shook her head again. "No."

"I hope she's all right."

She finally glanced at him. He seemed perfectly sincere. He was so...so...*sweet*. He probably assumed she was too.

If only he knew that some of the silver blood on her had not come from the bloodbat.

I shouldn't be here.

"I've missed your visits," he said.

No. You miss her visits.

The one who would return from those visits to a room as empty and alone as she had felt on the inside.

The one who had to drown her despair in her own blood.

The one who had given up everything she had left—which was only herself—not to be that person anymore.

That person was not the person sitting there next to Boden. That person was gone.

As was the naïve young girl who had come before her.

Boden smiled at her, and she pitied him more than she pitied herself.

It was working.

The first time a man other than Airell had brought her to his bed, she had been not-Ivana. Playing a part that wasn't her, just to survive.

In a strange reversal, that night, she would also have to play a part. But it wasn't the part of not-Ivana. No, this time, the part *was* Ivana. As much of Ivana that Boden thought he knew anyway.

She didn't know what she was. But she wasn't that same Ivana.

"I'm sorry," she said. "I thought it would be too awkward."

"I understand," he said. "And I don't mean to bring, well, that, back up. I just wanted you to know that I've missed you."

She met his eyes. *Oh, Boden. In another life.* "I've missed you too," she said instead. "Have you learned anything new and interesting lately?"

He relaxed. And Ivana settled in to play herself, perhaps for the last time.

Elidor was furious.

Ivana had never *seen* him so angry before.

He was cold. He sometimes snapped. He ridiculed. But this...this was more.

No sooner had the last embers died from the sky than Ivana

had excused herself, with thanks, from Grania and her family—and Boden. She ventured out into the streets to retrieve her cloak and dagger and return to Elidor's, hoping this had been one of those lucky years.

She had almost forgotten, in her flight from the scene of the assassination and subsequent sheltering with Da Grania and her husband, that things had not gone according to plan. And how livid Elidor had looked when he had sent her home.

Nothing had changed overnight.

She knew he was still angry the moment she stepped through the door, because he was in the front room waiting for her, pacing.

At any rate, she was still alive. For now.

"Where were you?" he growled the moment door had closed behind her. "I told you to come directly home."

"I had to find shelter," she said, a bit taken aback. Perhaps it wasn't the bungled job he was angry about? "I could hear blood-bane in the streets."

"Where?"

She hesitated only a moment. "With the family at that apothecary I used to go to."

He halted his pacing, turned, and looked at her as if for the first time since she had come in. His eyes roved to the bandage on her shoulder and then to the dagger at her thigh.

"The apothecary helped patch me up," she said. And before he could protest, she continued. "And don't worry. I discarded my dagger and cloak before I got there and told a story about being out in the streets looking for my lost cat."

"Lost cat," he repeated.

"They have absolutely no reason to think I would lie," she said. "You think average people will jump to the conclusion I must have been roaming the streets looking for someone to murder?"

His jaw jumped, but he conceded the point by ending the conversation. "Come with me."

"What? Where?"

"To meet our handler."

Ivana didn't know what this portended. Was this the reward for completing the job or the punishment for messing it up? Perhaps it wouldn't be Elidor who would administer the final judgment, but some higher power.

Ivana hadn't even changed; her shirt was still in tatters and stained with sticky red-brown blood.

Heedless, Elidor had grabbed her arm and was now dragging her across the city in the pre-morning dark, light enough to tell that their neighborhood appeared to have been spared the spawning of further bloodbane.

However, there was plenty of evidence to the contrary elsewhere. At one house a window had been smashed through from the inside. At another, four or five chickens had been torn to bits and scattered about the road. A foot here, a bloody pile of feathers there...

A half-dozen Guardsmen barked at them to stay back as they approached the entrance to one dead-end alley, as if the unnatural shrieking coming from the end weren't enough warning.

And then, of course, they passed one convoy of Conclave priests. They surrounded a cage on a cart being pulled by donkeys, inside which a man sat, staring out through the bars with hollow eyes.

This, Elidor and Ivana gave a wide berth.

Her attention was drawn back to the promised meeting when they approached and entered a small shrine. Ivana had never met their handler. She had picked up jobs and payment from secure locations, but she had never met the man himself.

Except...she had.

When the man who stood inside, waiting, turned around, she immediately recognized him.

"You!" she burst out, unable to help herself.

Elidor cast her a silencing glance; Llyr ignored her.

"Elidor," Llyr said, as calm as could be. "I hear payment is in order. A few extra bodies, but none that will be missed. Why did you summon me?"

"You," Elidor snarled, far more intimidating than her own affronted exclamation, "are never to set me or my apprentice on a Banebringer again, are we clear?"

"Yes, I heard about that," Llyr said. "A bit of a complication, wasn't it? My apologies." At that point, he finally acknowledged Ivana with a smirk. "But your apprentice handled the job, didn't she?"

"Are we clear?" Elidor repeated.

"The job does come with risk," Llyr said.

Elidor growled and took two menacing steps toward Llyr, who, to Ivana's satisfaction, flinched.

Llyr waved Elidor back with his hand. "Fine, fine. In the future, we'll warn you first. Fair enough compromise?"

Wait. Did Llyr know the target was a Banebringer or not? There was a subtext here that Ivana wasn't catching.

Elidor gave him a cold stare. "Where's the payment?"

Llyr tossed him a leather pouch. "Your apprentice looks as though she's been through it," he said, giving Ivana a once-over, and then a second once-over, far more probing than necessary.

She narrowed her eyes at him, trying to give him the same cold look Elidor had given him, and he snorted and smiled.

One day, she thought. *One day you will no longer mock me.*

Elidor jerked his head, and she followed.

She glanced back once at Llyr, who was still smirking at her. *One day.*

When they returned to Elidor's house, Ivana went to the kitchen to attempt to clean and change the bandage on her wound. Elidor followed her, but all he did was pace.

Ivana watched him, wary, while sitting on a chair in the kitchen, gingerly dabbing at the wound with an antiseptic-soaked cloth, waiting to see if he would speak.

At least, in the chaos of the night, the last thing on her mind was her first murder.

Finally, she couldn't take it anymore. "I'm sorry," she said.

Elidor turned on her. "Stupid girl," he snapped. "None of my anger is directed at you."

She blinked, startled. She knew he was furious with their handler, but she had assumed he was also angry with her for almost botching the job. "But I—"

"Did everything you were asked to do with perfect execution." He started pacing again. "No, it's *them.* A Banebringer! And they didn't warn us? It could have been worse, so much worse." Elidor's nostrils flared. "Reckless fools. At least the others weren't Banebringers as well."

Ivana digested that. So he wasn't blaming her for the near-disaster? Granted, the target was dead, and anyone who had seen was dead as well. But she was certain she had messed it up. "Surely, they couldn't have known," she said, though by the conversation she had been privy to, she suspected that wasn't true.

He jerked his head. "Oh, they knew. The Conclave knows."

"The Conclave?" Ivana said in disbelief.

Elidor sniffed. "Yes, the Conclave. Our masters."

Ivana sat, stunned. "I thought you worked for the government."

"I do, after a fashion. But my leash has been rented to the Conclave for a long time now."

"But why would they send us to kill a Banebringer? Don't they have Hunters for that?"

"Don't be naïve. A Hunter can't kill a Banebringer. A Hunter *subdues* and Sedates Banebringers. Anything else would undermine their own narrative."

That took her aback. "Their narrative? They don't Sedate Banebringers to keep the bloodbane population down?"

Elidor snorted. "The gods only know why they Sedate Banebringers. Whatever they say and however much truth there is to it, the real reason is certainly because it somehow bolsters their own power."

His words spawned a dozen more questions, but none of them were relevant to what she wanted to know the answer to the most. "But that still doesn't explain, why bother with assassinating a Banebringer?" Ivana pressed. "If Sedation is as good as death—"

"The weapon does not question its master!"

"But—"

"Obviously, they had something to gain by his death over Sedation."

"Why didn't they warn us?"

Air hissed through his teeth. "Because I would have refused."

Ivana blinked. "That's an option?"

"No," Elidor said, "but the only problem with creating a dangerous weapon is that you must have control over it. I am far too dangerous for them to chance losing control of me."

A moment of realization hit Ivana. "And, of course, I'm not."

"No. And at present, you are dispensable enough to chance losing you on a job like this." Elidor stopped pacing. Instead, he turned to look at her attempts at nursing her shoulder.

"Give me that," he snapped, yanking the rag out of her hand.

She let him finish cleaning and rebandaging the wound, afraid to say or do anything else while he worked.

The silence and sudden lack of frantic activity left time for her whirling mind to settle. It settled on reliving the events of the evening.

She had done it. She had actually done it. She, Ivana, had killed a target herself. She felt strangely dispassionate. In retrospect—other than the surprise of the target being a Banebringer—it had been mechanical. She had executed and applied the knowledge she had learned. And yet she wasn't wholly numb. Something still niggled at the back of her mind.

She found herself watching Elidor's face. "Do you think he had a family?" she asked, almost unbidden, and she immediately regretted the words.

He lifted his eyes to her, cold, aloof, but he said nothing. It wasn't exactly an invitation to go on, but now that the words were out, she felt the need to explain herself.

"It's just... My father. He wasn't assassinated, but he died on a blade. Murdered. After a fashion. I-I couldn't help but wondering..."

"A weapon does not think. A weapon does not wonder." He tucked the end of the length of bandage under itself. "Continue to clean it daily and change the bandages," he said, "or a wound like that will fester and sour. If it doesn't appear to be healing well, I'll see about a doctor." He turned to leave the room.

"Dal," she said, before he could leave.

He turned to look at her.

"Did I pass, then?" she asked.

"Yes. You are no longer a neophyte, but truly my apprentice." He gave a mirthless chuckle. "Congratulations."

With that, he swept out of the room, leaving Ivana alone.

A state she was, and would have to continue to be, very familiar with.

Culpable

After a terrible week of waiting, Ivana watched, helpless, while her mother continued to worsen until at the end, she was so weak and delirious she didn't even recognize her own daughters.

The morning after that, Ivana had a third corpse on her conscience.

She tried to be strong for Izel. She really did. But she was as scared as her sister, and the burden of the devastation that her choices had caused was almost too much to bear.

They spent the last of their coins on a proper burial for their mother, next to their father and Ivana's daughter. It had been a foolish gesture—why did the dead care? But Ivana couldn't stomach the thought of having her mother thrown into a mass grave or burned—which is what the landlord, panicked at the news of blood fever in his building, had wanted to do with her body.

Thankfully, he let them stay on. They still had over a week left in their prepaid rent, at which point he made it clear that they would either have to get out or pay up.

They didn't know what they would do after that. They had

little money left, nowhere to go, and no one to ask for help. They already were rationing their food and firewood to the barest minimum needed to survive, huddled together for warmth at night, and huddled near the tiny fire they allowed in the woodstove during the day.

The only upside was that they were talking again. For so long Izel had withdrawn from her, but with their mother's illness and death, they had had no choice but to set aside whatever was between them and work together to come up with options.

That was what they were doing one chilly morning, three days after their mother had died, and six days until their lease was up, as they sat as close as they dared to the woodstove. They had already discussed finding work, but they already knew from experience that no one would hire them.

Izel politely didn't say why. Instead, she proposed another option altogether. "Mama's family," Izel said. "In northern Ferehar. Didn't she contact them, after Papa..." She folded her hands in her lap. "If we could find a way to get there—"

Ivana was already shaking her head. "It's too dangerous." In fact, they had never met their mother's side of the family. Oh, their mother had talked about taking a trip, from time to time, but traveling that far with an entire family was expensive—unless one wanted to chance not having armed guards. And so the years slipped by, and now they barely remembered the names of their maternal grandmother and grandfather.

"More dangerous than staying on the streets here?" Izel countered.

"We don't even know the name of the village where they live," Ivana said.

Izel wilted. "Oh. Right."

And their father's extended family was no help. He was an only child, and his parents were both dead, several years back.

But Ivana wanted to be encouraging, even though she herself felt no hope. "But we might have to try."

Izel swallowed and nodded, toying with something in her hand.

"What's that?" Ivana asked.

Izel flushed and clenched her hand around it. "Nothing."

"It obviously isn't nothing. Come on. What is it?"

Izel sat stubbornly still for a few moments and then finally opened her hand.

It was her rose necklace.

Ivana blinked in disbelief. "You still have your rose necklace?"

"I-I just... Papa gave it to me."

Ivana found herself rising to her feet. Tears were shimmering in Izel's eyes. Ivana ought to stay calm, but her throat had tightened. "We sold everything, and you held on to that?"

"It isn't even worth anything! You wouldn't even understand. Papa gave it to me," she repeated stubbornly.

"And I sold his microscope!" The pitch of Ivana's voice rose at the end of her statement. She was losing the battle with calm.

Apparently, so was Izel, because she also rose to her feet. "His microscope? His *microscope*? Who cares about his stupid microscope!"

Ivana hugged her arms around herself and dug her fingernails into her arm. *Calm.* "I do. I did."

"You don't care about anything!" Izel retorted. "If you did, we wouldn't be here in the first place! But no, all you cared about was your precious Airell—and look where it got us! I told you. I *told* you, and you didn't listen." Izel clenched the rose pendant in her hand, the chain dangling from her fist. "So don't tell me I should have sold the last thing I have left. You have no right." Izel now faced Ivana as if they were about to have a duel. "This is all your fault!" She spat the final phrase out as though it were poison.

Ivana stepped back. The words hung in the air between them, thudded in Ivana's head, her heart, every part of her. *You think I don't know that?* she wanted to scream. *You think I don't tell myself that every miserable day of my life?*

And until now, Izel had never spoken it. Until now.

Choked by her attempts to suppress her grief and fury, all Ivana could do was hold out her hand. "Give me the necklace," she said through clenched teeth.

"No!"

She broke. She lunged at Izel, who unsuccessfully tried to leap out of the way. Instead, they landed with a thud onto the hard floor in a tangle of arms and legs. Ivana managed to pin her, pry her hand open, and wrench the necklace away from her. Izel looked up at her, daggers and hate in her eyes.

And there was a knock on the door, breaking the stand-off.

Ivana's chest was heaving. She shoved the necklace into her pocket, pushed herself up off the floor, and flung the door open while Izel rose behind her.

It was none other than the landlord...and Lord Kadmon.

Hope welled up in Ivana's chest. Had he heard about their predicament and come to rescue them? Did the old man have a kindly streak after all? Even if he would hire them as servants, they would be taken care of.

The landlord disappeared, and Ivana stepped back from the door to allow Kadmon in.

"Well, well." He inspected their apartment visually and then wrinkled his nose. "I heard about the death of your mother. So sad, so very sad. Well."

He didn't look like a man about to bring good news.

"Despite everything, you are both in good health, I trust?"

Ivana turned to exchange a glance with Izel, who looked mutually bewildered.

Ivana shrugged. "I suppose, my lord."

"Good, good." He stepped out of the door. She heard the murmur of voices, and when he entered again, two more men accompanied him, one bearded, and one clean-shaven.

Either way, they didn't look like kind men.

Ivana stepped backward, into Izel, and Izel clung to her arm.

"My lord?" Ivana asked hesitantly. "What is this about?"

"Well, you see, my dear, your father's wages were paid through the end of the month, and I'm afraid he passed near the beginning. I was generous in letting it go, at the time, given the circumstances, but…"

Ivana's mouth dropped open. This was an attempt to collect on a perceived debt?

"My lord," Ivana said, trying to ignore the surly looks of the other two men. "If you've come to collect from us, I'm afraid we have no money to give you. Therefore, if you would be so kind as to leave us to our grief in peace—"

"Oh, no, no. Of course you have no money." He nodded to the men, who approached the girls.

They stepped back again.

"There are other ways to recoup my losses, of course."

The men seized them by the arms, one for each of them. Izel screamed, and Ivana struggled in vain. "What is this about?" Ivana snapped, a burst of righteous indignation rising up from somewhere deep inside her broken spirit.

"You're to be sold as slaves. These men—"

"No!" Izel screamed again. She tried to step on the foot of the clean-shaven man, but he easily sidestepped her, then bound her wrists behind her back.

Ivana, on the other hand, sank down, limp, her earlier fire

extinguished in a moment.

Slaves. Burning skies, no.

"Ivana," Izel sobbed, trying to get to Ivana, any previous grievances forgotten.

The men had to drag them both out of the apartment; Izel kicked and screamed, and Ivana hung like dead weight from the bearded man's arms. He hadn't even bothered to bind her hands.

This was a fate worse than death. Slaves were beaten. Raped. Consumed and then discarded when every possible shred of human life had been sapped from them.

She had seen slaves before. They were either prisoners of war or sold to pay off debts. The latter in theory could eventually purchase their freedom if they worked long enough, but did a slave ever live that long? Was there anything left of life in them if they did?

Two wagons waited in the street just outside; Lord Kadmon stood by a carriage farther down.

No. They wouldn't be slaves. There had to be a way out of this. "My lord, please!" she pleaded while Izel's captor loaded her into the back of one wagon. "My father served you faithfully. This is how you repay him?"

Kadmon didn't reply. He wouldn't even meet her eyes.

The bearded man dragged her toward the second wagon.

She glanced desperately back at Izel, whose ankles were now being bound together and then chained to a metal hook on the side, so that if she tried to hurl herself out, she would end up crushed under the wheels of the wagon instead.

"Wait!" She dug her feet into the ground. "Why aren't you taking me with my sister?"

The man shoved her forward, and she stumbled and fell to the ground. "Different buyers. Get up."

No! Separated, never to see each other again? She couldn't let that happen, she had to do something, anything.

She disobeyed his order, choosing instead to remain on all fours while she thought. Izel's captor had moved down the street to talk to Kadmon.

Hers growled and leaned over to put a hand on her shoulder. "I said, get up."

And with the same righteous fury that had fueled a fist into the jeering face of a boy, she threw her fist back, up, and into his groin.

The man staggered back and fell to his knees, cursing.

It was all she needed.

He tried to grab for her as she rose and passed him by, but he missed.

She dashed back to the first wagon and tugged at Izel's bonds.

It was useless. The clean-shaven man was already sprinting back toward her and the bearded man rising to his feet; there was no way she could free Izel in time. She could save herself or neither of them.

Ivana met Izel's eyes. For a few beats, Ivana's heart felt heavy and slow.

Tears streamed down Izel's face. "Don't leave me."

"I'm sorry," Ivana whispered, her own face hot with tears.

For everything.

She spun and ran, just missing the grasp of the clean-shaven man. She ran, even though Izel screamed after her, calling her name, begging her not to leave her.

She ran, ignoring the shouts of surprised townsfolk as she passed by.

She ran until her head spun and her side hurt.

She ran, not knowing where she was going or how she was

going to get there.

    She ran.

Chapter Seventeen

Ivana lay on her stomach on the floor of a dusty and unused attic, her cheek resting on the back of her hands, bored out of her mind.

She hadn't practiced lying around *waiting*. She should have brought a book.

She lifted her head one more time to peer through the hole she had drilled into the board, in case she had drifted off and missed the target entering his rooms.

Still empty.

She sighed and craned her neck to look back at the trap door that led out of the attic.

Still cracked.

She put her head down again, resisting the urge to roll over onto her back.

Night had fallen, and the priest she was supposed to be assassinating *still* hadn't returned to his rooms.

She had been certain he had arranged the meeting with his associate in his private rooms tonight.

The door creaked open, and she put her eye back to the hole. *Finally.*

The priest entered his front room, and his associate—the poor man who was about to be framed for murder—followed.

Now she had to wait for their meeting to be over.

She stifled a sigh, put her forehead on her arm, and went back to waiting.

The hum of voices and clinking of glasses drifting from below lulled her half-asleep more than once, something she was sure Elidor would chastise her for if he found out.

Why was it that she couldn't see him lying around in an attic all afternoon to wait for his target?

But eventually, the sound of wood scraping against wood roused her.

She lifted herself to all fours and crouched down to look through the hole once again.

Yes, they were saying farewell.

Her heart leapt into her throat. What had been a tedious afternoon of waiting was finally about to come to a violent end.

She had killed four others by now, but since the first near-disastrous encounter with a Banebringer, Elidor had given her only jobs that required murder from afar, so to speak: three had been poison and one had been setting up a deadly "accident" and waiting for the target to walk right into it.

This was the first time she would be required to be more violent than that first knife in the back; this one had to look like a murder of passion.

She would be lying if she didn't admit to herself that she was nervous, for many reasons.

She needed to prove to Elidor that she could do this, too.

She didn't want to get caught.

She hoped she could go through with it.

The target's fellow priest finally left. Ivana waited for the target to lock the door, pour himself another drink, and settle down into an armchair. Ivana looked longingly at the drink. She much preferred poison, but sometimes it wasn't viable.

She crept over to the trap door, opened it, and, after checking below her to be sure someone hadn't snuck in while she wasn't looking, dropped into his bedchamber.

She tiptoed to the door, which was slightly ajar, and peered in.

Still sitting in the armchair, his back to her.

Just as planned.

She picked up the fire poker that was next to the hearth in his room.

She took several deep breaths, in and out, steadying herself.

Then she burst into the room.

He turned with only enough time for his mouth to form an astonished O before she cracked the poker down on his head.

He stumbled back, and she lunged at him and kicked him in the groin.

He went down on one knee but tried to get up, so she brought the poker down again.

He dropped to his hands and knees.

A final blow to the back of the head, and he collapsed, still.

She dropped next to him, set aside the poker, and rolled him over onto his back.

That was a mistake.

The Banebringer had already been dead when she had looked him in the face; this man wasn't dead yet. His eyes were still moving, bloodshot, disbelieving, and he used his last moment of sense to focus on her face, as though trying to determine if he knew her.

And then they went still.

The surge of energy born of nerves and the thrill of the attack that had been flowing through her rushed out of her all at once.

She swallowed fiercely and put two trembling fingers to his throat to confirm.

Yes. He was finally dead.

She stared down at the man, whose eyelids were still open, with unseeing eyes still looking in her direction. Blood seeped onto the floor from under the back of his crushed skull.

All at once, she had the overwhelming urge to vomit.

She had to get out of here, for more than one reason.

She hoisted herself back up into the trap door, closed the door, then squirmed out of the small attic window and dropped to the ground.

Sweat was trickling down her neck, even though the cool of an autumn night was upon them, and she loosened the hood over her head and let it drop back. She leaned her head back against the cool stone wall of the building and gulped in the air. Just for a moment. Just a moment, to calm down, to come to terms with what she had just done, and then...

"Ivana?"

The sweat on her body froze. *No.*

She pushed herself away from the wall and turned to face none other than Boden.

Her mind snapped from one mode to another, giving her mental whiplash. She turned her shock into pleased astonishment. "Boden?" *No!*

His face broke into a grin. "It is you! What are you doing

here?"

Her mind whirled. She could salvage this. She had to. "I might ask you the same thing!"

He chuckled. "We have a contract with the sanctuary here; I deliver supplies once a month. What about you?"

"Visiting a relative," she said, then changed the subject. "Are you headed out?"

He glanced up at the sky and grimaced. "I have one more delivery to make, and then I will. I've been caught up longer than I wanted waiting for a priest to return so he could sign for the supplies." He shifted from one foot to the other, and then blurted out, "It's so nice running into you again, after just a few months."

"It is, but unfortunately, I'm just leaving." Her meaning ought to be obvious. "Perhaps I'll see you around."

The corner of his mouth quirked up. "Yes. Perhaps in another couple months." He smiled at her again, more cordial, and less enthusiastic, and then walked away.

She let out a slow breath through her teeth. *Yes. Please. Cast me out of your mind.* Her stomach twisted in a way it hadn't in a long while.

She shouldn't have let him go. She knew it. He had recognized her at the scene of a job—in fact, right outside the very building where a murdered man lay yet to be discovered. Possibly waiting for the very man she had just murdered.

But he had believed her story. Hadn't she told Elidor last time, average people didn't assume you were prowling around finding someone to murder? He would never guess she had anything to do with it.

You've been compromised.

The words were Elidor's, but the voice was hers.

If he's questioned, he can place you here.

No. She knew Boden.

Elidor hadn't pressed the issue of her having gone to the apothecary after the sky-fire. It was fine.

This is different, and you know it.

She *knew* him. What was she supposed to do? She couldn't... She couldn't.

She pulled her hood back up, her hands shaking, and closed her eyes.

She could tell herself she had no choice, but that would be a lie. She could do what needed to be done, or she could not.

The only thing she could *not* do was go back to Elidor's without taking care of it, one way or the other.

Ivana heard Boden whistling before she saw him. Having discharged his duties, Boden was happily headed home, no doubt looking forward to a warm bath or a hot meal, or both.

Ivana felt sicker than she ever had before. Sicker than when she had watched a man die under her own crushing blows. Sicker than that first knife in the back.

Those were strangers.

This was Boden.

They had, for a brief time, shared a common interest.

He liked her. Truth be told, she liked him, after a fashion.

He *trusted* her.

Her breath was coming in quick, short gasps. This was not what she had signed up for. She had given up everything she had left in Elidor's service. Her morals. Her pride. Her own body. And the reward had been bittersweet. With every man and murder, another shred of who she had been was buried deeper until as she had hoped, the despair had retreated, and in its place was a blessed numbness.

And yet, she hadn't felt like she had lost her humanity.

Boden had almost reached where she crouched, hiding in an alley. She was on a precipice; either way she stepped, she had a feeling she would plummet into a chasm she would never climb out of.

For now, she tugged down her hood and stepped out of the alley to face him. If she went through with it, she would do it face-to-face. If she didn't, she owed him an explanation.

He halted and took a step back, hand on his purse. Then he peered at her face, and his hand dropped. "Ivana?" He hesitated. "I thought you would have long since arrived home."

"I was waiting for you."

He tilted his head. "Oh?"

"After we met again tonight, I was thinking." She took a step closer to him, her heart hammering. "I-I was thinking I owed you an explanation, and it couldn't wait. You should at least have the opportunity to..." She trailed off.

His brow furrowed. "What is this about?"

She swallowed. "The real reason I turned you down."

He was silent, watching her face.

She wasn't sure what prompted her to speak the next words. To punish herself perhaps? To make it easier to do what she had to do once he finally knew the truth and rejected her?

"I'm not pure, Boden," she said. "Anything but. And I think you deserve someone better."

He looked at her, searching her face, her eyes. And then his face relaxed. "Is that all?" He held out a hand to her. "Ivana."

She took a step back. "You don't understand."

"I understand. I know what people say about that sort of thing, and I know how that must make you feel. " He shook his head. "It's not so bad here in the city, and I don't care anyway. I like you Ivana. I *really* like you. Can't we just see where this might take us?"

She stared at him, horrified. That had *not* been the reaction she had been expecting.

"Look. It's late, and it's dark. Why don't we talk about this tomorrow?" He held out his hand to her again. "For now, may I walk you home?"

Why? Why, why, why? Why did he have to be so damn *nice*?

And no matter how she tried to push it away, no matter how hard she tried not to care, her deep and buried sense of guilt beat against her. *Your fault. Your fault. Your fault.*

If she hadn't pushed her hood off, he might not have recognized her. If she had been more careful. If...if...if...

Her eyes blurred. "Boden," she whispered, and the emptiness inside taunted her in a way it hadn't in a long while.

He took her dismay the wrong way, perhaps surmising she was merely grateful that he hadn't turned her away, and so he took her hand himself.

Something stirred inside of her. Something beyond the thoughts swirling in her mind, beyond the choice she had to make. Something she had practiced enough that it had almost become instinct. "I've missed talking to you," she said softly.

He hesitated and then drew her closer to himself.

"I've missed you, too," he said.

It took over. The person she had to be. The person she had become. The mask, the wall, the façade.

Behind all of that was only despair and pain. She could feel it eating greedily away at her, even now, gnawing on the raw emotion that had risen again to the surface.

She wouldn't go back to that. Not now, not ever.

She touched his chin with one hand, making sure he was looking at her face, and eased her dagger out of its sheath with the other. She then wrapped that arm around his waist.

"I am so, so sorry," she whispered.

She jumped off the precipice...

...and drove the dagger into his back.

His eyes widened, and he gasped. "I-Ivana?"

He swayed, but she held him there. Forced herself to see the betrayal, confusion, and pain. Forced herself to see it, and dismiss it, and in doing so, dismiss the same emotions that had roiled for so long within herself.

He staggered, and his weight finally forced her to let him fall to the ground.

She hesitated only long enough to cut his purse and take the coins, so that it would look like a mugging gone wrong, and to be sure he was dead. Then she left.

When she finally stumbled home, she found Elidor waiting for her in the front room. He had started doing that anytime she came back from a job that she had conducted independently.

"Well?"

"Can this not wait until morning?" she asked.

"No." He pointed to the armchair across from the couch he sat on. "Sit."

She gritted her teeth and sat, staring down at her lap.

"Report," he said.

She gave him all the details. All the details but one. The mortar on that wall was still too freshly laid. She was afraid if she talked about it, it would come crumbling down.

And then it would have been for nothing.

After she fell silent, he also was silent for a moment. "It sounds as though it went fairly well, and we will discuss areas of improvement in a moment. But first, what aren't you telling me?"

He was staring at her with his piercing eyes.

She could lie. She could say nothing. But he would know, somehow he would know, or find out.

She looked past him to a point over his shoulder and mentally reinforced the wall. "I was recognized."

He frowned. "I see. And how did that happen?"

"I let my hood down outside. After I eliminated the target. I was hot. I needed some air."

"Foolish. Get used to discomfort."

"Yes. I realize that now."

"And you took care of it?"

"I did." Her eyes flicked back to him.

His eyes narrowed, as if suspecting she was twisting the truth. "How?"

She drew her dagger from its sheath and laid it on an end table. It was crusted dark red-brown with dried blood. "He suffered a fatal mugging."

Elidor's hand relaxed. She hadn't noticed it tense, but she was certain it had been poised to draw his dagger should he discover she had deceived him.

"Who was it?" he asked.

She resisted the urge to lower her eyes to her lap. Instead, she met Elidor's squarely. That wall would stay up. Temoth help her, it would never come down again. "Boden. The apothecary's apprentice at the shop I used to frequent."

Elidor shook his head. "That damn apprentice," he growled. "I knew that would come to trouble."

She remained silent.

When she didn't respond, his mouth turned downward, and he pinned her with his eyes. "I trust you have learned through this that there is no one—*no one*—whom you must not be prepared to kill to preserve the integrity of a job," he said. "Even if it be your own flesh and blood."

"I have no flesh and blood left," she said, empty of anything but weariness. "Save, perhaps, my sister. But she's most likely dead at the end of a slaver's whip, so you needn't worry about that."

"You must not be so careless in the future. Do you understand?"

"I understand."

"Very well." He stood up. "Clean your blade and rest. I have a more complex job for you to begin tomorrow. It's time you started bringing together everything you've learned."

He moved to leave but stopped at the door and turned his head to look back at her. "You have done well."

She flicked her eyes to him, inclined her head, and he left her alone.

Her mouth was cottony, her head groggy, and her face tight with unshed tears—but she made no move toward her room. Instead, she stared at the dagger.

All she felt was dead inside at the sight.

She had killed more than one person last night. She had left the last of her former self lying there at Boden's side.

Part Two:

Sweetblade

Chapter Eighteen

Three years later

Light from the parlor filtered out through the shutters into the garden beyond, just missing where Ivana hid in the shadows. The room erupted in laughter as some drunk minor noble aimed to make himself look better than his peers.

She rolled her eyes, sighed, and sank back against the wall. Perhaps the worst part about lying in wait for the right opportunity to end someone's life was having to listen to all their drivel beforehand. The preening, the fawning, the compliments and lies...

Noble or commoner, rich or poor—it didn't matter. It was as though the lives that swirled about her day after day were one long parade of masquerade guests.

She straightened up. Her mind was wandering again. The last time that had happened, she had lost the opportunity and target, and nearly the entire job.

Finally—*finally*—chairs scraped against wood and some of the voices drifted away as people filtered out of the room. This party had lasted well into the wee hours of the morning.

A quick peek through the crack in the shutters confirmed that her target was still in the room and moving toward the garden door.

She slid to the side, farther into the bushes.

Her information indicated that after parties like these—and after his guests were gone—he would often exit through the garden door to tryst with his lover, who would wait breathlessly for him to emerge.

The body of his lover already lay behind the bushes, her eyes staring sightlessly toward the sky. He would be surprised tonight.

The door to the patio opened, and he was whistling, no doubt drunk and feeling pleased with himself for a successful dinner party.

"Telina?" he whispered.

When there was no response, he frowned and stepped forward, past where Ivana hid.

Ivana stepped in behind him, and before he had the chance to turn at her presence, she had put one hand over his mouth. A few quick stabs in the back, and he had joined his lover behind the bushes.

No one would notice he was missing until late morning when his servants would finally attempt to rouse him from drunken slumber. At that point they would go to search for him in the extensive garden—knowing his habits—and find both he and his lover sloppily stashed behind the bushes right next to the patio door.

In terms of ease of planning, this was a relatively simple job. She didn't have to make it look like an accident. She didn't even have to make it look like a robbery gone wrong or some such.

The Conclave had wanted to send a message to someone, and they would get it.

Ivana wiped her blade on the cuff of the man's trousers, stepped around the pool of blood, and slunk along the hedges, through the outer gate of the garden, and into the alley behind his house.

What had this man and his lover done to offend the Conclave? Spies for Xambria perhaps? Suspected rabble-rousers? Political opponents? *Or,* she thought wryly, *his wife*—whose beloved brother was a priest—*found out.*

It didn't bother her anymore. But she still hadn't reached the point when she never wondered.

She rubbed at her arm as she hurried toward the closest safe house to change out of her blood-spattered clothing before sunrise. The scars still itched on occasion. There had been no fresh cuts in over two years. At some point along the way, it had ceased feeling as though it were necessary.

She took that as a good sign.

A small crowd gathered on the street ahead of her, half a dozen blocks away from Elidor's. It was too early for most people to be out and about, so the commotion was surprising.

Naturally, she slowed to see what was happening.

Two horses with tack bearing the Watch's insignia were tethered outside a line of rowhouses, and a Watchman stood outside one door, keeping a stern eye on the curious crowd.

"What's happening?" she asked the first person she came to, a plump woman loitering near the back.

"They say there's been a suicide," the woman said, nodding as she spoke. She leaned toward Ivana and lowered her voice.

"But I say there're too many Watchmen about for that. Who really knows?"

"Oh my," Ivana said, putting one hand to her chest to feign shock.

"I live across the street," the woman continued. Apparently, Ivana's reaction had encouraged her to speak further. "Over the bakery. My sister runs it."

"Who was it?" Ivana asked, mostly out of her own curiosity.

The woman shook her head. "That whole row—all four of them—is owned by a woman who rents rooms to boarders. Could have been anyone; they're in and out every couple months." She clucked her tongue. "It'll be bad for business, mark my words."

Ivana nodded, murmured a polite assent, and then moved away.

Elidor was sitting in the front room reading, no doubt waiting for her return. He didn't look up when she entered and hung up her cloak. "Well?"

"It's done," she said.

He closed his book and set it aside. "Full report then."

She debriefed him each time she handled a job herself. The further she had gone in her training, the more he let her take care of all the parts of a job, from meeting with their handler to any research needed to the hit itself to collecting payment. She didn't know when exactly he would consider her apprenticeship complete—at which point the government or Conclave would move her somewhere else, whether somewhere else in Cadmyr or somewhere else in the Empire. But the more responsibility she took for a particular job, the more details he wanted to know.

And he was a critical master. He dissected her every decision and move for its merits and errors, despite the relative success of the jobs—and none of them had truly been failures, in the sense that she had been *caught*, or that the job had been compromised.

But nothing less than perfection was good enough for him.

So she sat down and spent the next half hour relating everything she could remember to him.

"You cut the timing far too close," Elidor said when she had finished.

"I didn't expect the party to go *quite* so long."

"This is something you struggle with. Since you had already eliminated his lover, what was your plan should it have chanced going till daybreak?"

His meaning was clear. She would have had no choice but to find a way to finish the job before sunrise, lest it be compromised.

"The party would not have gone that long," she answered.

He pressed his lips together. "And how do you know this?"

"Because his lover was *waiting* for him. He wouldn't have left his planned tryst till morning."

Elidor narrowed his eyes at her, silent for a moment. He didn't like to be contradicted, but over the years, he had begun to trust that she understood more about human nature than he did, to her benefit and his loss. "It still would have been wise to have a plan."

"For someone who is constantly badgering me that I need to think more quickly in a pinch, you are very set upon having backup plans." After backup plan. After backup plan.

"The two are not mutually exclusive."

"I had a backup plan. Just not for if the party went too long. Because it wouldn't have."

"No excuse."

She would lose this argument. He didn't understand. Instead, she inclined her head. "Yes, Dal."

He stood. "Very well."

That was it? He usually found at least two or three elements of her execution or planning to nitpick at. Granted, it wasn't as many as it used to be, but only one?

"Dal?" she asked.

"You're done, for now. I'll let you know the next time we have a job you can take."

He walked to the door of the room, stopped and then went back again to retrieve his book.

"Dal," she said. "Instructions for until then?" He usually assigned her some other task in between jobs, whether that be more training in a specific area, research to help him with one of his jobs, or mundane tasks like restocking the pantry and cleaning.

"Study something." He left the room.

She tilted her head. Study something? While she was happy to comply, that was vague for Elidor.

Something was bothering him.

Well. There was no point in trying to wrest it out of him. If he wanted to tell her, he would, and if he didn't, he wouldn't. If there was a way to manipulate or coerce him, she hadn't discovered it yet.

She headed to the kitchen to mollify her grumbling stomach.

Chapter Nineteen

wo weeks later, Ivana ran across another unusual gathering of people, this time on her way back to Elidor's
from a run for that night's dinner: a crowd huddled
around the public notice board for their neighborhood.

Ivana slowed her steps, curious as to what had, once again,
attracted so much attention.

The crowd was mixed: women jostled for position, craning
their necks to try to see around the men in their way, while
children slipped through legs to make their way to the front. By
the troubled expressions on the faces of those who turned
away, Ivana assumed it wasn't a notice announcing the dates of
the next traveling circus.

She clutched her groceries closer and squirmed her way
through the crowd. One advantage to being trained in stealth
was that she could slither to the front of any line easily.

The notice plastered to the board had large, bold writing

across the top, and then a smaller explanation underneath:

WATCH ALERT

The public is advised that the death of a local tradesman's daughter in the third district has been ruled a murder, perpetrator unknown. The Watch and family are requesting that persons having information regarding suspicious behavior or other evidence immediately report to your district Watch.

Ivana stepped back, and the writhing crowd gave way so that someone else could take her place.

Interesting.

In a city of over two hundred thousand people, there were bound to be murders, few of which had anything to do with Elidor, Ivana, or the other few assassins who worked for the Setanan government in various places around the Empire. In fact, the majority were overlooked altogether. No one cared about the random beggar or whore who ended up in a ditch somewhere after all.

Most people went about their business willfully ignorant of such things, as long as it didn't affect them and their families—or their livelihood.

In this district, the second district, which was neither part of the slums nor overly wealthy, violent crime was uncommon. Even so, the Watch didn't post a notice every time they suspected a murder.

Certainly, some of the attention had to be because of the identity of the victim. A merchant family would have enough power and means to demand justice. But what was done was done; why draw such attention to it, and so soon after the incident? Could the request for information not wait until next week's paper?

Ivana shrugged it off. If it were important enough, she was

sure she would hear about it sooner or later.

Almost two weeks later, Ivana stepped into a cobbler's shop in the sixth district and inhaled deeply through her nose.

Leather.

There was something warm and earthy about a cobbler's shop. From the musty smell of leather to being surrounded by shades of brown, it simply felt comfortable.

The cobbler was in the back of the workshop, humming to himself while working on a pair of shoes. "Be there in a moment," he said without looking up.

She waited with her hands clasped behind her back until he finally put the shoes aside, stretched, and came to the counter.

"May I help you?" he asked.

She set her pick-up slip down on the counter and glanced around the shop as though bored.

The cobbler glanced at the slip. "Ah," he said, his eyes flitting over her once. "Yes. Needed resoled?"

She nodded, and he bent down under the counter, lifted out a pair of boots, and set them on the counter in front of her for her inspection.

She picked one up and looked it over, sliding her hand around the sole on the outside and then into the boot.

She felt the tight roll of paper in the toe and pulled out her hand. She did the same to the other boot, and then opened her coin purse. "Looks to be in order," she said.

She paid him for the repair—and then some—and with a nod, tucked the boots into her satchel and headed back to Elidor's.

Not directly, of course. She stopped at a bar in the fifth district for a drink. Meandered over to the ninth district to pay her respects at the temple of Yathyn. Wandered down to a milliner in the first district to feign interest in a hat that she didn't end up purchasing, but she took a half hour to converse with the milliner about the merits of adorning hats with ribbons versus flowers.

It was sunset by the time she reached the public square nearest Elidor's again.

And a crowd surrounded the notice board. Again.

She stood on tiptoes to read the newly posted notice over the heads of those near the front.

WATCH ALERT

The public should be aware that two more murders occurred in the past twelve days. Though they occurred in the fourth district, they are believed to be linked to the previous. The Watch is doing everything it can to find the perpetrator; however, the watch urges anyone with information to step forward. Meanwhile, women in particular should be careful at night.

Three murders now?

Ivana stepped aside, feigning interest in the board, but really wanting to hear the circulating whispers.

Unlike the previous time, when the crowd surrounding the notice had been characterized by the silence of shock, a low murmur ran through the crowd—rumors being exchanged, worries being aired.

"I heard they all happened exactly at midnight."

"I heard they were all found in their own homes; don't know what good it does to warn us."

"But I heard they were found outside."

"Someone told me the last one was a man."

"No, they were definitely all women."

"Fereharian, I hear."

"Why do you suppose the Watch thinks they're related? Who are they?"

"Sick, that's what I tell you, sick. To think, our own daughters!"

Rumors were only that—rumors. They had to be taken with a grain of salt. Everyone claimed to have inside information, and yet half the information contradicted itself.

Still, it was never wise to ignore chatter completely. A stalk of truth usually grew among the weeds.

Today, Ivana's thoughts swirled around one of the statements in particular: the rumor about the women—and it seemed a safe assumption that the victims were women, given the Watch's warning—being Fereharian.

Cadmyr had a larger population of Fereharians than say, Fuilyn or Venetia, and the cities were more diverse, but it had to be more than coincidence that the victims had all been Fereharian. As she gazed out over the crowd, perhaps one out of every ten faces was the distinct bronze of her own skin. Another tenth were Fuilynian, another two-tenths, perhaps, from Donia or Venetia, and the remaining were from the three original regions: Weylyn, Arlana, and Cadmyr—or some mix thereof. If the rumor was true, that made it more likely that Fereharian women were being targeted rather than being victims of random choice.

Why Fereharian?

Any other Fereharian woman who stood in that crowd today would have fixated on that rumor simply because it would have struck too close to home. She, on the other hand, was annoyed. The last thing she needed was another reason for people to pay attention to her. Already, she could see how more heads turned toward the Fereharians in the crowd than normally would, subconscious reactions to the thoughts no doubt churning in people's minds.

Glad I'm not Fereharian.

Poor thing must be scared witless.

My neighbor is Fereharian; what if that draws the murderer closer to me?

She turned away and trudged back toward Elidor's. Her own thoughts took a different direction.

A serial murderer seemed to be lurking about the city; Elidor had to know something about it. He had access to sources that the Watch didn't typically rely on.

She determined to ask him at the next opportunity.

As it happened, the next opportunity was that same night at suppertime.

Elidor was eating with her tonight. He didn't always; in fact, he was often away. He tended to divvy out the jobs closer to home to her, probably so that he could better keep an eye on her progress.

"The Watch posted a notice in the square today," she remarked as they were finishing.

And when they did eat together, they rarely talked. The only acknowledgement Elidor gave was a twitch of an eyebrow. He didn't even look up.

"It was about two murders that occurred recently," she continued, as though he had inquired further. "Do you know anything about the situation?"

"I do not."

"There was another murder a couple weeks ago. The Watch thinks all three are related."

Still nothing more.

"There wasn't a contract you didn't tell me about?" she

pressed.

He did look up then, if only to cast her a disparaging look, and she took his point without need for further comment. If they had been hits ordered by the government—or Conclave—they would have done their best to be sure authorities stayed out of it—unless getting the Watch involved were part of the point, of course.

"There are those in our profession who don't work for the government," she pointed out.

"Indeed, and if that were the case, how would I know about it?"

She paused. An odd comment to make. He would know about it because the sources he used for his own jobs didn't only work with *him*. He would know about it because it was part of his job to be informed. True, he couldn't know everything, but these were murders near their own district, not the other side of the city. Surely, he would have heard something, even if only that it had happened, and the circumstances.

"Are you sure you don't know *anything* about it?" she asked. "The rumor is that the victims have all been Fereharian. I don't like how that might draw more attention to me."

He wiped his mouth and set down his napkin. "Sometimes murders happen. Perhaps a group of women were keeping the wrong company at the wrong time in the wrong place and discovered something they shouldn't have." He stood up. "I'll be in my study."

Women? She didn't recall specifying that the victims had been women. "Don't forget your boots," she said, jerking her head toward the boots she had removed from her satchel and set by the door for him.

He bent down, removed the scrap of paper from the left boot, and unfurled it, leaving the boots where they were.

His eyes skipped down the paper and then he stood, motionless, and stared at the paper.

"New job?" she prompted.

Still, he said nothing. A slight frown touched the corners of his lips—unusually expressive for him.

"Dal?"

He gave her a cursory glance. "I'll be in my study," he repeated. He started toward the door and then stopped, as if hitting a wall. He turned. "Actually, see me in my study." His eyes flicked to a clock on the sideboard. "In about an hour."

With no further explanation, he left.

Preoccupied again? She frowned. This was strange.

And identifying the victims as women?

Ivana sat back, sipped at her wine, and reviewed their brief conversation.

It could have been a thoughtless assumption, but Elidor wasn't normally given to thoughtless assumptions. More likely, he *had* already heard about the murders.

If so, why conceal that from her? Why was he hedging? Was it some sort of test? Was he the one behind them after all, and he simply hadn't told her about the job? Was that what that comment about the victims "learning something they shouldn't have" had been about? Or had they learned something about *him*, and it wasn't a job at all?

She swirled the last of the wine around in her glass. Whatever the case...

He was hiding something from her.

Chapter Twenty

Ivana drifted back to the tiny room she still occupied even after all these years. Elidor had no other spare bedroom, but there were ways in which hers could have been expanded to give her more space.

He had probably never thought about it.

She lit the lantern in her room and turned to the washbasin, her thoughts still on what discreet steps she could take to discover what Elidor was hiding. He wasn't one to play games with, after all.

She reached down to pick up her brush without looking, only to miss by a millimeter and instead knock it off the basin top. It clattered to the floor and slid under her cot.

She crouched and felt under the cot. She didn't immediately find it, so she sighed and knelt on hands and knees to look under the cot.

The brush was there—out of easy reach—and so was a long,

narrow box.

She stared at the box. She knew what it was, since she herself had put it there more than three years ago. She had forgotten it was there.

She reached for the brush, aiming to ignore the box, but instead found herself drawing out the box as well.

She didn't stand. Instead, she moved to a sitting position, leaned back against the cot, and opened the lid of the box.

There, lying on a bed of cotton fluff, was a rose pendant attached to a tarnished silver chain.

Her sister's.

It had lain on the lower shelf of the basin until that day she had decided she didn't need its constant reminder of who she had been. She couldn't, at the time, bring herself to get rid of it, but she had hoped it could be forgotten.

And she had, indeed, forgotten about it.

She tried not to think about her past. Most days, she succeeded.

It was hard to continue to mourn when she had so thoroughly desensitized herself to those sorts of feelings otherwise. She had to in order to do this job. She couldn't stop to lament every death, couldn't feel guilty, couldn't hesitate.

Her plan had worked. She wasn't sure if she liked what she had become, but at this point, her feelings on the matter, when she had them, were in so many ways irrelevant.

She couldn't leave this profession—nor indeed Elidor's service, before he deemed her training complete—even if she wanted to.

And she had achieved, or at the least, was achieving, what she wanted.

Death.

Death of the pain that used to consume her. Death of sorrow, death of despair.

Oh, she was no Elidor. She told herself those things had died, but they were merely locked away behind a wall she herself had built. The fact that she had drawn this box out—when she ought to have left it alone—was witness to the fact that she wasn't there yet.

But whoever she once had been: daughter of Galvyn and Avira, sister of Izel, Airell's plaything, almost-mother, street urchin...

She pulled up her sleeve and ran her fingers over the scars on her arms. Tormented soul.

No, the person who was all those things was long gone.

As if to prove it to herself, she lifted the necklace out of the box and fastened it around her neck. Why not? It meant nothing to her now, but it was a pretty bauble. She'd have to get the chain cleaned, of course, and if she lost it—it wasn't worth much anyway.

The shadows cast by the light of the lantern danced against the wall, and she looked up at the lantern. The flame was bobbing about as though a breeze had whispered through the room. She didn't think anything of it. It happened on occasion, as some unseen air current disturbed the flame momentarily.

Until she stopped to think about it.

She stood, set the box down on the basin, glanced at the lantern again, and then around her room.

Her room was tucked far enough into the house that the opening of an outside door shouldn't have reached her small lantern, and there was no window or other opening.

Well. No other *obvious* opening.

She carefully removed the shade of the lantern, exposing the flame directly to the air. Once it had settled from her jolting of the lantern, it shone steadily, with only a small sputter here or there. She picked it up and spun in a slow circle. The flame danced with her movement, of course, but once she stopped moving, so did it.

Something had to have caused that flame to move like it did. She stepped up onto her bed and held her lantern up.

The flame shuddered. She held still, hardly daring to breathe. It was bending ever-so-slightly toward the wall adjoining the broom closet next to her room.

Da Veryna used to keep cleaning supplies and such in there, as she recalled. She had always thought that, if he had been so inclined, Elidor could have knocked the wall out and given her a bit more space.

She put the lantern down on the bedside table and reached up to run her hands over the wall.

The wood was so knotted and creviced, it was hard to tell if there was anything unusual about it.

She jumped off the cot and poked her head into the hall, listening.

No sign of Elidor.

She set the glass back on the lantern, picked it up, and padded the few feet down the hall toward the closet.

She opened the door and stepped inside. It was tiny and now empty but for two buckets, a mop, a broom, and a few sponges. A small window was in the outer wall; one pane of glass had broken and someone had attempted to repair it by boarding over that section, but there was still a draft.

That answered that.

Like her room, the closet walls were plastered all around except for the one adjacent to her room.

She turned toward that wall now. Brackets to hang shelves still stuck out of the wall, but the shelves had either never been hung or had long since been removed. She stretched toward the top part of the wall, but without her cot to step on, she couldn't reach as high.

So she set her lantern aside, turned the bucket upside down, and stepped up onto it. She felt along the wall with her fingers, as she had in her room, and found a spot where one of the boards jutted out at the corner a bit. She pried at it, and it moved enough that she could squish the tips of her fingers into the gap, but it refused to budge any farther.

The board was above her head, even though she stood on the bucket, which made it awkward to pry at. She placed one of the unused shelves on top of the first bucket, turned the other bucket upside down on it, and tried again.

It was a precarious balance, but the loose board now came to eye level.

She dug her fingers into the gap again and pried at it, expecting it to remain obstinate.

Instead, it came out abruptly in her hand, and she lost her balance. She reached out to steady herself against the wall, knocking the mop over in the process. Her other hand shot out to stop it from hitting the door, but in the process she fumbled the narrow board itself, and it clattered to the floor.

She closed her eyes and held her breath, listening, hoping Elidor hadn't heard the racket.

After a moment of hearing nothing, she looked back at the much wider gap the board had revealed. She peered through the gap...

And into her room.

The slot was narrow. She would have never noticed the slit from where she sat on her bed.

She had no doubt as to its purpose. Elidor had been spying on her. Probably the entire time she had been staying here.

Had *that* been why he had taken her in? He had wanted his

own personal peep show?

That was unlike Elidor. She had never noticed any sort of lewd streak in him.

But what did she know about him, even after almost five years?

"I see you've discovered my little secret."

Startled, Ivana turned too quickly, and the entire contraption came down with a horrendous crash. But it hardly mattered because Elidor stood in front of the doorway to the closet.

She crouched down where she had landed, one hand on the ground to break her fall, and stared at the floor for a moment, collecting her thoughts.

"How did you find it?" he asked.

She rose, and he didn't move. His face was unreadable. "My lantern," she said. "I noticed a draft."

He nodded. "I'm surprised it took you this long to notice."

She narrowed her eyes at him. "You were here, not that long ago, weren't you?" Hence the sudden draft. Probably opening the door.

"Yes." He moved into the doorframe, blocking her exit.

A wayward thought flitted through her brain. What if he *had* killed those women, and what if it *hadn't* been collateral damage or cleanup? What if he had *snapped* for some reason and gone on a self-selected killing spree? Could that happen to assassins?

Her heart pounded as it hadn't since those first terrifying jobs, many years ago. Why in the abyss hadn't she waited until he was away to investigate?

Control, Ivana. She was being foolish. In all the time he had known her, he had never laid a hand on her in that way. In fact, he had hardly laid a hand on her in *any* way, inappropriate or otherwise. He wasn't affectionate, physically or otherwise, and though he could have a cold temper, any lashings had always been verbal.

If he had wanted to hurt her, why would he begin *now*?

She ventured to push him, if only to see his reaction—if indeed she could manage to get one out of him at all. "Elidor, if you want to see me unclothed—or frankly, anything else—do you think I would refuse your demand? You might as well ask me to wash clothes or weed the garden."

There was a long silence, long enough that he had to either be considering it, or considering how he would punish her for her cheek.

He stepped in closer to her, and light from the hallway filtered back in. Her earlier thoughts betrayed her body by causing her hand to twitch at her thigh, ready to draw her dagger.

His eyes flicked to the movement and back again, and she cursed inwardly, hoping he would take it as an unconscious reaction on her part and nothing more.

She forced herself to hold his eyes and wait for his response.

He lifted a hand and, for a moment, she thought he would touch her face. Instead, he lifted the rose pendant at her throat. "What's this?"

She raised an eyebrow. "A necklace?"

"It's not new."

"No. It was my sister's."

He let go of the pendant and lowered his hand.

"Your proposal is..." He paused, and the word hung unspoken in the silence. *Tempting.* But instead he gave a low, throaty chuckle. "Unwise."

He turned and stepped back through the door. "It's been an hour." With that, he disappeared around the corner.

She sank back against the closet wall, her mind racing. This was a revelation about his character that she had not known. His self-discipline may have prevented him from propositioning her, but it hadn't stopped him from a more discreet way of using her as an object of pleasure all these years.

The intrusion into her privacy was more annoyance than anything else—though she was glad he hadn't *actually* taken her up on her offer. Sleeping with a strange man was one thing. Sleeping with Elidor would be...awkward.

Nonetheless, she returned to her room before answering Elidor's summons, found an old shirt, and tacked it up over the hole.

Elidor responded to Ivana's knock on the door with a grunt, and she found him standing in front of that painting on his wall, his hands clasped behind his back, studying it.

"You wanted to see me?" she asked.

He turned around and went to his desk. He opened a drawer and drew out a slip of paper, just big enough to fit into the palm of his hand. He unfolded it, turned it around, and pushed it toward her.

"We have an unusual job."

She walked to the desk and read the slip of paper. It took a moment while she worked out the code, but finally she understood the gist. They wanted Elidor to find and *catch* the murderer? The same murderer they had been discussing over dinner?

There went the theory about it being collateral damage or some such. If Elidor had had to clean up some extras after a job or track down someone who knew too much, he would have informed Llyr. Had he truly not known about the murders then? That was still *so* difficult to believe.

There was always the other theory, of course. But that was almost as far-fetched. He was so composed and controlled. Assassin or not, he didn't seem the type to randomly snap.

She studied his face, but he merely gazed back at her, as if to gauge *her* reaction.

"That's peculiar." They specialized in assassinations, not bounties. "Wouldn't this fall under the purview of the Watch? Or better, a bounty hunter?"

"If I ventured a guess, I would say they're desperate."

"The Conclave? Why in the abyss would the Conclave care about a rogue serial murderer?" It wasn't as if the killer were going after priests.

"They wouldn't. This is the meddling of local bureaucrats concerned with public opinion."

"So..."

"So they've pled with higher powers to do something, and the government turned to their best assassin, who happens to be leased to the Conclave."

She became stuck on the middle part of his sentence. "Turned to their best assassin to not assassinate someone?"

"I'm assuming they believe I have special insight into the mind of a murderer."

Far-fetched as it was, she tested her second theory by choosing her next words carefully, infusing a touch of personal offense, only partially feigned. "*I* am a professional, not some crazed killer beset with untamed bloodlust."

It didn't faze him in the least. "Be that as it may..." He nodded toward the paper. "Our handler wants a meeting tomorrow night to go over the details."

Actual face-to-face meetings to discuss the details of a job were reserved for only the most complicated of cases—those requiring additional guidelines or setup. If it were a fast hit, it was a name on a slip of paper to start and the payment placed in a discreet location when it was done.

"And I want you to go in my stead," he continued.

She started. *"Me?* What would I know about catching a murderer?"

"No less than me, I'm certain." He rubbed a hand over his face. "It drains me to have to keep up a constant public façade, and I am certain this job will require more interaction with others. You have always excelled in that area more than me."

Was he *admitting* that she was better at something than him?

But he was right. He could act less anti-social, if need be. Over the course of her apprenticeship with him, she had seen that more and more. But she had also seen how, when having to do those jobs that called upon his ability to interact normally with people, he returned home more irritable and more withdrawn.

He hated those jobs; he gave almost all of them to her unless they required extensive travel.

"Be that as it may," she said. "I am more inexperienced than you as a whole."

He waved a hand, as if unconcerned, for once, by her lack of experience. "I'm certain you can handle whoever is behind this."

She met his eyes. He met them back. Cool. Calm. Collected.

Nothing other than what she expected from him.

She wrestled with her earlier thoughts. Would he really ask her to take a job to catch *him*? That made no sense. While much about the man was still a mystery to her, she knew self-preservation was top on his list of values, in addition to self-control.

Maybe he assumed she would fail, and sending her to fail was less complicated than having to pretend to catch himself.

The silence stretched out. Still, he didn't break the gaze.

Was he waiting for a response? An affirmation? Or was he taunting her?

She still couldn't shake the feeling he knew more than he was telling her, even if it wasn't her far-flung imaginings.

Well. Plying him about it would get her nowhere. If she wanted to find out what he was hiding, she'd have to do it in less obvious ways.

She inclined her head. "I will, of course, do as you command."

He gave her one of his cold, mirthless smiles. "I know."

Ivana knelt on a prayer mat to the side of one of the many shrines dedicated to Rhianah scattered around the city. Unlike the stone sanctuaries of Yathyn, the head god and Rhianah's husband, Rhianah's sanctuary was simple and unadorned.

It didn't need to be anything more. The walls were made of dark and luscious wood from the rysta trees native to Cadmyr, a statement of warm, common simplicity; the moonlight that shone through either one of the large, open windows to the east or west was the only light. A low-lying, wooden altar graced the front, on which a single wide-mouthed bowl had been set. The bowl was full to the brim with clear water: a place for worshippers to wash their hands in ritual cleansing before coming to the table of the matronly goddess of home and harvest in supplication.

Ivana, of course, had done no such thing. And all she did now was to bow her head in feigned prayer, waiting for their handler, Llyr, to show up.

She was early, as usual, and he was punctual, as usual.

Thankfully, she had only had to meet with Llyr a handful of times in the past few years by herself. She and Elidor had come together a few times. Most of the time, Elidor met with him and passed the job off to her if he wanted to.

Someone slipped onto a mat next to hers. She turned her head to the side enough to see the body of a man, hunched over hands clasped in prayer.

"Where is your master?" Llyr said to the floor.

"He sent me in his stead."

He shifted. "We were hoping for his assistance in particular."

"He felt I was more suited to the job," she said. Llyr could press it, of course, if he wanted. Insist Elidor take this job personally. Ivana almost hoped he would, just so she could bring that message back to Elidor and see his reaction.

After another long silence during which he was no doubt weighing Elidor's request, Llyr finally spoke. "Walk with me then."

The inside of the shrine was simple, but the outside was not. A well-tended garden sprinkled with fountains surrounded the shrine on three sides. Worshippers were encouraged to make their supplications and then meander along the path through the garden before leaving. It just so happened that the pervasive sound of running water made a pleasant mask for murmured conversation.

The two of them rose and left the sanctuary through the side door into the gardens. The garden was usually empty at night; even so, they walked close together, as though lovers taking a turn. Llyr even went as far as to put an arm around Ivana's waist to enhance the fiction—an unnecessary move, in Ivana's opinion. Another way in which Llyr would take any opportunity given to him.

"We need your assistance in finding and capturing a criminal," Llyr said once they had settled into a comfortable pace.

"So the note said."

He turned close toward her, and between their bodies he produced a tied and rolled sheath of paper. She took it and slipped it into her cloak pocket.

"This is a copy of the Watch file on the case. Study it, memorize it, and be prepared to assist the Watch."

"Assist?" She couldn't help it. Incredulity bled into her tone. They were assassins. They didn't *assist* anyone, except, perhaps, in their unique case, each other.

"Yes. You will work with the team of official law enforcement that has been assigned to this case. They will be told that you are an investigator who specializes in criminal apprehension."

"Official law enforcement? You say that as if I am some *other* sort of less official law enforcement."

"From a certain perspective."

Ivana snorted.

"When you're ready to catch the killer, we will assist in the actual arrest."

"You're going to send priests to arrest the killer?"

Llyr's jaw jumped. "Obviously not. The Conclave is involved in this merely as an intermediary between yourselves and those in the government who wish to see this resolved."

Elidor had been right on all counts then. This wasn't the Conclave's request, and he was not at all suited to this work. The idea of having to work with someone the entire time would have galled him.

"Any questions?" Llyr pressed, no doubt at her silence.

"Synonyms for *apprehension* seem to be key here," Ivana replied. "I'm not a bounty hunter."

"We don't have bounty hunters on retainer."

"So you're saying I'm cheaper."

"I don't know. Are you?"

Ivana pulled away from him. He had a suggestive grin on his face. "Would you say that to my master? If not, I would advise you to keep it to yourself."

He snorted, as though he didn't believe her implicit threat. "It's more that they would prefer to use a network we already have in place." He paused. "If you're concerned about payment, rest assured they are prepared to make this one especially generous."

"Very well," she said. As an apprentice, she received little of that money, so she didn't care. "I'll study the file, but the next time you have a body, let me know."

"The point is to catch the killer *before*—"

Ivana turned and gave him a piercing glare.

For once, he gave in. "We'll let you know."

Chapter Twenty-One

The next morning, Ivana made herself breakfast and settled down at the dining room table to eat while she read the file Llyr had given her.

There was nothing unusual about that. She often sat at the dining room table to work out the details of a job—after all, she didn't have a private study like Elidor.

All the better that there was nothing unusual about it, in this case. She continued to have the feeling that Elidor knew more about this job than he let on, so she was curious to see if he would take an interest in her work, and if so, what he would say or do about it.

And so she stayed there in her normal spot—her back to the door—long after she had finished her slice of cold ham and slab of buttered bread. Having pushed her plate to one side, she spread the pages of the file out in front of her chronologically.

The most surprising bit was that, in fact, there had been six murders, not three. The first had been the "suicide" Ivana had run across over a month ago, which the authorities now considered the first of the murders. Then there had been two more murders passed over in silence. Then there was the murder that she had seen the first notice about—the tradesman's daughter—and then the final two that the last notice had been posted about. Six murders over the course of about six weeks.

She had read the reports at least five times already. Frankly, there wasn't much there.

They really were desperate.

The Watch had considered multiple options. The first they had discarded: a series of hits by what passed for the underground crime scene in Carradon. If that had been the case, the murders would have taken place mostly in districts where those elements of society were most prominent. As it was—she checked the map they had provided with the locations of the bodies marked to confirm—they were spread out across multiple city districts.

The second theory was that it was someone out for revenge. But the apparent lack of connection between the victims made that a questionable theory, especially as the murders multiplied.

They had finally decided it had to be a single killer targeting partially random victims—perhaps someone with a grudge against Fereharians—and had thrown up their hands in despair at ever being able to solve such a crime or find such a criminal.

That, apparently, wasn't good enough for local authorities, who were starting to feel some public pressure.

She slid aside one of the sheets to uncover a related report.

It was at that point that a Watchman from outside Cadmyr had been brought in to organize the haphazard investigation—

one Ruios Xathal from Fuilyn. Ruios was an honorary title, not a promotion, given to a soldier or member of the Watch when they had performed some exceptional service to Setana, above and beyond duty. The report did not state, however, what Xathal's "exceptional service" had been.

Whatever it was, someone must have thought it qualified him to head up this investigation.

She set that report aside and turned back to the matter at hand.

Despite the seemingly random nature of the murders, there *were* commonalities. For one, the timing was consistent. Apparently, the murders had all taken place exactly one week apart from each other.

In addition, the victims were all women, they were all Fereharian, and none of them, save the fourth, had family or friends in Carradon. Xathal had noted in his initial report that the last wasn't unusual for this sort of criminal—nor was targeting women, nor even women of a particular look.

According to him, it was the *method* of murder that was the most infuriating and problematic part of the case because there were too many differences.

The first victim had initially been ruled a suicide. She had been found with wrists slit, blood on her hands and on the knife, and on the floor near her bed. But she had been a boarder. No one knew her. It had been quickly forgotten.

The second victim was similar. She, too, had been a nobody—a beggar off the streets. Her wrists had been slit, but instead of having died on the ground in a pool of blood, it appeared that her body had been moved from elsewhere in the area to the pile of rags that sufficed as her bed and then arranged as if sleeping. Too little blood stained the rags for her to have been killed there.

That was, of course, the clue to the Watch that this had been murder. But, this one, also, had been filed away. The beggar had received hardly more than a footnote.

The third victim, best they knew, had been an independent prostitute. She had had more than slit wrists. Her body showed some signs of assault before death, according to the medical examiner—though, interestingly, given her occupation, not sexual. Bruising on the arms, as if grabbed and shaken. A broken jaw, as if hit. The watchman who had written that report had surmised that she had resisted and the injuries were the sign of the struggle. But once again, she had died of blood loss through her wrists, and had been arranged on her bed in her tiny apartment after being murdered in the only other room. Once again, she had no connections. Once again, the case was barely glanced at. Sometimes things went bad for whores, after all—especially those with no connections to a larger organization.

The fourth victim had the only common factor in all the murders beyond gender and home region: slit wrists. She was also arranged on her bed, which was, the report said, *becoming* a common factor. It didn't appear, however, that she had fought back as the third. In fact, in this case, it almost looked like the woman had been restrained and tortured prior to being killed. She had slashes all over her body, as if her murderer had been determined to bleed her to death from a thousand cuts before finally giving up and making short work of it.

This victim had something else *not* in common with the other three: she was not an unknown. The notice had been correct; she had been the daughter of a respected tradesman in the district.

It was at that point that they revisited the first cases in earnest, including the supposed suicide, and linked them to the fourth.

And then the spree had continued. The fifth and sixth victims had been from the poorer parts of their respective districts. They, too, had the commonality of slit wrists and the arrangement of the bodies. They, too, would have been overlooked had the fourth victim not been murdered first. Now, the Watch couldn't deny that they had a bigger problem on their hands.

That had been the end of the reports. They had no other evidence, no eyewitness accounts, and not a single person had stepped forward to offer information.

It was so clean. So tidy. No loose ends.

Ivana's eyes flicked up to Elidor's empty chair on the other side of the table.

Impossible. That made absolutely no sense. These were crimes of, as she had once put it, untamed bloodlust. It did not fit Elidor's personality at all. Nothing about him was untamed, and he had no lusts that she knew of...

Or didn't he?

She splayed her hand on the final sheet of paper. She had *thought* he had no lusts until she discovered he had been spying on her for who-knew-how-long.

And all of the victims were not only women, but Fereharian. Like her.

Still, not a single victim had displayed evidence of sexual assault. So if *that* were it...

She shook her head and looked down at the report under her hand.

It was a single brief included by the chief Watchman for their district in which he noted his opinion that people were getting both nervous and irate; they demanded justice for the tradesman's daughter. They demanded answers before more of their own daughters were killed. The report had been submitted to the city administration, probably along with like reports from other districts.

Hence where Xathal came in.

And apparently, Ivana.

She flipped the last sheet of paper over onto the stack, straightened it, and pushed it away.

She hadn't the faintest idea why the "government" thought assassins would be the people to put on this case. How should *she* know what would drive someone to kill like this? She might be a professional killer, but that didn't mean she had the urge to go around offing people for no good reason.

Granted, she might not be the best standard to judge by. She had met one other assassin in her time with Elidor, about a year ago, a freelancer. He had been beyond strange to the point of downright unhinged. What was it he had said, as she and Elidor had been leaving the dive they had met him in? *"Got a sweet one there, Elidor. Bet she tastes nice."* And then he had licked his dagger and winked at her.

Burning skies, *that* one, she'd have believed the murders of in a heartbeat, but he didn't work in Carradon. The look even Elidor had given him before whisking her out of the back room of the inn had been unmistakably one of disapproval. No, Elidor was peculiar, but not deranged.

Right?

She leaned forward, cupping her chin in one hand, and stared at the top report, unseeing. Then again, what if his disapproval had been of the other assassin's lack of restraint, rather than of his intent?

Elidor was nothing if not restrained. But who knew what that restraint hid underneath?

She flipped absently through the stack again. She had counted herself lucky at the time, that if she had been fated to be plucked off the street by an assassin, it had been Elidor, and not someone like the other.

"Is that your copy of the file?"

Her hand jerked and scattered a few of the papers across the table. She turned to see Elidor standing behind her. "*Must* you do that?" she asked, masking her nerves with annoyance.

He said nothing, so she gathered the wayward papers and spread the file out again. "Yes. Would you like to see it?"

By way of answer, he moved one step to the side so he could look over her shoulder.

And look over her shoulder he did. Silently. For several minutes.

She pretended to look over it again with him. She thought she had lost her gift for youthful imagination back when she had first speculated what sort of torture devices he might keep in his study, but apparently it had merely been waiting for the right opportunity to rear its head. Was he grasping his dagger in anticipation of what he might do next at that very moment?

"I find the third and fourth women interesting," he said, startling her once again.

Burning skies, she was jumpy all of a sudden. "And why is that?"

He leaned over her to pull those two reports forward. "Because they have anomalies. The third was assaulted, and the fourth was apparently tortured." He traced the relevant sections of the reports with his finger. "And then the perpetrator goes back to the more cut-and-dry approach."

She turned to look up at him. "Cut and—was that supposed to be some sort of deranged joke?"

He just blinked at her.

"Never mind," she muttered, and she turned back to the reports.

He, on the other hand, didn't move. He was still hovering behind her, even closer since he had leaned over to point at the reports. Close enough that she could feel the brush of his shirt against her own as he breathed.

It would be nothing for him to catch her throat in the crook of an arm. Nothing for him to draw a dagger or produce a garrote.

If he were the murderer, it would be absurdly easy for him to strike again.

What was she thinking? Obviously, Elidor was a murderer—whether he had killed those women or not—and always had been.

Even so, his presence was making her neck prickle, an uncomfortable feeling she didn't often have.

She might pay for it in his anger, but perhaps she could make him go away.

"How old were you when you became an orphan?" she asked.

"I don't see what relevance that has to the task at hand."

"No relevance. I'm just tired of you lurking behind me. It's disconcerting, with a killer on the loose and all." And a good excuse as to why she was so unusually jumpy.

Elidor made a soft noise in his throat. She wasn't sure if it more resembled a grunt of amusement or annoyance. Either way, it accomplished her goal of getting him to move away from her.

Not, however, in getting him to leave. He moved over instead to the chair at a right angle from hers, though he didn't sit down.

"Surely, by now you are confident that you could handle yourself against some common criminal," Elidor said. "To meet such an end, after your training... How humiliating."

"Yes. Humiliating. That's exactly the word I would use." She doubted he would catch the sarcasm. "Anyway, I hardly think whoever is behind this is some 'common criminal.'" She held herself still and kept her face placid, avoiding anything that might suggest she was trying to assess his reaction to the latter comment.

The poke didn't seem to disturb him. "Are you concerned that I would let anything happen to you while under my charge?"

"Elidor. That's almost touching. I didn't know you cared."

"I care about the time and money I've invested in your training. What a waste their loss would be."

Was *that* why he hadn't murdered her? Because it would be wasteful? She could almost believe that would be the way his mind would work. Better to slake his thirst for the blood of Fereharian women on whores and beggars.

The idea of Elidor having to slake his thirst for anything almost made her laugh aloud. It was just so *not* him.

And in the end, everything came back to the same question: after almost five years of living with him, why would he do this now? It was a pressing question that punched the largest hole in her wavering theory, and it irritated her so much that she almost asked him.

Before she could do or say anything so foolhardy, she changed the subject. "In any event, I can examine all the details of these murders, and I still know nothing about the killer himself—other than, apparently, he likes Fereharian women and...beds." She snorted. "And that could be said of a lot of men. I don't know how I'm supposed to catch him on that."

He didn't respond, and she swept the papers in front of her into a pile and stood up. "If you have any revelations about the killer, I wouldn't turn down hearing your thoughts," she said.

"Otherwise, I'm going to go occupy my mind with something else for a while."

She had almost reached the door when he spoke.

"Five."

She turned. "Pardon?"

"I was five when my parents died."

She stared at him. She had never expected him to answer her question.

He tilted his head and looked back.

Not knowing what else to say or do, she inclined her head and left the dining room.

It was only after she had returned to her room, tossed the file on her cot, and plopped down next to it that a chilling thought occurred to her.

What if that had not been an answer to her original question, but a response to her later ruminations? Her need to know more about the killer?

Was he *toying* with her?

Her imagination?

She swallowed and glanced at her bedroom door, which was cracked.

She didn't know, but she would find out.

Chapter Twenty-Two

Ivana didn't have a chance to investigate her theory further because Elidor left for a job the morning after their discussion. She had been hoping to follow him if he left around the time another murder ought to occur; instead, she spent the rest of the week with the house to herself before she finally received the message that the murderer had struck again—or so they thought. She had a slip of paper with an address and the word "probable." It had been exactly one week since the last body had been found.

She was pulling on her boots when another pair of boots, already on their owner's feet, appeared in her vision.

"You're home," she said without looking up. She hadn't heard him come in last night, but then again, that wasn't unusual.

"I arrived late last night," he said.

How convenient. The body was found in the fifth district, on the other side of the city. Had he stopped for a treat on the way home? There was no way of knowing.

She tucked her smaller dagger into the sheath secured to the lower part of her right calf, laced up her final boot, and stood up. "There's another body," she said. "I'm headed to meet the chief investigator at the scene."

He stood aside so she could grab her fall cloak from the peg behind him. The weather had finally turned chilly enough that she needed more than long sleeves.

She turned to leave, but he was still standing there, so she paused. "Was there something you needed?"

"Be on your guard. Don't give the Watch a reason to look into who *you* are."

She raised an eyebrow. "Obviously." She threw her cloak around her shoulders, nodded to him, and left.

If she had any doubt as to the house she needed to go to, it was washed away when she reached the corner of Fourth and Cedar in the fifth district. Two horses with saddles marked with the insignia of the Watch were tethered to a post outside the rowhouse, along with a carriage and its horses. The front door was open, and a small crowd of onlookers was being held back by two Watchmen, presumably the owners of the horses.

She approached the door, only to be stopped by one of the Watchmen.

"Sorry, Da, you can't go in there right now."

"I'm here to see Xathal," she said. "My name is Ivana. Just tell him I'm here."

The Watchman looked dubious, but he gestured to his partner and disappeared into the house.

While she waited for him to return, she glanced around the area. A man leaned against a building on the other side of the street, reading a newspaper. The top of the paper flipped down, and he met her eyes.

Llyr. He nodded, folded the newspaper, and strode away.

Making sure she showed, she supposed.

The Watchman returned. He jerked his head toward the door. "Up the stairs, to the left," he said, and then he returned to his share of the crowd-control duties.

She entered the house and took his directions.

The first door to her left was guarded by another Watchman. Before she could open her mouth to speak, a gruff voice spoke from within the room. "Let her in."

The Watchman made no move to stop her, and so she stepped into the murder scene.

It was almost surreal. She supposed this was what happened after some of their jobs—especially the higher-profile ones. But she was usually long gone before any *real* law enforcement showed up.

And here she stood, right in the middle of a crime scene, surrounded by them.

Well. Sort of. She shook her head and turned toward the only other person inside the room itself. The stark contrast of his light skin compared to anyone else she had encountered so far that day marked him as a Fuilynian; she assumed this was Xathal.

Xathal stood next to a double bed, his back partially toward her, and between his profile and the post of the bed, she couldn't see much yet. He made no move to invite her farther in, so she took it upon herself to move to the other side of the bed.

She looked down at the body that lay there.

She expected a young, Fereharian woman with slit wrists. Instead, the body was a middle-aged Fereharian man.

His wrists weren't slit.

He had no visible bruises.

Only one large, bloody stain on his shirt in the center of his chest.

That was unfortunate. If it were Elidor, why would he have changed tactics so drastically? Six Fereharian women, and now a Fereharian man, who wasn't even killed the same way? Perhaps she had been too hasty.

Xathal shoved his hands into his vest pockets and looked up at her from under the rim of a round felt hat. He studied her face for a moment, and then his eyes made one critical sweep over her before returning to her face. Whatever his first impression of her was, it was hidden behind a perfectly impassive expression.

"Da Ivana, I presume," he said.

She inclined her head. "Ruios Xathal."

He directed his attention back toward the body. "Initial thoughts?"

Straight to the point then.

"He's not a woman," was what came out first, only because she was still surprised. "And his wrists aren't slit."

He remained silent, no doubt waiting for more, since that much was obvious.

Ivana leaned over the body to pull back the hole in the shirt. The wound was smooth and clean. She had seen many of the same. "He was stabbed with a sharp blade," she said.

"That was my conclusion as well."

She let the flap of the shirt fall back into place and rolled the body onto its side to look at the back. The stab wound didn't go all the way through. "No other signs of violence?" she asked, letting the body roll back.

"None."

"This doesn't fit the pattern."

"Correct."

"So what makes you think this is connected to the other murders?"

Xathal gestured toward the body and the bed. "It's been about a week, he *is* Fereharian, and he was killed elsewhere and then put in bed. Even though this one is a man, at this point, I don't want to overlook anything." His lips tightened. "They've already overlooked far too many."

"The first three?" she asked, thinking of the boarder, the beggar, and the whore.

"The first *six*," Xathal replied.

"There were only three in the file before the merchant's daughter—at least the file I received."

"That's because only this morning was I made aware that in fact there were three more murders prior to that first one—the one the Watch initially ruled a suicide—that might also be related."

"Slit wrists? Found on a bed?"

"No. Two were strangled, one had taken a vicious blow to the head. Two more beggars and another whore. They were left on the streets, presumably where the killer found them."

"Other injuries?"

"The first two had bruising, likely where they were grabbed, but nothing like the third victim from the report you have."

"Timing?"

"They didn't find the bodies as quickly as the latter murders, but the medical examiner placed the times of death close enough to a week apart that we can suspect they are related."

She considered that. "Then since there is no other commonality, they must have been Fereharian women."

"Yes, all three. The change in method is strange, but once the second woman was found dead, it should have raised eyebrows.

The third?"

"No one cared," she said. She already knew why.

He gave her an acknowledging nod. "They might as well have been scum on the bottom of your shoe. An afterthought. A more than *two-month* afterthought. And the last two before him"—he gestured toward the dead man again—"would have been quickly buried in the files of unsolved murders, were it not that someone of value was killed in the interim."

The vehemence with which Xathal spoke surprised her, given his initial rigidity.

She regarded the man more closely. His face was beginning to show its age. The skin was crinkled, and the sun had shone one too many times on his pale face. His salt-and-pepper hair fell to right below his chin, curled under at the edges, but it was dry and brittle-looking. His frame was fit, but his hands were wrinkled. She would put him late sixties, perhaps older, if he bore his age well. Probably called out of retirement.

"And why you, Ruios?" she asked. "What did you do to deserve the title 'Ruios' and be sent our way?"

He rubbed at his eyes, and both the stiffness and passion fell away to reveal a man who merely looked tired. "I once hunted and found another killer, some twenty-five years ago, up in Fuilyn. He was popularly known as The Painter because of the way he would use the victim's own blood to paint landscapes on their bodies." He removed his hat, ran one hand through his hair, and then set it back on his head again. "I suppose they thought I was the only living 'expert' on this sort of criminal." He snorted, as if doubting his own words, and then his eyes raked critically over her once again. "The more mysterious question, Da, is why *you?*"

She was reminded of Elidor's warning. Had he heard of Xathal—or The Painter—before? The events Xathal spoke of had taken place before she had been born, but Elidor may have already been in the service of the government then.

Before, Xathal's face had been impassive; now, his eyes were narrowed in thought. He was no doubt noting that she was a woman, Fereharian, and far too young to be a "special investigator," in his opinion.

He could have once added "orphan," "beggar," and "whore" to his list of attributes.

Given his earlier speech, he might have been the only person to care had she gone missing after Elidor had taken her in.

She crafted her response carefully. "Because I could have been one of those women at one point in my life, Ruios, before I was resurrected into something else entirely. And I will see justice done." She raised her eyes to meet his own. "For *all* of them," she added.

It was in no way an answer to his question; instead, it was a mix of truth and smooth words that contained exactly what he needed to hear so that he would never question who she was and why she was here again. All he needed to believe was that she was a kindred spirit.

He held her eyes for a moment, probing, and then nodded, seeming satisfied. "Well then," he said. "Have you any other thoughts?"

This murder was a wide departure from the others in several key ways, which gave her pause. "It seems so strange that this victim is a man. Why the change? Could it be unrelated?"

"I'm not ruling the possibility out," Xathal said. "But let's work under the assumption that it's connected for now." His eyes were on her again. "After all, does it matter in this moment? A man is dead, we're here to investigate a murder, therefore, we will do so."

She checked herself. She couldn't seem apathetic about the

corpse lying on the bed in front of her. Xathal seemed a no-nonsense type, but he also didn't seem the sort who would take in stride that his colleague in this investigation was a killer herself.

Whether she was right about Elidor or not, she needed clues as to why the killer was picking the targets he was. She needed to be able to predict his next target—or perhaps goad him into choosing someone in particular—so she could trap him there.

The fact that this was not a Fereharian woman complicated matters, but that didn't mean she couldn't learn about the killer from it.

"Very well," she said. "Where did the murder occur?"

Xathal gestured around the room. "Why don't you tell me? I'm interested to hear what you conclude without my bias coloring your search."

She gave him a curt nod and did a circuit of the bedroom. It wasn't large, but there was no pool of blood in the room, which should have been there due to the manner of his death.

There was, however, a smear of blood on the wood floor leading into the room.

Without saying a word to Xathal, she followed the trail of blood out of the room. It went past the Watchman on duty, continued down the hallway in the direction opposite that which she had come, and into the next room over, which looked to be a sitting room or study.

A desk was pushed into the corner, its chair askew and a window ajar next to it. She walked to the desk.

There was the blood she was looking for, in between the chair and the window. A dark crusty stain on the lighter floorboards, some already dry, some still congealed where it had ceased soaking in. Had the victim been sitting at the desk when the killer had struck from behind?

But the wound was on the front of the man; inflicting it from behind would have been awkward and inefficient. Why not strangle him? The killer had apparently done that twice before.

No, the killer more likely had been facing him.

She glanced around the room, searching for all possible points of entry. There were only two: the door she had entered through and the window she had already noted. The window seemed the most obvious, but was it ajar because the man had wanted fresh air, because the killer had entered through the window, or because the killer had left through the window? Or some combination thereof?

She moved closer to it, inspecting the frame and sill. No bloody footprints, no bloody handprints—not a spot of blood at all, in fact—on the frame, window, floor in front, any or all of which she would have expected had he left through the window.

Unless the killer was exceptionally fastidious, of course.

She pushed the window farther open, poked her head outside, and looked down. There was nothing of note that she could see on the walls or ground, either, though she ought to take a closer look at the ground once she was back outside. So where *had* he exited?

She frowned down at the bloodstain on the floor and imagined that this man had been a target. The killer had entered, perhaps, through the window, finding the man at his desk. But the window wasn't far enough from the desk for the killer to be able to surprise him. The man would have seen the killer, risen from his chair in shock and faced him...

Closer in to the window?

That didn't make sense. Why would the man have risen from his chair on the side *closer* to where the killer would have entered—unless, perhaps, he thought to attack him?

She turned and walked to the door. The location of the bloodstain made more sense if the killer had come in through the study door. He had made some noise, or something else had caught the victim's attention at the wrong moment, and the man had turned, and, seeing the stranger, rose and put the chair between himself and the killer, perhaps even contemplated jumping through the window. Then the killer had drawn his weapon and stabbed him, just like that?

There was no sign of struggle. It had been quick. No bloody footprints where the victim had trampled in his own blood, nothing knocked over or broken—only the smear of his blood where the killer had dragged the body into the bedroom the room over.

Had the victim *known* the killer or otherwise been expecting him?

None of this fit the profile. Was this even related? And yet, the body had still been arranged on the bed, which was such a strange thing to do, and it was exactly a week after the previous murder.

She spun in a slow circle, scanning the rest of the room. A ball of yarn with knitting needles still stuck in it sat on a work table on the other side of the room. The table was laid over with embroidered linen, and a vase arranged with wild flowers had been set in the middle.

A book lay open, and Ivana walked over to peer at its contents.

A silt novel.

Nice.

She flipped absently through the pages of the novel. This was a modest rowhouse with a family, not a boarding house or sleazy inn.

This man was someone's husband, perhaps someone's father.

Her hand stilled.

If the killer were going to deviate, that was a curious choice.

She took one last look around the room and then followed the trail of blood, still hoping to find where the killer had exited.

She was so focused on that trail that when she reached the door, she nearly ran into Xathal, who was leaning against the doorjamb, watching her.

"Find anything?" he asked.

She tossed him a glance. "Excuse me," she said, and he moved out of her way.

She retraced the blood back down the short hall and into the bedroom. A double bed, she noted anew. Married?

The trail ended at the body on the bed. Other than that, there was no blood anywhere. The window to the bedroom was closed. She opened it, repeated her actions from earlier, and then closed it again.

Still no hints as to where the killer had made his exit.

"Where was his wife?" she asked without turning, guessing that Xathal had followed her back to the room.

She was right. "Out," he said.

"Children?"

"Two adolescent daughters. Both were in their bedroom, next room down. It was the younger who found him."

Right again. And not merely *someone's* father, but the father of two daughters.

Her hand went to the pendant at her throat.

Two sisters.

Was it too much of a coincidence that after he had killed six young Fereharian women, six women much like herself, the killer had then chosen to kill someone that reflected a piece of her own past? Right after *she* had been put on the job?

Was his little comment this morning about not letting the Watch find out more about her supposed to be some sort of a hint that the murders would start being about her in a more specific way?

Was she jumping to conclusions?

Her instincts were screaming at her that she knew the answer, but her brain needed more. It wasn't enough.

She dropped her hand, walked back to the doorway, and walked the trail of blood toward the bed as though it were a path. She noted this time that the boards creaked several times along the way. She retreated, and then tried walking the path again twice, slightly to either side each time. Still creaked. The trajectory of the blood smear suggested the killer would have had to walk right over the creaky boards.

The killer had snuck in, killed the man without a fight, drug him to his bedroom, and snuck out, all without alerting the girls in the next room over? Hadn't he even cared that there were people in the house who might catch him? Or perhaps one of the girls had been the real target, and the father had caught him sneaking in, so the killer had panicked, killed him, and fled?

But this was not the scene of a panicked killer. There was no trace of blood suggesting his place of exit. It was as though he had killed without treading in the not-insignificant amount of blood spilled, nor without touching it.

Even she would have had trouble being so meticulous.

She pressed her lips together. Elidor could have done it.

"Well? Thoughts?" Xathal said, breaking into her concentration.

"Where did the killer exit?" she asked.

"I haven't been able to determine that."

"What about at the other crime scenes?" Now that she was thinking along these lines, she didn't recall reading anything in the reports about this issue.

"No determination there either. Very tidy, just like this one."

She blew a few stray strands of hair up on her forehead. No evidence of entry or exit. No sound. No mess, other than the blood spilled by the victim. *Damn it all.* There was no way around it. "This crime scene has the fingerprints of a professional."

"Obviously, the man is a serial murderer—"

"I didn't say someone who had killed before. I said a *professional.*" She ticked off her fingers. "He moved in and out without a trace or sound, not even alerting the girls in the next room over, despite"—she bounced up and down on the balls of her feet, causing the boards to creak again—"the difficulties associated with such a feat. On top of that, he killed without tracking a spot of blood anywhere else." She waved her hand. "Any moron can kill someone. It takes quite a bit more skill to do so without leaving *any* evidence other than the body."

The veteran Watchman was attentive and still. "Are you suggesting this was a *paid* kill?"

Unlikely. A brute hired to bash someone's head in wouldn't have cared about finesse, and she and Elidor were the only government-sponsored assassins in Carradon. But she could hardly say that. "A professional would not have taken the risk of sneaking into an occupied house without good cause," she said, "so I doubt it."

Still, though she didn't know of any in Carradon, there *were* freelancers, and it was theoretically possible that one had traveled to the city for a single job. However, it was then odd that they would have imitated this killer by way of moving the body to a bed, unless that was part of the terms of the job.

She was reaching.

"All the same," she said, "it might not hurt to look into his connections to see if anyone might have had a legitimate reason to want him dead."

Xathal raised an eyebrow. "Is there a legitimate reason to have someone killed?"

"I said a legitimate reason to *want* someone dead," Ivana said, giving him a side eye. "I could think of a few without trying."

He inclined his head. "Point taken."

"But assuming this is connected to our other murders, I think that the person we're looking for obviously knows what he's doing. In other words, you're not looking for a drunken bum off the street. You're looking for someone who could look like you or me, even be working a respectable job."

Xathal passed a hand over his face, looking unsettled. "I see." "What did the victim do for a living?"

"He was an assistant professor at the university," Xathal answered.

Ivana's breath caught in her throat.

A married man with two adolescent daughters—*perhaps* that could be considered coincidental.

But also a scholar?

It was one too many "coincidences."

She spun on her heel and walked back to the study. She didn't know what she was looking for, other than something, anything to corroborate what every part of her—other than the tiny bit of her brain that wanted *proof*—already knew.

She rummaged through the victim's desk drawers. Flipped through a file folder. Looked beneath the work table.

It was there, tucked underneath the table, that she spied a wooden crate. The words *University Property* were stenciled on the side.

Curious.

She pulled the crate out, lifted the top off...

And closed her eyes. There was no longer any room for doubt. It had to be Elidor.

Inside the crate, nestled in a pile of soft cloths, was a microscope.

"What is it?" Xathal's voice said from behind her.

She opened her eyes, remembering she wasn't alone.

Xathal appeared at her side and peered inside the crate himself. "Is that—?"

"Yes. A microscope."

Xathal scratched his chin. "Huh. Heard of them, but I don't think I've ever seen one before."

Had Elidor put it there?

A piece of paper was attached to the lid. She ran her eyes over it; it was a form indicating that the professor had checked the microscope out for the foreseeable future.

So that meant Elidor hadn't planted it himself—only found someone who fit her father in as much detail as he could manage.

Xathal was staring at her, no doubt waiting for some sort of conclusion.

She had none she could give him; to expose Elidor in this moment she would have to reveal that she had a connection to him—and *that* she could not do.

She set the lid back on the crate, straightened up, and shook her head. "It's perplexing. A respectable, settled man, with a family—the only connections being the timing, the region he's from, and the curious habit of depositing the body on the bed. What do you think? Is it the same person?"

"In my experience, the nature of victims and the"—he grimaced—"methodology were the two most common factors. Up until now, we've at least had the gender of the victim to tie them together. Now…" He removed his hat and ran a hand through his hair. "Your thoughts?"

"Frankly, I don't know. It could be someone else, I suppose, copying some vague details they'd heard to try to send us down the wrong path." She shrugged. "I think we're going to need more evidence." And more time to think.

"But there isn't anything more."

"By that I mean, more bodies."

He gave a little awkward half-chuckle, as if he weren't sure if she were trying to make a morbid joke. "Forgive me, Da, but there aren't supposed to be—"

"Do you have an idea yet of where to find the killer or how to catch him?"

Xathal hemmed a bit.

"I didn't think so," Ivana said. "Have a copy of the updated file made for me and I'll stop by to pick it up in a few days." She turned away. "In the meantime, send a message the next time someone ends up dead."

Chapter Twenty-Three

When she returned to Elidor's house, Ivana didn't immediately go inside. Instead, she came at it from a back way and now crouched in the shadows of the alley across from the house, her eyes trained on the front door.

She was thinking.

Going over everything she knew, everything she had learned. There was one glaring omission in her knowledge.

Why? What was his goal? What was his motive?

He had permission to kill. It made no sense that he was doing it to satisfy mere bloodlust.

No, it had to do with her—but what? After all, if he had the desire to kill or hurt her, he had had ample opportunity. Not merely over the past few years she had lived with him, but even in the past few weeks since the murders had begun.

Her original, almost flippant theory that he had snapped and gone on a murderous rampage didn't make sense. The kills were evenly timed. The crime scene she had just investigated had been remarkably tidy. And the detailed attention to her own past was too meticulously planned.

There was no evidence that he had lost control of himself in any way other than committing murders unrelated to a sanctioned job.

She clenched and unclenched a fist. Did she go to Llyr? Would he think she was crazy?

Or did she confront Elidor? Was that what he wanted? Was that why he'd left such an obvious trail? And to what end?

He could have taken the job himself and sent the Watch on a wild goose chase while he laid plans for escape. Instead, he'd given it to her.

He had to have had a reason for that. She didn't know what it was. That was perhaps the most chilling realization of all.

Confronting him was dangerous—doubly so when she didn't understand his motivations. And she still wasn't sure she could best him in a face-to-face conflict. But she *was* certain that if she ran, he would come after her.

No, if all of this was going to lead to him coming after her anyway, she'd rather it be on her terms than his. The best option was probably to go inside, play innocent, and see what happened.

She drew her dagger under her cloak, just in case, and crossed the street.

The house was dark and silent. Ivana stood on the threshold after she had closed the door, straining her senses for any hint of another presence in the house.

Nothing.

She removed her boots.

Still nothing.

She padded down the hall and stopped in front of his study door. No light shone from underneath, but she knocked anyway. "Elidor?"

No response, and a thorough search of his study and then the rest of the house confirmed that he wasn't there.

The possibility that he might not even be home hadn't crossed her mind.

That meant he knew exactly where she was likely to be, and that any move would be on his terms.

She rolled her shoulders to release the tension she could feel building there. Well. At least she could use the time to make some plans.

And to make plans, it wouldn't hurt to do some research.

Seven days later, Elidor was still mysteriously absent. Ivana was beginning to wonder if he was planning on coming home at all.

Even so, she had made herself scarce during the day. At night, she locked her bedroom door, the hinges of which she had stripped clean of any oil. It now shrieked every time it opened. Never had she been so glad that her room did *not* have a window.

She also kept her dagger on her at all times.

Today, seven days since the last murder, she was expecting a message from Xathal, so she stayed in. She sat at the dining room table, which was covered in reports, books, illustrations—anything she could get her hands on to try to make sense of the pattern, or lack thereof.

She sat in Elidor's chair, her back to the wall, where she could see both doors and the window.

She glanced up at the hall door, certain she would see

Elidor's profile appear in it at any moment.

It remained empty.

She sighed and went back to her books.

The whole string of murders had started normally. The Butcher of Arlana, for instance...

She pushed aside one stack of papers to an open book and turned it to look at the facing pages again.

Fourteen women dead before they caught him. All young—between sixteen and twenty years old or thereabouts, though the region didn't seem to matter. In that case, they had thought at first they'd been dealing with a kidnapper, because the women had disappeared—no bodies. It hadn't been until the last brave and enterprising woman had left behind clues on the way to her death that the authorities had found him—and the slaughterhouse he had kept the bodies strung up in like meat ready to go to the market, earning him his name.

Ivana flipped a few pages to her next bookmark. And then there was The Painter, the killer Xathal had apparently caught, though the book didn't use his name. Women, again, but all Fuilynian. Their pale white skin made a gruesome canvas for his impressive paintings, all done with his victims' own blood. He had been caught when a woman involved with the investigation had volunteered to be bait. Fortunately, they had caught him. Unfortunately, she hadn't survived.

Ivana wrinkled her nose and pushed aside the book.

She had lost track of the number of people she had assassinated by this point. Some deaths had been bloodless. Some hadn't. But they had all been efficient. She was a tool in the hands of her Conclave masters. A sword, as Elidor had once put it.

But this was different. She was thankful, at least, that Elidor had thus far been a bit more conventional in his methods. No butchering or painting here. Even she, who had seen and caused so much death, couldn't help but feel a bit disturbed at such brutal and twisted carnage.

She supposed that meant that despite everything, she had still retained some semblance of her humanity.

But none of this helped her. It might not matter in the end, but then again, it might. She wanted to know why he was doing what he was doing, and none of these killers' apparent motives fit.

The dining room door creaked.

She had cleaned that one, too.

She didn't look up right away. She wanted to play this carefully. Project as unconcerned of an air, as possible, until she knew where he stood.

He would notice the change in the door, so she mentioned it before he could. "Huh," she said. "Apparently, the hinges need oil." She finally looked up at him.

He stood in the doorway, framed by the lantern she had left lit in the hall. He had no weapon in his hand, but that meant nothing. He eyed her, and then the table. "What are you doing?"

"Research," she said, and then she dared to look back down.

The only signal that he had moved closer to her was the faint rustle of his clothing. His footsteps were silent. She couldn't even hear him breathing.

But he stopped at the edge of the table, within her peripheral vision, to survey the spread of papers and books.

"Ironic that a professional killer needs to research other killers," he said after a moment.

"It's all about motive, Elidor." She tapped two fingers on the cover of the closest book and glanced up at him. "I am *not* one of these monsters." She had chosen the word deliberately, but he gave no sign that it had any effect on him. "I don't do what I do for the high of the kill or bloodlust or to satisfy some perverted fantasy of mine, so I'm trying to understand." She paused, raised an eyebrow, and tilted her head. "Why, do you have some insight you wish to share?"

She almost thought she caught a flicker of amusement behind his eyes, but it might have been her imagination.

Too much?

"Have you made progress?" he asked.

"Hardly," she said. "The last victim was a man. Completely broke the pattern in almost every way. Fereharian, but not a nobody. He had a family—a wife, children—and his wrists weren't slit. But the body had been moved to his bed, so that's why they think it's connected." She paused. "The killer knows what he's doing. He came and went without a trace."

No reaction.

"And how did he die then?" he asked.

Like you don't know. Did he really not realize she knew, or was he playing along because he had no intention of killing her yet? "Stabbed through the chest."

"Mmm. And does it bother you?"

She started. That had been unexpected. "Pardon?"

"A father, so much like your own, leaving behind children."

She raised her eyes to meet his. No. He knew.

Her muscles went taut with anticipation. "I'm sure I've eliminated my share of fathers," she said, her hand creeping toward her thigh.

He didn't look, but he saw. "You've taken to wearing your dagger inside?"

"One can't be too careful with a killer on the loose."

He was more experienced, but he was also aging. She had the advantage of faster reflexes.

Would it be enough?

His hand twitched.

In one smooth, fluid motion, she stood, kicked back her chair, and drew her dagger.

And then blinked in astonishment.

In one likewise, smooth, fluid motion, he had simply *fled*.

She darted after him—out the hall door he had come in through. The front door was halfway open. She cursed, sheathed her dagger, and flung open the door.

Only to be brought up short by an adolescent boy standing on the stoop, who took a step back at her appearance.

Elidor's cloak disappeared around a corner in the distance.

She pounded her fist once against the door frame. *Damn.*

The boy's throat constricted and then he bowed. "Da," he said. "I have a message for you." He shoved out a hand grasping a letter, as though eager to be rid of it.

She took it, and he tipped his hat and took off in the opposite direction from Elidor, not even waiting for a tip.

At least she had had the presence of mind to sheath her dagger before throwing the door open.

She glanced around the street. Thankfully, there was no one around who could have viewed the spectacle. Only once she had closed herself inside the house again did she look at the seal.

The Watch. Xathal had another body.

Chapter Twenty-Four

E lidor hadn't broken the time pattern, anyway. He must have committed the murder that night or early that morning before returning home.

She had enough time on the way to the scene—just over in the fourth district—to wonder what her plan should be now, but not enough time to arrive at an answer. So for now, she would move forward as if nothing had happened.

This time the message directed her to an apartment over a shoemaker's shop, but the victim wasn't the shoemaker. The husband and wife who owned the shop itself had divided the living space into two smaller spaces and rented one of them out after all of their children had moved away.

That was what the Watchman at the door told her when she arrived.

"Why is this important?" she asked him.

The Watchman shrugged and jerked his head up the stairs.

"The shoemaker and his wife are up there now, talking to Ruios Xathal."

"Thank you." Ivana took the stairs and entered the apartment on the left.

It was a small space indeed. The apartment had one main living area divided into three by moveable partitions. Still, though it was small, it was comfortably furnished. Firewood was stacked in the corner, attesting to the family's preparations for the encroaching fall chill. The wood floor was swept clean, and it smelled of apples and cinnamon.

Xathal stood speaking with a man and a woman—presumably the aforementioned shoemaker and his wife. The husband's face was drawn, and the wife was leaning on him, not weeping openly, but wiping her eyes occasionally on an embroidered handkerchief.

"She was such a nice person," the shoemaker was saying. "Just couldn't afford a bigger place, that's all. Never had any issues. Quiet. Clean. Well-behaved little girls."

"I can't believe it," the wife murmured. The way her husband patted her arm told Ivana that it wasn't the first time that phrase had left her mouth.

Xathal noticed Ivana standing in the door, and he gestured her over. "This is Da Ivana, my associate."

Ivana inclined her head to the couple. "Where is the body?"

The wife turned to her husband with an exclamation and buried her head in his arm.

Oops. Sometimes she found that Elidor had rubbed off on her a bit *too* much. She was playing a part here.

Xathal gestured to one of the nearby partitions. "On the bed."

Of course. She started to duck behind the partition, but something the shoemaker had said stopped her. She turned toward the shoemaker and his wife, who were preparing to leave. "Pardon," she said. "You spoke of girls."

"Yes," the wife said, dabbing at her eyes. "Two sweet little girls."

Two daughters again. "Where are they now?"

"We took them in, of course," the shoemaker said. "At least until other arrangements can be made. We're trying to find other family, but..."

"It was so hard on her, raising them on her own," the wife put in. "We gave her this space in exchange for work at the shop, but it's a lonely business nonetheless." She shook her head. "What a horrendous thing, as if it weren't bad enough for them after their father was taken by the same illness."

Illness? Was this a murder or a hospital deathbed?

Ivana inclined her head again, and the shoemaker and his wife left.

She ducked behind the partition with Xathal. As he said, there on the bed lay a woman. Fereharian, but older than the other female victims, who had all been young—around Ivana's age or even younger.

Every part of the woman's exposed skin was covered in open sores, but there was no visible sign of injury, though they must have had some reason to suspect murder other than that she was found in bed.

"Cause of death?" Ivana asked, certain he wouldn't say whatever illness had struck her.

Xathal put on a pair of gloves and turned down the lace at her neck. Bruises: red, purple, and the marks of fingers.

Strangled.

Xathal flipped back the lace and pulled off the glove. "Well. Now what do you think?"

"Was she strangled in bed?"

"We assume so." He grimaced. "Her children found her when they woke up this morning."

Ivana ran a hand over her face. If there had been any doubt left in her mind—even if she hadn't had the chance to see Elidor before this—it was erased now. A Fereharian woman with a serious illness? Two daughters, their father already dead?

But what could she say to Xathal? "What makes you think this is related to the other murders? Surely, the fact that she was found in bed would not be unexpected given her pre-death state."

Xathal nodded. "Admittedly, we are now stretching. The killer—if indeed it is the same person—now has chosen a method of murder other than, well, shall we say, knifework. But we *are* back to a woman."

"But not a young woman."

Xathal sighed. He looked tired. "But still Fereharian. In bed. Exactly a week later. And we mustn't forget the first two women were strangled before the killer apparently developed his preference for a blade." He shuffled his hat off and on his head. "Violent crime is rare in this district—given the recent spree, it's too coincidental to discount."

Ivana nodded. "I don't disagree. But this is becoming stranger with each body." And *why*, for Temoth's sake? Was he taunting her? Flaunting her presumed inability to catch him? Or was he baiting her? "What is he gaining out of these murders?" she mused out loud.

"Gaining?"

"As you noted in your initial report, choosing young Fereharian women—women who look similar—is typical of these sorts of killers. Similar-looking victims, even similar modes of death, after those first few—the slitting of wrists. The assumption would be that something about those victims attracted him.

The bloody method of murder suggests that something about *that* attracted him. But the previous murder—the man—broke the pattern of the type of victim, and this murder breaks it even more, in it being bloodless—though we are returning to females once again."

"There is still the possibility that one of the daughters was the intended target at the last house."

"But the family situation didn't make sense. None of it makes sense." She decided to voice the connections she had made. "Is it coincidental that both this victim and the prior had two daughters, and that both times the killer timed it in such a way that the daughters would find their bodies?"

Xathal stared at the corpse, his brow furrowed. "That does seem more than coincidence," he said after a moment. "But how are we supposed to catch him if we can't even nail down what victims he prefers?"

She shook her head. She knew what these victims signified. "Signs of sexual assault?"

"No."

"Never," she murmured. "That's consistent at least." Also consistent with what she knew about Elidor, other than his voyeurism as it pertained to her.

"As is the Fereharian origin," Xathal said. "I have considered whether he had been wronged by a Fereharian sometime in his past and simply snapped, but it doesn't seem to fit that sort of crime."

Ivana furrowed her brow. "Agreed. It's too methodical. Too planned. If it were revenge gone mad, it would show signs of passion. He would likely find the most Fereharian-populated district and go on a wild killing spree until he was caught." She paused. "But this man doesn't want to be caught. He's now slipping in and out of risky places: an occupied house, an apartment over a shop.

"It's almost like he's toying with us. Playing games." Yes, that was it. Playing games. She clenched and unclenched one fist at her side. But what were the rules?

Presumably, she won if she caught him. But under what terms did he win? When he had exhausted everyone in her life who had mattered to her and was now gone. Then what? And *why*?

"Games. As in taunting us or leaving clues?" Xathal pressed when she was silent for too long.

Clues? That could be. Was he daring Ivana to try to prove that it was him? Even to catch him? "Either. Both, perhaps."

"Why would he leave clues if he doesn't want to be caught?"

She tapped the bedpost with one finger. Xathal was an ally, yet a half-blind ally; she couldn't tell him everything. "What has changed since the murders started breaking the most recent pattern?"

"Da?"

"Us. The Watch brought in two outsiders to help. He knows we're stepping up the search, so perhaps he, in turn, is stepping up his game."

"An interesting theory, and if true, it raises the level of madness of this individual."

She could absolutely believe it of Elidor.

She closed her eyes. A part of her had hoped that her theory would be proven false. Not because she cared about Elidor's fate. Because she cared about her own.

She turned away. "Make me a copy of your interview with the shoemaker and his wife. In fact, make me a copy of your reports of any questioning done if you can. I want to explore the possibility that this has turned into a game for the killer. And if there are clues we're missing, I want to find them. We need to beat him at his own game."

She had to catch Elidor before he finished whatever game he was playing with her, and to do that, she might yet need Xathal and whatever resources he could bring to bear. But how could she utilize him safely, without compromising herself?

As much as she hated the idea, she had a feeling it was time to go to Llyr.

Chapter Twenty-Five

Ivana was being watched. Not by human eyes, but divine. Obsidian eyes peered out at her from the nine reliefs carved into the stone walls around the small shrine to Yathyn, so different from his wife's. Someone had created them so that a visitor would have that impression. Probably to help the visitor feel the weight of their recent guilt, or at least dredge up some sin to feel guilty about.

She supposed a normal person would find it unsettling. For her, it emphasized the depths of depravity these supposed holy men fell to. A government keeping a few assassins on retainer? Sure. A religious order? Damn hypocrites.

The stone gods couldn't watch for Llyr, however. Ivana's own eyes turned back to the solitary entrance to the shrine from her place in the dark.

And so, unusually, she saw Llyr before he saw her.

Who was he anyway? Was he another pet of the Conclave,

doing their bidding in a different way? Or was he a priest himself?

His eyes swept the inside of the shrine twice before he spotted her in the shadows and moved to stand in front of her. "Well?"

She didn't move. She had propped herself up into the corner of a stone bench set into the wall, one foot on the bench with her knee drawn to her chest, and the other dangling off the side. "I know who the killer is."

Llyr's eyes flicked down over her casual position, and then his lips pressed into a line. "Good. Why are you bothering me? Do what you need to d—"

"It's Elidor."

His face spasmed in shock and then smoothed.

So. He *didn't* know. The thought had crossed her mind while she'd waited that this could have all been some sort of sick final test on their part, such as setting Elidor on people to see how far she would go. If she would turn on her master if need be.

"Did I hear you correctly?" he asked.

"It's. Elidor," she repeated.

There was a long silence, and then, "You're certain?"

"Yes."

"How do you know?"

"It's complicated," she said. "But I realized he's been playing a game with me. His first victims were all young Fereharian women, like myself. Then he killed a man, clearly meant to represent my father. The latest victim was an older woman, clearly meant to represent my mother." She swung her leg down to join the other and stood up. "One of your tools has gone rogue, I'm afraid." She crossed her arms. "What do you want me to do about it?"

Llyr swore under his breath and then passed a hand over his

face.

She was glad he didn't question her for more details. She didn't want to have to explain her entire life story to Llyr so that he would understand.

"Does he know you know?" he asked.

"Yes," Ivana said, "but he fled when I went to confront him. I haven't seen him since." She smirked at him. "Could be lurking in the shadows outside the shrine, for all I know."

In fact, she had checked the shadows outside the shrine thoroughly, as well as any shadow on the way. Still, it hadn't escaped her that Elidor could be keeping a close eye on her. She felt mildly comforted by the logic that if he intended to kill her now, he could have already done so.

Llyr, on the other hand, took her comment with obvious discomfiture. He tried to hide it by glaring at her, but his hand had begun tapping against his thigh.

Ivana was more amused by his distress than she ought to be, given the circumstances, and she made no effort to hide it. It felt good to be the one in control.

He didn't like the reversal. He leaned toward her, his face inches from her own. "You realize that your livelihood, indeed, life, is in my hands? I can send you where I want." He leered at her. "Do with you what I want."

She snorted. "I'd like to see you try."

"You're walking a thin line, sweetheart."

She shrugged and brushed past him. "Fine. Deal with him yourself. That should be entertaining."

"Stop," he said.

She stopped but didn't turn to face him again.

"If you have the opportunity to eliminate him without suspicion, do so. Otherwise, continue whatever plans you're enacting or planning to enact with the Watch. They may be of use to you in pinning him down; find a way to give them what they need, and no more. When the arrest is made, I'll make sure my people will be in place to take custody before he can be questioned. We'll deal with him from there."

Eliminate Elidor or manipulate the Watch. Which would be easier? In exactly five days, Elidor would kill again; that gave her little time to plan, but she had an idea of where to start.

"Very well," she said to Llyr, left without another word.

How closely was Elidor watching her? Did he know, for instance, that at that moment she was breaking into his safe and stealing from him?

"Stealing" was a strong word, of course. If he were here, he would have given her what she needed. Bribes weren't cheap, after all. But he wasn't here, and she had heard or seen nothing of him since she had confronted him two days ago.

Three days ago, now. It had slipped past midnight during the time she had spent with Llyr and traveling back to Elidor's. Ordinarily, she would have left this until the following night, giving herself a little more time to think and plan on a full night's sleep. But she didn't have time.

Elidor's meticulous attention to detail was useful in this case. He had stacked four shallow wooden boxes on top of one another inside the safe, each containing an equal amount, with coins sorted by denomination. It made it easy to count out what she thought she would need, and then add a little extra to be on the safe side.

She dumped the coins into two coin purses, secured them to her belt, relocked the safe, and headed back out into the night.

***

The door of The Drunken Rabbit slammed shut behind Ivana, shutting out the stench of the garbage rotting in the alley and closing in the smell of unwashed bodies and ale.

She had only been here twice before, both times with Elidor, long ago. She had never come back by herself; of all of their sources, this one tended to demand the most for the least information, and the environment made it less than pleasant to deal with him.

However, when he had information to give, it had always been good. She didn't have time to waste on false leads.

The place hadn't changed. Same stench, same filth, same seedy-looking customers, half of them half-drunk, the other half all the way drunk.

And despite the fact that it was just after two in the morning—it had taken her almost two hours to wind her way through the city and to the tavern situated on the outskirts of the slums that spilled outside the northern wall—the place was packed.

Her arrival didn't go unnoticed, but people were used to minding their own business here.

Most of the time.

She pulled the hood of her cloak down, sauntered to the bar, and set six silver selmas on the top.

A middle-aged man wearing a dirty apron appeared almost instantly to claim her coins.

She jerked her head toward the cauldron being kept warm over coals in the center of the room. "Mug for some velca," she said.

"One mug's only three selmas," he said, looking her over dubiously.

How honest, she thought drily.

She looked pointedly toward the sign above the bar, on

which was scrawled the day's special: bottomless mug of velca for the price of two. "That not today's special?"

He looked her over again, grunted, and shoved a mug her way.

She wiped it out on the hem of her cloak, grimacing internally, and went to the cauldron to scoop herself out a mugful of the wretched stuff before taking it back to the bar and finding a seat. She had no intention of drinking the entirety of even the mug she had taken, let alone more than two, but she had to shatter the perception that she was more helpless—and therefore gullible—for being female before she would get anything out of him.

Unfortunately, that was an area where Elidor had it easier than her.

Not that she was the only woman in the place. Aside from a server and the two leaning on a burly man throwing dice in the corner, a tall, lithe woman sat alone at a table with her feet up, glaring at anyone who came close to her, and another woman sat at a table of men, downing velca like it was water.

But they'd already earned their places.

The barkeep helped two other customers and then started wiping down the counter behind the bar lined with bottles of varying shades of amber, red, and brown liquids—for all the good it did since he was using a rag already mottled brown with who-knew-how-many spills he'd cleaned up. The surface even sported a blot of what looked suspiciously like dried blood.

She sat, nursed her mug, and waited.

The barkeep was keeping an eye on her in what he probably thought was a discreet way, but he didn't come over again.

Eventually, some half-drunk, misguided male sat next to her, as she had counted on.

"Hey, sweetheart," he said, draping one arm around her

shoulders. "Can I buy you somethin' better than that piss-water?"

In response, she feigned taking a long draw on the mug, and said without turning to face him, "No, thank you, but you can remove your arm from my shoulder."

He laughed. "Hey, hey. Just an offer. Don't have to get all hoi-ty-toity about it." He pounded his free fist onto the bar, as if he amused himself. "We got a reg'lar little lady here," he said to the man next to him.

That one glanced his way, grimaced—no doubt at the stench on his breath—and moved a stool down.

"I note," she said calmly, "that your arm is still on my shoulder, and I've asked you to remove it. Not to mention," she added, as if it had just occurred to her, "you stink."

His smile evaporated, to be replaced with a half-smirk, half-sneer. "What right you think you have to be talkin' to me that way, eh? Just tryin' to be nice."

She was baiting him on purpose. It didn't take much with his type—especially drunk. The barkeep had taken notice of their quiet disagreement and had drifted closer.

"I'm going to ask you one last time to remove your arm from my shoulder," Ivana said.

"Or what?" he sneered, pressing his hand flat to the table. "You think you're somethin'? Lemme tell you, bitch—"

It was glorious how rapidly he went from beating his chest to yelping like a kicked puppy. All it took was a quick sleight of the hand, a flash of silver, and a little blood, and his entire attitude changed.

His arm did drop from her shoulder, then, to tug at the boot knife she had just driven between his index finger and middle finger and into the wooden bar beneath, nicking the webbing between them.

"Filthy bitch!" he screamed at her. "Barkeep, you see that?" He finally managed to wrench the knife out of the wood, and before he could turn it on her, she had her dagger pointed at him and her other hand out.

His nostrils flared, and he gripped the hilt of her knife as though considering returning the favor. In the end, however, he turned it and slapped the knife hilt-first into her palm.

"I'll ask you to quit vandalizing my bar like that, Da," the barkeep said, tossing his filthy rag to the man.

"There," she told the man, who was dabbing his wound with the rag. "I knew I could give you a good reason to do as I asked."

He glared at her, shoved his stool back so hard that it fell over, and went back to the table where his companions were slapping their knees and guffawing.

The man, on the other hand, was watching her with dark, dangerous eyes, his upper lip curled in a permanent snarl.

She sighed. She'd have to deal with him later. That one wasn't letting it go.

"All right," the barkeep said, "you've made your point. Do it again and I'll kick you out."

Ivana sheathed both blades and inclined her head. "My apologies, Dal." She produced a setan. "Will this cover the damage?" It was ludicrous, of course. The bar top was so beat up that she had already lost track of which notch was hers.

He snatched the setan up anyway. "What do you want?"

"I was hoping you might have heard some things I might be interested in."

He grunted. "What sort of things?"

"They say there's a killer on the loose in the city," she said. "Someone might pay quite a bit for some information on that."

"I don't know nothin' 'bout no killer," the barkeep said, sliding curiously into street inflection he hadn't been using a moment ago.

"That's funny," she said. "You usually know something about everything."

"Don' know where you'd get that idea," he said.

"Burning skies, man," she said, sighing heavily for emphasis. "Do I need to trot out the tired-out lines?"

His brow creased, but he didn't say anything.

"Here's one to get us started." She leaned over. "I can make it worth your while."

"Sure you can," he said, and in response, she set another setan on the bar top.

He snorted. "You're gonna have to do better than that," he said, except this time, she repeated the line out loud right along with him.

His mouth opened, as if to speak again, and then closed.

She gave him a broad smile. "It's like we both read the same script, isn't it?"

He stared at her.

Temoth, this was tedious. "Can we skip to the part where you tell me what I want to know, I give you copious amounts of gold"—she put an entire purse on the counter; it wasn't her money anyway, she had another one, and she knew where to get more—"and we both go away satisfied with the transaction?"

"All right, all right. Just..." He held up one hand in placation and pocketed the pouch with the other. "Look, there isn't much to tell. But your killer—the one who likes Fereharian girls?"

Close enough. She nodded.

"There's some chatter that a shadow's been slinking about round the warehouses down by the docks."

She cast him a dubious look. "That could mean anything."

He held up a hand. "That same shadow's been seen talking to

slavers who sometimes sell out of an abandoned warehouse down there. If you ask the slavers, they'll say it was asking about Fereharian women."

Slavers. So his next victim would represent her sister. She could have deduced that, but it was good to have confirmation—and a location.

"Anything else?" she asked.

"Nope." With that, he turned away to find a new dirty rag to wipe his counters with.

Ivana left her mostly-full mug of piss-water on the bar and left The Drunken Rabbit feeling both invigorated and annoyed.

Invigorated because that had been mildly entertaining on all fronts; she clearly didn't have enough human interaction.

Annoyed that the only way to be accepted by a bunch of arrogant assholes was to stoop to their level.

The drunken man followed her for a block before he tried to assail her. She put him where he belonged: laid out in a garbage heap.

Something was different. She knew it the moment she stepped through the front door at Elidor's.

A light was coming from Elidor's study door down the hall, which was cracked, and she had neither left the door open nor a lantern burning.

She eased the front door shut, keeping the handle turned until it shut all the way so the latch didn't make its quiet *snick* when it caught.

And then she drew her dagger and flattened herself against the wall.

She stood there in complete silence for a moment, holding even her breath so it wouldn't interfere with anything she might hear around her.

Nothing. She exhaled silently.

Elidor hadn't attacked her when he had that first opportunity. Instead, he had chosen to flee. Ten days had passed since then, and still she had seen or heard nothing of him.

But he was either here now, or he had been here.

She crept down the hall one soft, silent step at a time, stopping every few steps to listen once again.

Finally, she reached the study door and peered through the crack. She saw nothing from her vantage point, but that didn't mean he wasn't in there. Again, she listened.

Again, nothing.

She tapped her dagger gently against her thigh. What if the study were merely a trap, a way of luring her into a dead end?

But why go to all that trouble when he could have more easily murdered her while she slept?

No. His next target would be a Fereharian slave meant to represent her sister, and she felt fairly confident that that meant he didn't intend on coming after her—yet.

Still, she kept her dagger drawn as she opened the study door and moved into the study.

She halted inside the door, taken aback. The painting on Elidor's study wall—*The Execution of the Last Aife*—hung in tatters. It had been slashed, not once, not twice, but multiple times, as if someone had taken out their anger on the inanimate object.

After a cautious glance around at the empty room, she approached the painting. She pushed one ribbon of the painting back up into place, pairing it with its match. A portion of the horrified faces of the crowd stared back at her.

She let the scrap fall back down. Anger at the inanimate object, or what it represented?

He had always been fascinated with that painting, and she had never understood why.

As she had never fully understood Elidor himself. She had become more like him in many ways—in the ways she had wanted—but they were like jars of glass and clay that were painted on the outside to look identical. Someway, somehow, their innate *substance* was still different.

And that knowledge didn't help her now.

She popped her head into his safe room to be sure he wasn't hiding down there, and then came back to his study to open his safe and deposit her remaining bag of coins back in it.

To her surprise, the safe was unlocked.

To her even greater surprise, it was empty, save a single rose lying on the bottom of the safe. The stem still had its thorns, and a strip of paper had been pierced through and stuck to the rose stem with it.

She reached for the rose and then hesitated. Could he have poisoned the thorns, hoping she would prick herself?

She tugged on her gloves as an extra layer of protection, gingerly removed the rose from the safe, laid it on his desk, and pulled off the curl of paper.

One line was written on it in his bold script: *What is a chain to one.*

She laid the slip of paper back down on the desk, baffled. It was the first half of a well-known axiom, the full saying being, *What is a chain to one may be freedom to another.* Parents liked to trot it out when their children were complaining about doing chores or schoolwork or some other "burden" of childhood, to remind them that some children would be grateful to have chores and schoolwork to do. She remembered her own father and mother using it on multiple occasions.

But in this context, it made no sense. Was he trying to give her his own clue that the next victim would be a slave?

Still, what good did that do her? It didn't tell her where to find him—or his next victim—before he struck again in exactly four days.

Or did it?

She opened Elidor's drawer, found a sheet of paper and a pen, and scribbled a note to Xathal on it. She glanced at the clock on Elidor's desk. It was half-past four; she would walk it to the first district precinct herself at dawn. She knew how she could use him.

Chapter Twenty-Six

"Dal! We have him!"

Ivana stopped pacing and turned to face the Watchman who had burst into the small office at the back of a third district warehouse. Ivana recognized him as Lann, a member of one of the teams of three they had scattered around the area.

Xathal shot off his chair and onto his feet.

"Where?" he demanded. "In custody?"

"No, no." Lann stopped to take a few gasps for air. "But Judoc saw someone with the right height and build entering one of the warehouses down by the docks, one of the ones with all the chains, like you said—"

"And, and? Nothing remarkable about that," Xathal cut in, impatient to hear the rest.

"And he was carrying something big on his shoulder. It looked like a big rug—or something wrapped in a big rug. Judoc sent me to get you, and he sent Marwyn to get the next closest team. Judoc went in after him."

Xathal swore and grabbed his hat off the desk. "How long ago? No, never mind. Just go! Now!"

Lann was already out the door, Ivana close on his heels.

They quickly lost Xathal, who wasn't of an age or condition to keep up with a young, fit Watchman and an assassin pelting through the twilight.

Lann stopped at an intersection three blocks over and flung his arm toward a warehouse kitty-corner to them. "There!"

Ivana gave him a sharp nod. The aforementioned Judoc, if he had followed Elidor into that warehouse, was almost certainly dead. It was better she go in first.

"Wait for Xathal." She trotted up to the warehouse and pulled up short right outside the door. It would do no good to burst in if he was waiting for her just inside, but the warehouse had no windows except far above her, so one way or the other, she'd be going in blind. At least the sun hadn't fully set yet.

Conscious of Xathal finally limping toward them far down the street, she drew her dagger and pushed the door open.

Across the warehouse, a cloaked figure knelt next to a young woman chained to the wall. The body of a man lay nearby, uniformed and bearing Watch insignia.

The warehouse had only one other door, and it was closer to Elidor than her.

She didn't wait for him to look up. She would recognize that profile anywhere.

She had the advantage of surprise. Elidor wasted a few precious seconds in looking up, taking stock of the situation, and making a decision about where to go. Meanwhile, she darted toward him, but with a slight trajectory toward the other door.

They collided and crashed to the ground in a tangle of cloak and arms and legs. His dagger hit the stone floor next to her head with a hard clank first, and then bit into her upper arm next. She thrashed her legs, trying to land a blow near his groin, but his greater strength won out. He shoved her away, sprang to his feet, and turned back toward the door in one movement. But as he did, he stepped on the hem of his own cloak, and fell back down hard on one knee. She drew her blade and lunged at his back, but he curled in on himself at the last moment and she went over him instead. She rolled, but her hand smacked against the ground, and her dagger went skittering across the floor. She drew her boot knife as she rose to a crouch.

She was now between him and the back door. She glanced over his shoulder to see Lann dart in and block the door she had come through. Xathal followed and skirted the wall, heading toward the woman chained at the other side of the ware-house—and the unfortunate Judoc.

Elidor seemed to know what was going on behind him. He gave her that cold, mirthless smile he so excelled at. "You're too late," he said.

"Even so, I can keep you from doing it again."

"Still a marionette? You could do so much better."

As he spoke, he was turning so that he drew ever-closer to the unguarded door. In a face-to-face confrontation with Elidor, the odds were with him. However, he was favoring one leg. She could tell as he moved. It might be enough to give her an advantage.

Her eyes went to Lann. If she could pin Elidor, could he come to her aid fast enough to take over?

Her left palm tickled, and his eyes flicked down to it. She became dimly aware of an ache in her upper arm where he had stabbed her; his blade had caught the flesh and nothing more, but it hurt, and it was bleeding.

She didn't dare tear her eyes away from him long enough to look at it, but she had seen that look in his eyes before.

Maybe she had another advantage.

She lifted her left hand and turned it so that the blood ran across it instead of dripping onto the ground, hoping it would distract him as it did once before.

And it almost worked. Unfortunately, in the same moment that she stepped closer to him, preparing to launch, anger danced across his eyes.

She recoiled instinctively, but she had been preparing to attack him, not flee herself.

He dove toward her, grabbed her by the wound in her arm, and dragged her up against himself.

She bit her tongue to keep from crying out as she struggled to free herself from his grasp, and Xathal shouted from across the warehouse, as if in a belated warning. Lann drew his sword and ran toward them, but it would be too little, too late. Elidor's had sheathed his dagger, and his other hand was already closing on her throat.

Yet he didn't constrict it any further. Instead, he met her eyes. His fingers dug into her hurt arm, her own blood seeping out around his hand as it sought a way beyond the compress.

"Well," she whispered. "You have what you wanted. Don't tell me you're having a spasm of conscience *now*."

Without warning, and right before Lann reached them, Elidor let go of her throat, curled his fingers around the necklace there, and shoved her away from himself, hard. The chain snapped, leaving the rest of it, including the rose pendant, in his hand. She landed unceremoniously on her rear, and by the time she scrambled to her feet and ran to the door, he was gone.

Lann skittered to her side. "I thought he had you, Da," he said. "What happened?"

She put a hand to her throat and shook her head.

She had no idea.

She glanced over at Xathal. The old Watchman was kneeling at the side of the body of the woman, his head bowed.

Ivana waved off Lann's attempts to tend to her arm. Meanwhile, several other Watchmen appeared at the warehouse door. One of them cursed and ran to Judoc's body.

Ivana walked toward Xathal.

Xathal rubbed his eyes. "It was all in vain, I'm afraid. We were too late for her, lost Judoc, and didn't catch him. And so close, too." He looked up at her. "I assume, at least, you had a good look at his face? His back was to me." He sounded weary. This investigation was wearing on him, no doubt.

"I would recognize him if I saw him again," she said. "We can have a sketch made when we get back." She knelt next to him, and together they looked down at the body of the ill-fated young woman chained to a wall.

There were many ways in which the murder returned to the theme of the earlier crimes. The victim was a young woman—Fereharian, of course, which was the single commonality. And her wrists had been slit again. But this time, she had been chained to the floor and wall. Literally.

A series of metal loops were bolted into the floor and wall at the far end of the warehouse. The owner used them to chain boxes together, either to discourage theft or to keep them in place.

Xathal was talking with the warehouse owner outside while Ivana continued to examine the body by the light of several lanterns, the wound on her arm now cleaned and wrapped snuggly with a fresh bandage.

Elidor had used the chains to bind the woman to both the floor and wall. She sat propped upright, both ankles chained to loops, but, curiously, only one arm chained. Had that been when she had interrupted him? Or when Judoc had interrupted him perhaps?

Ivana ran her fingers along the chains. They weren't tightened excessively. Merely enough that the woman wouldn't be able to escape them. And yet her skin was raw and angry everywhere the chains crossed her flesh, evidence of a struggle against her bonds.

Ivana sat back on her heels. So the victim had been alive when Elidor had chained her, however briefly. That made sense. The amount of blood suggested that the woman had died from the slit wrists right there in the warehouse.

Ivana hoped that Elidor wasn't about to take a turn for the more macabre. If she had to start cutting down bodies from slaughterhouses or examining blood paintings…

Well, she probably didn't need to worry about that. If he was following a course dictated by her own life, he was running short on subjects.

Ivana peered closer. There were shallow slices on the woman's forearms. Similar to the scars that she herself bore, but these were fresh. One other victim had had cuts like this, but they had been all over her body, not only her forearms.

Ivana's knees were starting to ache and her feet tingled from crouching in that position for so long, but she couldn't tear her eyes off those cuts.

"Well, what do you think?" Xathal asked from behind her. "Does this give us some clue as to where he might strike next?"

She stood to face him. "I think this is by far the strangest yet. In some ways, a return to earlier crimes, and yet in others, a departure."

Xathal nodded. "No bed. And why the chains?"

Ivana kept those thoughts to herself. She had told Xathal that she had obtained information on where the killer might strike next, and, given that they had no other options, he had followed her lead. He knew nothing more.

Xathal continued his questions. "Do we know who she was? Where he found her?"

By way of answer, Ivana lifted the woman's chin, as her head had lolled to the side, and as she did so, the woman's hair fell to one side, revealing a crimped ear.

"A slave," she said. Ivana didn't know unequivocally that her sister was dead. She had been alive the last time Ivana had seen her. Screaming for Ivana not to abandon her.

Her hand went to her throat, where her sister's necklace had rested not even fifteen minutes before.

Ivana pressed her lips together and stood up. That necklace wasn't supposed to matter.

Xathal moved around to look, ran a hand over his face, and then shook his head. "Well. A new kind of nobody." He sighed and bent down to examine the woman's other ear, neck, and face.

Ivana stood up and stared at the corpse. Something niggled at the back of her mind, like two pieces of a puzzle that seemed like they ought to go together, if she could just turn them the right way.

Those cuts.

"Why is one arm free?" she murmured.

"I assumed you—or more likely Judoc—interrupted him while he was chaining her."

A plausible explanation, yet it still bothered her. The cuts on her arms were fresh, not crusted over as they would have been had he tortured her first and then brought her to the warehouse. He'd begun to chain her, had been interrupted by Judoc, and after dispatching him, had commenced with his torture before he had finished restraining her?

Why would he leave a possible way for her to gain an advantage, however small?

She moved to the other side of the woman to lift her arm. She turned the hand over and pried open the stiff fingers. Of course, her hands were covered in her own blood, so there wasn't much to observe.

From the vantage of behind the woman, Ivana peered again at her cuts. She frowned and crouched down again. "Can we unchain her?" she asked, fingering one of the locks.

"Well, I suppose, if you're done with your initial observations. Let me go get help."

Xathal disappeared out of the door.

She didn't need help, but she was in no hurry. She had no urgent reason to reveal to Xathal that she could pick locks. So she waited, unmoving, until he returned, her mind whirling.

She waited while he and one of the other Watchmen fretted over the chains and locks, and then called in yet another Watchman. Finally, they freed the victim's arm, and while they worked on her ankles, Ivana pushed the body forward a bit and moved behind it. She crouched down again and laid the body back against her own chest so it didn't fall over.

She turned the woman's right forearm over. There were cuts, but they weren't as consistent. As though they had been made by someone else, like she might expect.

She then held her arms out in front, as if they were the woman's, and pretended to draw a knife across her forearm with the woman's free hand—her right hand. They were exactly as they should have been had the woman made them herself.

She stood up, and the woman's body fell to the floor. She

hardly noticed.

Burning skies. Burning skies!

Of *course.*

His spying on her had never been about voyeurism in the ordinary sense. He had been watching her *harm* herself.

And then she had stopped. True, that had been years ago, but she had caught him still watching her not even a month ago. Watching, waiting, and hoping, perhaps?

It might very well have taken years for the loss of his sick fantasy to finally erode his self-control until he had finally snapped. And perhaps knowing he couldn't kill or injure *her*, he had lashed out at others who looked like her—at least initially. Perhaps the first ones had been his initial frustration. And then he had evolved to trying to recreate a bit of where he had watched her, in her bedroom.

But then what was the point of all of *this*? Why allow her— ask her!—to take this job? She had felt all along that perhaps he was waiting until the end, playing some game, where the final kill for him would come full circle, back to himself.

But if that were the case, why had he left her alive? He could have killed her today, and he didn't.

There was no one left. Her father. Her mother. With her sister, the last of those she had once cared about had been taken from her.

She jerked her head up. No. There was one other.

Rhianah.

Had she ever mentioned the child to him? Her father, her mother, yes, even her sister, but...

She closed her eyes, straining memory. It was so many years ago.

Yes. Yes, she had. When she had been training with Da Lavena.

"Do you have something?"

Xathal's words jerked her out of herself. His voice was curious, perhaps a little nervous.

Well, she had just been cradling a dead body.

"Yes. The next victim will be a baby." Xathal paled, but she continued on. "I want you—you personally—to scour the temple records for recent births in the area. Concentrate on the second district. Fereharian women only. The more recent, the better. I want a complete list, as soon as you have it." If they could narrow it down to one or two women, they had a real chance. They wouldn't have to spread out their resources so thin and could have a large enough team prepared to take him down—and save the next victim.

She couldn't tell Xathal anything about how she knew who the next victim would be, of course. That would expose more than just Elidor to Watch scrutiny, and the Conclave would deny involvement with her faster than a bloodcrab could snatch a fisherman from his boat—and then probably have her eliminated.

Xathal was staring at her. He hadn't moved a muscle since she had issued her—she was sure from his perspective—random pronouncement and bizarre orders. She expected a flood of questions, but perhaps he had grown to accept her taking charge. After all, her last mysterious lead had turned out correct.

"Why only the second district?" was his only question.

That, at least, she could justify. She crouched and drew an invisible square with her finger. "The locations of the murders were fairly random and spread out at first," she said. "But once we started investigating, and he began his game, the murders have been on a trajectory." She pointed to the rough location of districts on her invisible map. "Fifth district. Fourth district.

Third district."

"The next is the second," Xathal said.

She stood up. "Correct." Also, their own district, which made a certain amount of sense, if this was his last move. "We have a week. I want your report much sooner, so we can plan."

"Da, might I ask...?"

"No. It's a suspicion, and a strong one." She turned her eyes on Xathal. "Do it, and I think we might just win his game."

Sometimes it still seemed strange to simply walk through the front door of a precinct. Ivana had spent years working under the nose of the law. To be working *with* them was, in some ways, the ultimate charade.

Xathal had no idea his "special investigator" was a killer herself.

The man at the front desk nodded her into the back. They recognized her by now.

This was the end of her time in Carradon—and likely Cadmyr itself—and hopefully not because Elidor would see to it himself. She was now recognized by far too many people who might one day investigate other more *off the record* jobs. Not to mention, while Xathal and the Watchmen hadn't seen Elidor's face yet, if the Watch managed to arrest him, people would. And someone would eventually make the connection with the man Ivana had lived with.

But would the Conclave simply move her somewhere else? Other possibilities had flitted through her mind.

For instance, perhaps this was their final job for her. Perhaps they intended to discard her, seeing her usefulness as at an end. Worse, perhaps they would view her as a liability, and once Elidor was dealt with, have her eliminated as well.

Regardless, her time in his house, in this city, would be over soon. It wouldn't hurt to be prepared for a sudden flight.

"You wasted no time, I see." Xathal was already standing next to the door of the meeting room. She entered and he followed, closing the door behind them for privacy.

Ivana settled down in a chair next to Xathal at the small table in the room.

"What do you have?" she asked.

He plopped a thin stack of papers in front of her. "As you requested. A copy of all recent Fereharian birth records kept by the temple in the second district."

"A copy?" she asked, untying the twine holding the sheets together. "I hope you didn't delegate this task."

"No. I did it myself, as you asked. Frankly, there weren't that many. Fereharians are a relatively small percentage of the population in the second district, and then you were asking for an even smaller percentage of those."

Xathal fell silent, watching and waiting while she paged through the dozen or so records and separated them into two piles: definite no, and maybe.

Seven went into the "no" pile because the mother was married. He had, thus far, been as accurate as he could be, given what he knew about her past and, no doubt, given his options. He wouldn't choose a child whose mother was married, not when he had several others to choose from that were closer to her own situation.

She hesitated over the five that were left. Had she mentioned the gender of her child? She didn't think so. Still, it had been an off-hand comment, and she wasn't certain of that. Either way, she had better not use it as part of the criteria.

She set two more aside. The mothers were both older than she was now by at least a decade, let alone than when she had given birth. He could do basic math. He knew how long she had been with him. He would know she would have had to have been young.

That left three. She spread them out in front of her, side by side.

Their ages were sixteen, nineteen, and twenty-one.

Their children would be six months, nine months, and several weeks, respectively.

The fathers were all listed as unknown.

She rubbed a hand over her face, and then slid aside the middle woman. The child *and* the mother were older.

That left the sixteen year-old with the six month old, and the twenty-one year-old with the newborn.

Would he choose the child closer in age to the one she had lost, or the woman closer in age to herself?

She closed her eyes. It would be the younger child. The victims he had chosen so far had all been attempts to mimic the people whom she had lost, and she had specifically mentioned that she had lost the babe soon after she had been born.

She set aside the sixteen year-old and stared at the paper in front of her. It made sense to her now, but that didn't mean she couldn't be wrong.

She put a finger on the paper and slid it toward Xathal. "I think it's this one," she said. "His next victim, that is."

Xathal stared at the record as though it were a bloodbane. "How do you know? I still don't—"

"I don't know. Not for certain." She slid out the other two women, her second and third choices. "These are two other possibilities. Have someone survey all three options, so that we can gather a bit more information. But we don't have a lot of time, so it needs to be done quickly. And I cannot stress enough, *discreetly.*"

Xathal stared at her. "Survey? I thought the point of this was so we could protect potential victims."

Ivana stared at him incredulously. "Do you *want* to catch him?"

"Of course I want to catch him."

"Then the last thing you want to do is put anyone under obvious Watch protection. If you alert the victims, you will alert him. Then he'll choose another victim—one we *don't* have under protection—and not only will someone else die, but we'll lose another chance to trap him."

Xathal stared at the paper containing Ivana's first choice, then laid the paper down. "You want me to knowingly put these women in danger? Without even *telling* them?"

"Do you see another way?"

He shuffled his hat on and off. Then he rubbed his eyes. "What's your plan?"

Chapter Twenty-Seven

Ivana and Xathal had been biding their time in an empty room across the ally from the house where the presumed next victim lived since midnight on the seventh day. It was now closing in on eight o'clock, and still there had been no sign of Elidor. The woman, along with her baby, had been in and out throughout the day. She was out now.

Xathal had been fidgeting for hours: pacing, tapping, removing and turning his hat in his hands. Ivana, on the other hand, had sat motionless against the wall during that same time. As darkness fell, they had kept the room dark and had spoken little.

Waiting was always the most tedious part of her job, but she was used to it.

Xathal dropped his hat and looked more intently out the window.

Ivana straightened up. "Something happen?"

"She's home again. This time she has another child with her, a little older."

"What?" Ivana frowned and crawled over to the window to look through herself.

Indeed, she could see a young woman moving about in the room, just a small boarding room. She carried an infant on her chest while an older girl clung to her skirts.

"How did the fact that she had two children not come up in our survey of the three women?"

"Maybe the other child wasn't there, like she wasn't for most of today? Maybe my man didn't think it was important? Maybe it isn't her child? I...don't know."

She pressed her lips together. If she could have done it herself, she would have. But if Elidor had seen her anywhere near the homes of the three women in question...

No matter. It was what it was.

But where was Elidor? If he were coming here, surely he would have been here by now. Technically, he still had four hours, but why wait until so late?

Something wasn't right.

Twenty-one. Sixteen. Newborn. Six months old.

Ivana had gone with the younger child.

But what if...

"Damn," she whispered.

"That's not what I want to hear," said Xathal.

Elidor seemed to have chosen the other victims based on their similarity to the people in her life he was representing. She had assumed, then, that the child being the other person in her life whom she had lost, he would choose a child closest in age to hers, lost only a few hours after birth. But what was a few months in the age of a baby to a man like Elidor?

But it wasn't about the child. It was about her, this time. *She* was the girl.

"You still have teams waiting nearby the other houses?"

"Yes, but—"

"Someone would have alerted us if they noticed anything, correct?"

"Yes, but—"

"Then we might still have time." She stood up. "This isn't the right woman."

"That is *not* what I want to hear!"

"Get to the second team now. I'm going straight in; stay near, but give me five minutes before moving in." She might still have a chance to take care of this herself, especially if she could catch him by surprise, but she wanted the backup if she needed it. "Do you understand?"

He nodded.

Ivana disappeared into the night.

The house was dark when she arrived. Unlike her first choice as a victim, who had lived in a boarding house, this girl shared an apartment with two other women.

Ivana already knew the girl's housemates would be out. Xathal's man had noted that they worked staggered shifts, so that one of them would always be home with the baby.

She had found a support system. She had done something Ivana had not even been able to do for herself, let alone herself and a child. A sort of fierce pride swelled in Ivana's chest, surprising even herself.

Ivana brushed it aside. She felt, rather than knew, that she was short on time. The silence and darkness of the house unnerved her.

She scaled the wall and then inched along the roof until she reached a window that led into the apartment. She leaned over as far as she dared to see inside.

Only darkness.

She ran a hand over her face. She didn't have the time to fully assess the situation.

She turned and dropped herself over the edge of the roof, lowering herself down until she found purchase on the windowsill. The window was already cracked open, which seemed unusual, given the time of year.

Had Elidor entered here? Worse yet, had he entered here and then left it open for her deliberately?

She made sure she had her balance, opened the window all the way, and then dropped inside.

She found herself in the main living area. A woodstove and pantry on one side, with a small round table in the middle, and then a few chairs and a row of shelves on the other side.

Near the window, a door led into another room. It was partially closed, but light shone through the crack.

Ivana crept closer to the door, staying away from the line of sight from within the room.

She dared to peek.

"You're later than I expected. Did you get lost?"

Ivana froze. *Damn.* So much for surprise.

"Why do you hesitate? Come in. We have a guest."

The last, she felt, was said to someone else, which was a positive sign, she supposed.

She glanced out the window. It would have taken Xathal a few minutes longer than herself to get to and instruct his team. She had maybe another six or seven minutes before they arrived.

She entered the room.

Chapter Twenty-Eight

The woman was gagged, sitting on the bed with her wrists tied behind her back to the bedpost. Her shoulders were low and her head was bowed when Ivana first walked in, making her wonder at first if she was still alive. But at the sound of Ivana's footsteps, the woman's head jerked up.

Ivana halted inside the doorway. "Woman" was a strong word. Ivana was struck at once at how young the victim looked. Sixteen, the records had said; the youngest of all of Elidor's victims, and she looked it. Just a girl. A girl like she had been.

And the girl was a mess. Dirt and tears smeared her face, the corners of her mouth were rubbed raw, and her hair was a tangle. Despairing eyes flickered with hope when she saw Ivana, and she struggled against her bonds again.

As for the child...

He sat at Elidor's feet, innocently unaware of what was going on around him while he played with a cloth book. At his mother's renewed struggles, his head swiveled to look at her, but the newcomer was more interesting, and so his gaze soon turned toward Ivana.

Unknowing that above him stood a madman with a sharp blade in his hand.

Elidor had been watching her. He only spoke now when her eyes had turned away from the girl and the babe and toward him. "I've been expecting you."

Ivana let out a slow hiss through her teeth, meeting Elidor's eyes. This was not a situation she could safely eliminate him in. Now, she had to stall him long enough for Xathal's men to arrive. "And you weren't last time?" Her eyes roved to the girl and back. "Things seem different this time. Why?"

He laughed, his empty, mirthless laugh. "Which do you think would be worse? To kill the woman first or the child?"

"Put the knife down, Elidor. Or better yet, let her go, and let's finish this, you and I. That's what this is about anyway, isn't it?"

He ignored her, instead choosing to crouch down beside the babe. The child glanced curiously up at him.

The mother shrieked through her gag and hurled herself against her bonds.

Elidor looked up at the girl, studied her for a moment, and then glanced at Ivana. "Yes, clearly, the child. You see, I'm learning."

Come on, Xathal. It had to have been five minutes. How long had it taken him to get to the team?

She took a step toward the child, but Elidor's eyes grew hard, dangerous, and she froze.

"Oh, no, I don't think so," he said, bringing the knife too close to the child.

"Why are you doing this?" she asked. "It makes no sense, not for someone like you."

He closed his eyes. "Someone like me," he repeated. "What does that mean? What am I?" He opened them again. "Does it bother you?" he asked, not for the first time, except this time he was dangling a knife over a babe's head.

"No," she said, and it was mostly true.

"You lie. You're not like me." He picked up the child and rose to his feet, and then walked over to the girl and sat next to her on the bed. He balanced the child on his lap and ungagged the girl with a free hand.

"Put him down!" she shrieked. "Monster!"

He ignored her and instead shifted the child farther away from the girl.

She changed tactics. "Please," she said, addressing Ivana. "Please help me."

Elidor cocked his head and spoke only to Ivana. "Does it tear at you? Rend you? What are all those words people use?"

"What is this about?" Ivana asked. "Why are you doing this?"

"Let my son go. Take me, but let him go," the girl whimpered.

"Does this break your heart?" Elidor continued, unmoved. "What does *that* feel like? Tell me!"

What did he want from Ivana?

She glanced at the girl, whose body was trembling, and yet, her eyes still flicked to her son, as if to make sure that in the midst of it, he was still alive.

Where. Are. They?

"I don't understand," Ivana said.

"I know you do. Or you used to." He drew a thin chain out from under his tunic and let it rest on his chest. Her sister's necklace. "I saw it every time you took out that blade."

She frowned—and the door to the room burst open.

Amidst the shouts of Xathal's men, Ivana lunged toward Elidor, which was just as well because he shoved the child toward the edge of the bed and dove for the window.

Ivana cursed, caught the babe, and handed him to his mother, who had already had her bonds undone by one of the Watchmen.

Another was standing at the window, his head out, looking up. "He's on the roof!"

"Move!" she shouted, and the Watchman moved aside just in time for her to step up on the windowsill. A quick glance told her the path Elidor had taken. She flung herself to an external wooden stair outside the next apartment over, darted up the stairs as far as they would take her, climbed up on the railing, and jumped for the lip of the roof.

She caught it and heaved herself up in time to see him hurling himself across the gap between this building and the next—a narrow alley below—and land on the other side.

He would *not* get away this time.

She took a deep breath, sprinted across the roof, and leapt across the gap in pursuit.

Elidor was slowing. Ivana could tell. She had pursued him across the rooftops of the second district for close to five minutes, and she had gained on him, now landing on the roof of a building before he had jumped off to the next.

And he had stumbled, briefly, the last time he had landed from yet another jump.

They were coming out of the dense residential area and closer to the main thoroughfare that led to the city through the southern gate. He was soon going to run out of buildings close enough together that he could leap.

She didn't know where he intended on going, but—

There. He had reached the end.

He halted at the edge of the building and stared across the street to the one on the other side, as if gauging the distance.

He couldn't make that jump. He knew it. She knew it.

He turned and lowered himself over the edge of the wall to climb down, but his hesitation had allowed her to close in on him.

She couldn't lose him in the streets. He had too many places to hide.

She drew her dagger and hurled herself toward him, lashing out at the fingers still gripping the edge of the roof.

He let go of the roof with the hand she had aimed for, causing her to miss, but the leg he had braced against the side of the building, the same one that he had fallen on a week ago, gave way, and he lost his grip with the other hand.

She grabbed for his other hand, and he scrambled for purchase, found it, and then lost it. She was forced to let go, lest she be dragged over the roof herself. He half-slid, half-fell against the wall toward the ground below.

She didn't wait to see what happened. She sheathed her dagger and turned to climb down herself. The sound of an impact and a grunt came from below her, but by the time she made it down and turned, the hem of his cloak was already disappearing around the corner.

She ran to the corner, rounded the edge—

And found herself being dragged backward into the darkness of the alley beyond, a knife at her throat.

"Here!" she screamed. "Xathal!"

He growled and hurled her against a wall—the dead end of an alley.

She hit it, gasped, and fell to her hands and knees.

He stood above her, a menacing shadow blocking the only way out.

She was trapped.

She stood, and when she made to reach for her dagger, he moved closer, his dagger held out and ready to strike.

"Don't!" he said. "Just tell me!"

They were back to this again? She held her hands out to either side. "All right. Just relax."

His eyes were wild and angry; she had never seen him look so out of control.

He divested her of her own dagger and threw it out into the street.

She had to calm him down, get him talking again, to give Xathal and his team time to find her. "I really don't understand."

"You can remember. You remember what it feels like."

She was becoming exasperated now. "I don't *want* to remember. That was the whole point of all of this, Elidor. You know that. Or you would if you had been paying attention."

He stepped in close and dug the point of his dagger into her neck. "Tell me! Tell me what you felt!"

Her fist clenched reflexively. "It hurt," she spat out.

His eyes were hungry. *"Tell me."*

She closed her eyes and then opened them again. How to make him understand? "Very well. Imagine that after a long, hard fight, you've been bested in hand-to-hand combat," she said. "You lie flat on your back, wounds smarting, feeling so tired that you can hardly move.

"Your victor stands over you and laughs. And rather than honorably reach down to help you up, he deliberately puts the heel of his boot on your chest and starts grinding it down." She touched his chest, and he didn't move. "Slowly. Painfully. You feel the gravel pressing into your back. Your lungs begin to lose air. Your vision blackens."

The anger had drained out of his eyes. Instead, they had glazed over. She lifted her hand and pushed the dagger away from her throat. "All you can feel, all you know is the certainty that this is the end. And yet it isn't. The pain of the boot heel goes on, and on, and your arms are lead, you have no strength to move, you're helpless to get up, until..."

She tugged up the sleeve to one arm, baring the scars that were still visible, even if the wounds themselves had healed long ago. "Until you would gladly find any other lesser source of pain to distract you from the agony."

His eyes roved to her arm. His lips parted. Something almost pained flickered across his eyes. "You are," he whispered, "the closest thing I've ever had to understanding."

And in that moment, she finally understood as well.

He really didn't get it.

He had been living despair vicariously through her, via the only connection he understood: blood. Physical pain. Violence. He had never experienced his own emotional pain as he ought to have, given his past, and perhaps he knew he should have. Perhaps this had been his way of doing so.

It may have started as mere fascination, perhaps at her plight and obvious misery when he found her in the streets. But it had evolved into more. Since the time he had first seen blood on her fingers, he had discovered his muse and succor.

And then she had learned to kill. She had learned to wall off the pain, control her anger, bury her hurt. He had lost his medication.

But she also understood in that moment that no matter how tall and thick those walls were, she would never be like him.

Not truly.

Had he been trying to goad her into harming herself again? Was that what all of this had been about? Perhaps it had started as a lashing out, a release for his anger—but then the Watch had unexpectedly asked them to become involved. Had he then seen an opportunity?

Had he played this entire game in a vain attempt to return her to her previous state of pain? It hadn't worked, of course. It had been unsettling, the similarities—but these were strangers to her. She had been trained far too well to let their deaths affect her. She had no connection with them. He didn't understand. He had never understood.

But he had been trying to, hadn't he? That picture, on the wall. His obsession with their faces. His insistence that she dine with him.

Tell me.

She leaned down and pulled out her boot knife, and, her eyes never leaving Elidor and his dagger, now held loosely in his hand, she skimmed it across her forearm.

And as her own blood welled up, it was as though some of the memories she had tried to bury beneath thick skin, now cut, were trying to seep out as well.

But his hand lowered.

"Why did you kill those first women, Elidor?" she asked softly.

He licked his lips. "I...didn't want to," he said. "Not really. I just wanted to see them bleed. And they wouldn't—they wouldn't cooperate." He licked his lips again, appearing at a loss.

She had never seen him appear so helpless and out of control. He had even *stuttered*. "But you knew that you couldn't then leave them alive after torturing them."

His shoulders straightened with resolve. An excuse—justification, perhaps? "Of course not," he said.

He had killed those women to satisfy a lust that had gone

unsatisfied for years, because *she* had ceased harming herself.

Those women—and a man—had all died because of *her*.

A long-suppressed voice now found a place to emerge. *Your fault*, it whispered.

No.

They had died because of Elidor's sick obsession with her, and that was it.

"But it wasn't the same, was it?" she asked.

"No," he said, seeming downcast. "It wasn't the same."

"Of course it wasn't," she said, speaking as though she were soothing a toddler who had skinned his knee. "But you don't need them." Her eyes flicked up behind him, and he was so lost in his own thoughts that he didn't even notice. She gently took his hand in hers and removed the dagger from it. "I'm here now."

"Yes," he whispered, his arms falling to his side.

She stepped to the side as three burly Watchmen barreled into him from behind and flattened him face-down on the ground.

They shouted and demanded and bound his hands behind his back and did all the things lawmen liked to do upon catching their prey. She slunk around them and back out into the street.

Xathal was waiting there.

She met his eyes. Wiped off her knife. Returned it to her boot. Picked up the dagger Elidor had thrown and sheathed it back at her thigh. Straightened her cloak and pulled it back around her.

"That was quite the pursuit, Da," Xathal said softly when she had finished. "I feel as though there is more to you than meets the eye—perhaps more than I've been told."

Her hand came to rest on the hilt of her dagger under her

cloak.

He gave her a side eye. "No. Don't tell me. There are some things I simply don't want to know."

She released the hilt of her dagger. Unnecessary, and problematic anyway, with three Watchmen in the alley who had only moments ago seen him very much alive.

"The mother and child are both unharmed," he continued. "Well done."

Ivana flicked her eyes to the alley. The Watchmen were dragging Elidor out. "You have your killer, Ruios. Congratulations. This is where my work ends."

With that, she bowed and walked away from him. She crossed two intersections and then looked back.

Xathal was still watching her. He tipped his hat to her and turned away.

She turned the corner and breathed deeply of the late fall air. It was cool and moist, decidedly un-suffocating.

"Very good," a voice said from the shadows. A cloaked figure stepped out.

Llyr. She had expected him.

"Meet me three nights from now. Usual spot," he said.

He left without an affirmation from her.

Alone in the night, she lifted her still-glistening arm to the moonlight and examined the blood almost dispassionately before wiping it off.

Yes. Decidedly un-suffocating.

Chapter Twenty-Nine

The underground hall was empty but well-lit. Nonetheless, Ivana stayed toward the wall, in the shadows.

Llyr had changed the location of their meeting at the last moment to a little-used hall in the underbelly of one of the larger temples to Yathyn. The change made her uneasy.

Her time in Carradon was done. Too many people would recognize her now, and there would be too many questions about the man she used to live with and his disappearance.

But what exactly did the Conclave intend?

She had no good will toward the Conclave. In fact, she was tired. Tired of doing the bidding of others, whether that be Elidor or their Conclave handlers. Tired of being jerked around by shadowy masters whose motives she could only guess at.

Oh, it wasn't that she cared whom they decided needed to be assassinated or why. But the entire group was distasteful to her. She supposed some of the lowest of priests were sincere, but those with any sort of power were corrupt, through and through. She didn't know whether they even believed in the gods they purported to worship.

She wanted out from under their thumbs. She doubted they would ever let her go in any other way than at the bottom of the river.

Footsteps echoed down the silent hall at last. Ivana looked in their direction to see Llyr striding down the hall.

And him. Oh, how she hated him.

His snide remarks. Crude comments. Suggestive looks.

Ugh.

She moved out into the open, halting him.

"Good," he said. "You're here." He removed a leather pouch from his waist and tossed it toward her.

She caught it easily—and frowned. It was far too light.

"This," she said, raising an eyebrow at Llyr, "is 'well-paid'?"

"Yes," he said. "About that."

Ivana narrowed her eyes at him. She wasn't in the mood for this. She had spent the last month playing games with a serial murderer, all the while being reminded of a past she had taken up this life to forget. She wanted her money, she wanted to know their plans for her, and she wanted both now.

"What," she said through clenched teeth, "is the problem?"

He raised an eyebrow, and she met his eyes coldly back.

"Those who wanted Elidor on this job insist that the original amount was quoted for Elidor's assistance." His eyes slid over her. "Not his apprentice's."

Ivana's jaw twitched and her ire rose. "You fools would have paid the killer had I not been the one who took the job."

Llyr's upper lip curled in a sneer, but she cut him off before he could make whatever snide comment he had at the tip of his tongue. "I caught your killer. I want the agreed upon amount, and I want it now."

"But it didn't turn out as we expected, did it? And since you didn't manage to eliminate him, we had the additional hassle of getting him back from the Watch before they could interrogate him."

She didn't have to take this from these people. She could snap this arrogant man's neck if she wanted to. She stepped in close to him. "Do you really want to spar with me?" she hissed.

He didn't seem at all flustered. "You're being transferred to Arlana. Go back to your home and await further instructions." He raised an eyebrow. "Unless, of course, you have some further objection to raise?"

He met her eyes smugly, as if knowing he had her, and there was nothing she could do about it.

She glared at him and turned away.

He sniffed and began to move past her. "I always did think you were a little too *sweet* to be a hired blade," he whispered in her ear as he passed, and his hand brushed her thigh.

Her barely contained rage snapped.

Her dagger was in her hand and shoved into his gut in a split second, and then she shoved him backward before he bled all over her.

He stumbled back, his eyes wide with shock, his hands to his stomach, blood staining the cream-colored rug beneath their feet.

Then he fell—and she finished the job with a quick slice to the throat.

After a moment, he lay still.

Ivana looked down at him, bloody dagger still dangling from her hand. "A sweet blade," she said to his corpse. "Appropriate. Thank you."

She divested him of a second pouch of coins, wiped the blade on his tunic, and then sheathed it.

Well. So much for Arlana.

Epilogue

The wind was cold. Winter was on the threshold, and Ivana had hundreds of miles to travel before she could find a place to disappear for a while—give the Conclave time to give up the search, and more importantly, forget they had ever employed an assassin's apprentice named Ivana.

Both good reasons to move on as quickly as possible.

Even so, her steps tarried on the way out of the city that night. She found herself drawn to the burial grounds at the outskirts, and then to the wall where those who had chosen to have their remains cremated had their urns interred.

She walked along the wall and then stopped at one plaque in particular. She ran her finger along the engraved words, which were difficult to make out in the dark, even with a clear night and a half moon.

But she knew it was the right one. She had been here once before, three years ago, when she had attended the funeral as a family friend.

Boden, the apothecary's apprentice.

She wasn't sure what she intended to find or feel, standing here again.

A test, perhaps?

As it was, all she felt was the night breeze trying to find its way through crevices in her cloak.

And yet...

"After all this time, you still grieve that boy?"

Ivana stilled, but she didn't turn. "*Grieve* would be a strong word," she said, and it was. There was nothing so intense left within her walls. "But perhaps there is still room for regret."

Finally, she turned to face him. "You escaped."

Elidor stood about ten feet from her. Not close enough that she couldn't defend herself against a sudden move, but neither was it far enough that she could easily run from him.

The corners of his mouth curled up in that same smile that never reached his eyes. A learned reflex. "*Escaped* would be a strong word. It would be better to say exiled and repurposed."

She shook her head. It all amounted to the same thing. They had let him go. Why?

It didn't matter. All that mattered was why he was *here*.

"You betrayed me," he continued. "I always wondered if you would in the end."

She snorted. "As if you care."

"You know me too well." He lifted his face to the sky and studied it, as though the stars held some hidden meaning for him. "And, perhaps, you learned from me too well, to my own undoing."

She knew his meaning. He had sought to undo her training, her self-control, her resolve, by tormenting her with her own past—for his own sick purposes. She hadn't bent, and instead he was the one who had lost control.

"Where are you going now?" he asked, when she didn't reply.

"I'm afraid I may have upset the delicate balance between myself and our former masters," she said. "So somewhere—anywhere—else."

"Ah, yes. I heard about that incident."

She shrugged. "No great loss."

"And what will you do?"

"I haven't decided yet." Her knowledge and training could open several business opportunities for her. "Private investigator. Bounty hunter." She smiled faintly. "Innkeeper."

"I always thought you would do well with freelance work."

She raised an eyebrow, a bit surprised. He was speaking as though they would bid farewell and she would walk away, but she didn't believe he would let her do that so easily. "Freelance work," she repeated.

"In fact, I would suggest it strongly. As long as I know you're out there somewhere, drawing *someone's* blood, I think I can be content."

That settled that. "Freelance work would do as well."

He moved closer to her, and she put a hand on the hilt of her dagger. But he merely held out his hand. Dangling from it was her sister's necklace. "I believe this belongs to you."

"Keep it."

"I insist."

She frowned and held out her hand, and he dropped it into her palm. "So you're content to leave me alone."

"I am content." He smiled again, and this time it was of a quality that reminded her who she was speaking with. "For now."

He inclined his head to her, turned, and walked away.

Ivana splayed her hand against her thigh. So that was it.

Once again, she found herself alone.

But unlike before, not defenseless.

She glanced at Boden's plaque and was satisfied at the genuine lack of any overwhelming feeling within her.

No. Not defenseless at all.

Her fingers curled around her sister's necklace.

For now.

ABOUT THE AUTHOR

Carol lives in the Lancaster, PA area with her husband and two energetic boys. She loves reading (duh), writing (double-duh), music, movies, and other perfectly normal things like parsing Hebrew verbs and teaching herself new dead languages. She has two master's degrees in the areas of ancient near eastern studies and languages.

Also available:
Banebringer (The Heretic Gods #1) – May 2018

For more information on upcoming books, visit
www.carolapark.com